SOUTH OF JUSTICE

S.K. MUSKAT

For Jason.
This book, and all of them.

ONE

THE SOUND of the bass was so deep it could bury the dead. Smoke hung in the air, heavy with the stench of sweat and cheap perfume. Laser lights swept the dance floor like searchlights. The strippers moved ghost-like through the haze, eyes dull, smiles fixed. Ryan Inglis leaned against a chipped concrete pillar, motionless except for his eyes.

From the outside, Club Persephone looked like it used to be something else. A fish-packing warehouse, maybe. Or a cantina that outlived every liquor license it ever had. It was located in the Zona Playitas, a dimly-lit, slightly decaying neighborhood of Ensenada, a few streets inland from the sea. Tourists came here by accident. Cartel affiliates came here on purpose. Deals were made in booths where the sound system drowned out even the worst intentions.

He turned his head, taking in both exits and the rusted spiral staircase that led to the VIP area. The high rollers in this town were entirely different beasts from the ones back home. Here, they didn't carry Louis Vuitton handbags or lap dogs, just nickel-plated Desert Eagles tucked into holsters and stares that dared you to test them.

A pair of locals—day laborers from the look of their dirt-caked work boots—moved toward the bar. One of them nudged the other, gesturing toward Ryan. *"No hagas pendejadas, güey. El Muro está ahí."*

Don't do anything stupid, man. The Wall's right there. They were talking about him. The name had been floating around for a while now—*El Muro*. The Wall. He didn't mind the nickname. In fact, he thought it kind of suited him. Walls don't feel. Walls don't care who you used to be. Both the men laughed, but not loud. The second guy glanced over at Ryan, then away just as fast. *"¿Ese cabrón? Ni parpadea."*

That bastard doesn't even blink.

Ryan didn't react, he just returned his focus to the room around him. Back when he wore a badge, this place would have been a raid waiting to happen. In his two months of working as a bouncer in this particular doorway, he'd learned three types of people come here. The ones who want to forget. The ones who want to be seen. And the ones just killing time until they kill someone.

Behind the bar, Marisol, a pretty bartender in her twenties, her black hair in a thick braid, mopped up yet another spilled drink. She'd lasted three whole weeks here, which made her a veteran in Ryan's book. Marisol sometimes gave him that slow, careful smile that invited a man to imagine things. Ryan imagined them—God, he did—but he always shut the door on the thought. A single touch might undo him. A single kiss might burn through the discipline he'd built, brick by brick, since his life went to hell. That didn't stop the need for a woman living under his skin like a low-grade fever. But letting it loose felt like inviting disaster.

A string of English expletives cut through the din. Ryan tensed. The voice was slurred, but unmistakably American.

His gaze swept across the room until he found the source: a lanky gringo by the bar, sweat blooming dark across his t-shirt, pupils blown wide. High on more than the cheap liquor. He was looming over a stocky local, swaying hard enough he looked ready to either punch the guy or pass out.

The local wasn't planning to find out. His hand drifted toward the pistol tucked at his lower back.

The American didn't clock it, either too stoned or too stupid. He slammed his plastic cup onto the bar behind him, spilling booze across the counter. Then he shoved the other man hard, and Ryan watched his hand close around the gun.

Marisol, who'd just finished wiping up the last mess, sighed and moved across the bar to start sopping up the spill. Ryan played the scene out in his mind. If the man drew and fired, she would be right in the line of fire.

He moved. Not fast, not loud. Just a wall, shifting into place.

The local caught sight of him first. Ryan shook his head once, slow and deliberate.

The man froze, one hand still hovering at the small of his back. A quick calculation behind his eyes. Not worth it, not tonight. He let go of the pistol. Hands raised in a tight arc, frustrated, he backed off into the crowd.

The American wasn't so smart. He turned, wide-eyed, and for half a second, Ryan saw something sharp behind the fog of drugs.

Recognition. Or maybe just the spark of a man grabbing at half-formed memories.

Ryan's gut twisted hard. He'd had nightmares about this exact moment. There were still posters of him up in the States. His face was on websites, side-by-side with words like "traitor" and "disgraced deputy U.S. marshal." And the story behind why was still doing the rounds on TV on slow news days. If someone recognized him here, it wouldn't just end his exile. It could get him killed.

The American's mouth opened, slow and stupid. "Hey... You —you look like..."

Ryan was already moving. He caught the man's wrist, twisted it cleanly, and slammed him chest-first into the bar.

A grunt of pain, a slurred curse. Nothing intelligible. The tension broke as fast as it had built.

Ryan crouched low, voice just for the idiot's ear. "Pick another bar. Pick another town."

The American blinked up at him, dazed, barely coherent. Whatever flicker of memory had been there was already gone. Ryan let go, stepping back before adrenaline made him careless.

The drunk staggered past him, pushing other patrons out of the way in his desperation to get to the door.

Ryan watched until he disappeared onto the dark streets of Ensenada. He straightened, breathing steady but his pulse still hammering behind his ribs.

The bullet he'd dodged wasn't lead tonight.

It was memory.

***

He turned back to the bar. Marisol slid him a bottle of water over the counter. The incident appeared to have barely fazed her, which was a skill Ryan wasn't sure if he admired or feared.

"El Muro," she said, then added in heavily-accented English, "personality of one, too."

Their eyes met for a second, hers amused.

He took the water. "You want me to make conversation or keep the idiots from bleeding out on your floor?"

"Long as you do the second one, you can stay mute all you like."

Ryan nodded and returned to his post by the door. This place was purgatory, with tequila. But no matter how monotonous the nights were, how predictable the actions of drunks with weapons, he never let himself become complacent. Never let himself while away the hours scrolling his phone or take a few drinks to dull the edge of his boredom.

Because he knew if someone ever came for him, it'd be here.

The crowd shifted, pressed tighter by a new beat pounding through the speakers. Ryan adjusted his stance again by the concrete pillar. Habit. He hated this part—the way the crowd moved like a living thing, all heat and noise and blurring shapes.

It was too easy to lose track of threats. Too easy to miss something.

He felt it then, the slightest tug against the hem of his jacket. His hand closed reflexively around his pocket. But there was nothing unusual. No wallet lifted, no weapon drawn.

Then a voice came from behind his left shoulder, just loud enough to be heard over the music. *"Para ti. Él dice que te recuerda."*

Ryan spun around, his pulse thudding in his ears. He scanned the bodies surging past, their faces glazed with drink–grinning, shouting, oblivious.

Or pretending to be.

Keeping his movements easy, he shifted one hand inside his jacket. His fingers brushed something smooth and hard, a plastic USB drive slipped into the inner pocket of his jacket.

It hadn't been there a minute ago.

He didn't freeze. He just straightened against the wall, scanning the exits again. Trying to pick out who was watching.

Because someone was.

Near the back of the room, a man raised a phone, pretending to film the strippers, maybe. But the lens wasn't pointed at the stage. It was pointed at him.

And when Ryan stared the man down, he melted into the throng, swallowed by the bass and strobe lights.

He slid the drive deeper into his pocket. Later. For now, he just kept breathing. Kept pretending everything was normal. Which was hard when the words he'd heard behind him kept echoing in his head.

For you. From someone who remembers.

TWO

RYAN LIVED in a one-room walk-up above the club. It was barely bigger than the mattress he slept on and about as homey as a bunker. Cracked tile floors, a barred window that didn't open, and a fan that buzzed overhead like a dying wasp. A tiny bathroom, not much bigger than a closet. The air smelled of tequila and old cigarettes.

He locked the door behind him, bolted it and slid the chain across. Then shoved a chair under the handle for good measure.

He sat at the table, his laptop in front of him, the flash drive pinched between his fingers like it might bite. The cheap overhead bulb flickered once, twice, before settling into a dim, nervous glow.

Typical. Club Persephone could keep the tequila flowing but couldn't keep the lights steady.

Ryan slid the drive into the port. One folder. One video. No label.

His hand gripped the mouse, and he clicked.

A video screen sprang open and immediately began playing. The footage showed a small blue and white house set back in a well-tended yard. A child's bike lay abandoned in the grass. Around the side of the house, a woman was hanging laundry on a line. The video looked like it had been taken on a phone, from across the street. The camera was steady, so Ryan guessed it had been shot from out the window of a parked car.

A boy ran into frame. The camera snapped to attention, panning until it had him fully in shot, then zooming in close. The kid was seven, maybe older. Soccer ball under his arms. Messy brown hair. Skinny limbs.

Ryan leaned forward, squinting. He didn't recognize him.

The camera shifted its attention abruptly, focusing instead on the woman by the clothes line. The footage blurred for a second, then sharpened. The woman had turned to face the boy—and the camera—and was calling something out to him. She was in her sixties. Long grey hair, big green eyes, high cheekbones.

Ryan's chest went tight, breath catching. His hand squeezed the mouse like a trigger.

It had been many years since he'd laid eyes on his former mother-in-law, Diane Carmichael. But there was no mistaking that face.

She looked just like her daughter.

Kylie. His ex-wife.

Dead two years now, brutally murdered by cartel enforcers back in the States. She'd been caught in the crossfire of a world he thought he'd left behind. The guilt never left him. Neither did the rage.

Ryan leaned forward, stomach knotting. His eyes followed the camera as it panned back to the boy.

It had to be Noah. Kylie's son. Her only child.

The resemblance was unmistakable, his mother's auburn hair, her wild freckles scattered across his cheeks.

The footage zoomed all the way out again, taking in the quiet suburban scene. A boy playing with his soccer ball, his grandma hanging out the laundry.

Ryan kept watching, confused. Then he heard a soft, sinister chuckle. He could tell it was coming from whoever was shooting the video.

The screen went blank.

Ryan didn't move. The silence felt thick and pressurized. His pulse thumped loud in his ears, like it was trying to fill the room.

He stared at the laptop. Waiting for something else. Another message. A command.

But there was nothing.

He stood up, fast. Paced once, then twice, rubbing a hand down his face. He wasn't breathing right.

It wasn't just the footage. It was the angle, the steadiness of the camera. The way it zoomed, not with curiosity, but with precision.

He sat back down at the table and gripped the edges with both hands. They'd found Diane. They'd found Noah. They'd found *him*.

And they hadn't said a single word. There were no demands, no ransom, no names. Just a video and a laugh.

That was the message.

———

He stood, went to the door and rechecked the deadbolt. He shoved the chair harder under the doorknob, then crouched and slid the Walther PPK from the holster beneath his mattress.

He checked the mag and the slide, then he secured the holster under his shirt and slid the pistol into place.

The tequila bottle on the shelf looked tempting. He poured a shot, let it sit untouched. Instead, he went to the windowsill and unscrewed the lid of the dented coffee tin. Peeled back the foil false bottom.

The cash was still there. Enough to buy a bus ticket out of town, out of state, maybe even out of the country altogether. South—he would go as far south as it would take him to fall off the face of the earth.

He shoved the money back inside and closed the lid. Turned back to his laptop on the table. It felt like it was watching him.

Ryan didn't trust the laptop. It was old—secondhand—bought

in cash at a flea market south of Rosarito. But still, he'd plugged in *their* flash drive. That was a mistake.

He powered the machine down, pulled out the battery, and unscrewed the casing in three practiced motions. Snapped the hard drive from its slot and cracked it against the bed frame until it split open with a metallic crunch.

He tossed the remains into a grocery bag, then removed the chair from the door handle, unlocked the chain and deadbolt. Keeping his head down, he strode down the hallway, then down the backstairs that led to the rear door of the club. He unlocked it, then slipped out into the night.

The stink of the dumpsters greeted him from half a block away. They were behind a Chinese restaurant and Ryan guessed they were due for emptying. He gave the street a thorough sweep in both directions, then slipped down the side of the restaurant, lifted the lid and slung the grocery bag with the shattered laptop inside.

Then he made his way back to the club, glad for the hard lump of his pistol at his waistband.

Safely back in his room, he turned his attention to the flash drive.

It went easier. The plastic cracked like a wishbone between his fingers. The metal piece he dropped into the rusted drain in the bathroom floor. The plastic shell he burned over the gas flame of his stove.

By the time he was done, it was like the message had never existed.

But it had. And no matter how many times he cleaned the room, counted his cash, or wiped the sweat off his palms, he couldn't stop seeing Diane. That house. The kid.

When he closed his eyes, he could picture Kylie on the last day he'd seen her alive. She'd been six months clean and sober. She'd looked happy. She'd looked like the girl he'd married on a bright fall day in Tellico Plains, East Tennessee.

His mind skidded forward to the last time he'd seen her, strangled to death in a dog crate. It had only been in a photo, but the image was burned into the back of his mind like a hot poker.

The fan buzzed overhead like it was shorting out his thoughts. He lay down on the mattress and stared at the ceiling. One arm behind his head, the other pressed flat against his chest like maybe he could keep whatever was breaking inside from leaking out.

He had no proof the boy was in danger. No name. No voice telling him what to do.

Just a video. And a memory that wouldn't stop replaying.

THREE

BEHIND THE SHUTTERED taco stand on a forgotten stretch of the I-35 corridor, past an alley that reeked of uncollected garbage and dog shit, there was a door. No bell, no sign, just a slab of steel in the concrete wall.

Deputy U.S. Marshal Tomás Gates pushed it open, stepped inside and let the door close behind him. It was so dark inside it took a second for his eyes to adjust. There were three booths, and only one was occupied.

Gates slid into it, across from a man in a DOJ windbreaker. They didn't bother with a handshake. A file sat open on the table between them. The man was older, with a heavily-lined face and eyes that were too close together. It reminded him of something his ex-wife used to say about men with that particular facial feature: that they were shifty.

This guy was, probably, or at least, no shiftier than anyone who worked in their world.

"You're late," he said.

Gates said nothing, just sat back in his seat.

A flat pause. Then he said, "Heard you're running point on the northeastern corridor. Joint task force with the federales, right?"

Gates didn't respond.

"Still don't get why they brought you in on the Inglis case," the contact said. "We had it covered."

Gates scoffed. "Your 'coverage' has had him missing two years."

The man flipped a page, ignoring the comment.

"As you know, back in '23, former Deputy U.S. Marshal Ryan Inglis illegally accessed WITSEC files. He breached one of our highest-level vaults. He was looking for one name: Jessica Meeks. Federal witness in the *La Mano Negra* case."

Gates nodded. He already knew every frame of this story but let the man unspool it anyway.

"Inglis used her location to negotiate with the cartel because *La Mano* was holding his wife, Kylie. And he broke protocol, broke the law, to try and get her back."

"He got her back dead," Gates said flatly.

The man blinked, as if surprised by Gates's insensitive take on the matter. Then he continued as if he hadn't been interrupted. "Once the damage was done, Inglis tried to get Meeks to safety. But she figured it out along the way and ran before he could explain. Got picked up anyway. Cartel had her for two days. She survived. Barely." He flipped another page. "Inglis disappeared. Burned his IDs. He's been Marshals Most Wanted ever since." The man sat back, one finger tapping the corner of the file. "Hell of a fall. The guy used to teach ethics and inter-agency cooperation."

"I'm not here for a postmortem," Gates said. "I'm here to find the kid."

That got a reaction, a small tilt of the contact's head, not sympathy, but understanding. "Noah Carmichael," he said. "Still missing?"

"Three days. Picked up from his grandmother's place in Tennessee. No forced entry, no ransom note. Just gone." Gates pulled up a photo on his phone. A seven-year-old boy, red hair, crooked smile. A school portrait, the last one taken. "We think he was smuggled south," he said. "Into México."

The contact narrowed his eyes. "He Inglis's?"

"Not biologically," Gates said. "But close enough to matter."

The man whistled under his breath. "So you think he'll come out of hiding for the kid?"

Gates didn't answer. He just stood and headed for the door, taking the file with him.

"So what is this really?" the contact called after him. "A child recovery op, or a rogue marshal clean-up job?"

Neither, Gates thought but didn't say. He just pushed open the door and stepped back out into the Texas heat.

FOUR

THE COFFEE at Club Persephone tasted like it had been filtered through motor oil, but Ryan drank it anyway. At least the taste distracted him from the image of that kid on the screen.

The sky outside was a flat, lifeless grey. It wasn't even noon, and the heat was already pressing in. A fly buzzed against the barred window. He sat at a small table near the back of the club—off-hours, dead quiet—and opened a second burner phone. One of two he kept in a cloth pouch in a lockbox under the floorboards upstairs.

If they were watching the boy, they were watching for a reason. And if that reason had anything to do with Kylie's death, or the men who had used her and discarded her, then he was already running behind.

The phone felt heavier than it should've in his hand. He stared at the screen for a full minute before scrolling to a number he hadn't used in over a year.

Mark Lyman. One of the few people who might not shoot him on sight. Or worse, turn him in for a promotion.

Emphasis on the *might*.

Years back, they'd worked together in the Caribbean fugitive unit. They'd shared six months of late-night stakeouts, heatstroke and impossible cases. Mark had once taken a bottle to the ribs in Curaçao, and Ryan had been the one to patch him up with a stolen first aid kit and a hotel towel.

In return, he'd helped Ryan out of his own tight spot a year ago, when he'd lent him his car to drive to Panama City Beach and find a woman named Jessica Meeks.

That was the last time they'd spoken. It was also the last time Lyman had ever seen his car, but that was a whole other story.

He was more than a colleague. Maybe not quite a friend. But back then, Lyman had looked at him like he was someone worth backing.

Ryan rubbed his hand across his mouth. This was a risk. A real one. If Lyman was wired, if the number was monitored, if someone even flagged a ping off a tower, Ryan could have a drone over his head before sunset.

He knew he should leave it alone, that he should pack his bag and disappear south. But Noah was just a kid. Kylie's kid. A kid being watched, maybe worse. And Ryan had very few allies left. So he hit "Call."

One ring. Two. Three. It clicked. No voicemail. Just dead air.
Then—

"This number is not in service." The mechanical voice cut sharper than expected.

Ryan stared at the phone. Hit redial. Same result. He tried the old work cell Lyman used to carry. Nothing. Then his backup contact, the Gmail they'd used for dead-drops.

Login failed.

He tried again.

Password changed.

He exhaled, feeling a sharp pain in his chest. Then he closed the phone and sat still for a long time. The kind of still that didn't feel strategic. Just…empty.

The walls felt like they were closing in now. He pushed away from the table and paced once across the room. His boots thudded softly against the floor.

He poured himself another cup of the sludge-coffee and sat again.

Think.

He ran through a mental list of names. One he knew for sure was a no-go: Tomás Gates. They'd come up together at Glynco, friendly rivals through the academy, always neck and neck on quals. Later, they'd served on the same task force, back when Ryan was second-in-command of the Two Rivers Violent Fugitive Unit. Gates, ever the poster boy, had headed it. He'd always been the kind of guy who knew how to play politics, keep his nose clean and his boots polished. Ryan could still picture him, leaning against his SUV, in the humid Tennessee dusk. That easy laugh, the one that made you forget how sharp the guy really was. Once, Ryan would have trusted him with his life. Now? He wouldn't.

The silence in the room pressed in. He was a thousand miles from anyone who knew him, and even farther from anyone who gave a damn. He had no backup. No flag on his badge to fall back on. The brotherhood was gone.

He felt it then: the tipping point. The moment when his old life finally stopped being a resource and started being a liability. He stared at the phone on the table for another long minute, like it might ring on its own. But it didn't.

The club was still quiet as he made his way back upstairs. Just the distant thump of someone restocking bottles and the low hum of the AC unit that never gave off any cool air.

He climbed the narrow back stairwell and unlocked the door to his room.

Inside: stillness. The mattress. The fan. He turned the bolt, slid the chain across, set the chair back under the handle.

Then he lay down on the mattress and stared at the ceiling.

He didn't have a plan, or even full understanding of the problem. He had the memory of a face on a screen, and a threat wrapped in silence.

And now he had one less person to call.

FIVE

THE STREETS of Puerto Escondido blurred into dust and shadow as the sun bled out behind the hills. The restaurant sat right on the shoreline, three cracked tables outside, salt-stained walls, the smell of frying oil in the air.

Lucía pushed the door open, relieved to find the place nearly empty. From the kitchen, the cook waved her in without pausing her dance between the burners.

"*¡María!*" she called, voice rough from smoke and years. "*¡Entra aquí!*"

Lucía ducked her head and stepped into the kitchen's sweaty warmth. She'd been living under the name María Torres for eighteen months. Long enough for it to almost feel like hers.

She dropped her bag onto a milk crate. Pulled out her battered laptop. She wasn't here to wait tables or clean dishes. She was here to keep the books.

The real ones.

Two sets of numbers lived in this restaurant: one for the tax officials who came sniffing around with greasy palms and badge-shaped threats. And one for the kitchen, for the people who cooked and scraped and survived. Lucía kept both balanced, neat and untraceable.

It wasn't just a job, not least because it barely paid her anything. It was a way to make something clean, controlled. If she could keep the numbers straight, maybe the rest of her life would follow.

And it was also a small act of rebellion. A sliver of control in a world that had stolen everything else from her. And a way, however insignificant it sometimes felt, of repenting for her many sins.

On the street outside, a scooter backfired.

Lucía flinched before she could stop herself, fingers tightening around the laptop.

She waited for her heartbeat to steady. Then she opened the laptop, faked a smile for the cook. And got to work.

Hours later, she packed up her things, said goodbye to the cook, and stepped into the thick coastal night.

The sea was a black smear against the dark, the ocean's breathing a low, restless thing at the edge of town. She turned east, the streets thinning as she left the coast behind. Music still bled from bars near Zicatela, bass thudding, tourists laughing too loud, scooters coughing past in tight packs.

But four blocks inland, the world shifted. Lights dimmed. Storefronts pulled their steel shutters tight. Dogs slunk through the alleys, their nails tapping against the broken pavement. The rhythm of the city slowed and turned in on itself.

Lucía kept to the sidewalk, steps quiet, head down. She took a shortcut through an alley, past cracked stucco and sagging wires. Every sound—laughter, a slammed door, a motorcycle backfiring—seemed to hit sharper here, like it was stripped of cover.

A car crawled down the street behind her, music low but deliberate. As it neared, she dropped her head and hunched her shoulders, old instincts kicking in.

The car slowed, just enough to make her skin prickle. Then it jerked forward and rounded the corner.

She waited a beat.

Two.

Then she straightened, blowing out a shaky breath. She'd never been the kind of girl that men hollered at from car windows. She wasn't unattractive, she knew that much. But nor was she the kind of pretty that stopped anyone mid-stride. That realization had stung when she was younger. Now, it was a blessing—one of the few she still counted.

She kept it that way deliberately. Her long dark hair was tied up in a messy knot. Her makeup was minimal, her clothing loose and colorless, in shades of black and navy. Nothing that caught the eye. She hadn't dressed to impress anyone in a long, long time.

She dressed to disappear.

Ahead, her apartment block leaned tiredly into the dark, as if it, too, was ready to collapse. A set of metal steps led to her door. The lock clicked into place behind her. Two deadbolts. One chain.

She leaned her forehead against the door, breathing slow, letting the night's noise bleed away. The heat stuck to her skin like wet paper.

The apartment smelled of mildew and old plaster. Barely two rooms: kitchen, bedroom and living space in one, cramped bathroom in the other. A plastic table, a sagging couch that she folded out every night to make into a bed, and a temperamental refrigerator that clicked on and off at whim—a trick it liked to play on only the hottest days.

This place wasn't a home. She hadn't had one of those in many years.

Inside her bag, the emergency passport pressed against her side like a loaded gun. Every night she told herself she'd use it. Every night she stayed.

Because even a half-life in the grime and heat was better than dying on her knees back in México City.

She sat cross-legged on the sofa, laptop balanced on her knees. Her muscles ached from the walk, her mind still circling that car on the corner, the scooter backfire, the thousand tiny wrong notes only a seasoned survivor could hear. It had been so long since she'd felt like she could relax. Since she'd felt any sensation other than anxiety.

She couldn't even remember the last time she'd laughed out loud. Or cried over a sappy movie. Or, God forbid, felt that little tingle when catching a man's eyes and making him smile.

She exhaled and tried to focus on the screen in front of her. She ran her usual checks first: dummy email accounts, offshore proxy layers, message boards where no one posted under real names. It was a routine she'd repeated a million times, and it never failed to calm her nerves.

The same patterns. The same safe silence.

A thousand safe nights had trained her finger to move fast, a habit born from the life she used to live, the life that taught her how easy it was to hide numbers where no one thought to look. The trick wasn't just encryption. It was misdirection. Layering. Making the lie clean enough that no one ever thought to doubt it. Lucía knew how to hide a ledger better than she knew how to hide herself.

She opened the restaurant's back-end accounting site, the one she'd encrypted twice over.

And there it was.

A message. Buried inside the vendor payout list under a fake supplier code.

MARÍA TORRES: I SEE YOU.

Lucía froze. Her breath caught sharp in her throat. Her heartbeat surged against her ribs like it wanted out.

She sat motionless, one hand leaving damp fingerprints on the trackpad, the other curled into a fist at her knee. The fan above spun in lazy, useless circles, dragging sweat from her skin. She blinked. Rebooted the system. Pulled her alternate browser. No change.

She ran a basic sweep of her network logs. Then an advanced one. The IP list came back clean, but too clean. Cleaner than she ever kept it.

"Shit," she whispered.

She launched her encryption check script. It hung. Glitched. Then returned all systems stable.

That wasn't possible.

It should have taken thirty seconds. It had returned in ten. That didn't happen unless someone had already swept through, either to protect her…or to watch her. The keyboard suddenly felt cold against her fingertips.

She slammed it shut, heartbeat hot in her throat. Then she sat in the dark, breathing through her nose. Counting backwards from ten. Training her pulse back to something she could control.

Her phone buzzed once. A notification. Battery draining at double rate. 17%. She'd last charged it an hour ago. A surveillance app? Something embedded without her seeing?

She grabbed it from the sofa, popped the back, and pried the SIM out. The card snapped in half between her fingers. The phone followed, battery pulled, motherboard cracked against the edge of the table.

Still, her hands didn't stop shaking.

She had options. Her escape bag was packed. The passport was waiting, and she had money in her crypto wallets. She could be on a bus by midnight, gone by morning.

But she didn't move. Maybe the message was a bluff. They hadn't used her real name. Maybe they were just casting a wide net, hoping to spook her into making a mistake.

If she ran now, she'd leave a trail. Noise. Attention. And the first rule of surviving was simple: never run until you're sure you have to.

SIX

LUCÍA YANKED ON HER BOOTS, tucked her go-bag under her arm, and stepped out into the walkway. The night outside was thicker than it had been an hour ago. The moon, once full above the roofs, had disappeared behind a stack of slow-moving clouds.

She headed for the edge of town, toward the only internet café that didn't require ID and took cash up front. She walked fast and kept her head down, but her paranoia walked faster.

Somewhere behind her, footsteps echoed. Not urgent. Just… wrong.

She ducked into a corner *tienda*. Pausing at a rack near the door, she pretended to look at nail polish. The footsteps passed. She glanced up, muscles tensing, ready to bolt if necessary. It was a man with a limp and a blue baseball cap. Only when his back disappeared out of sight did she allow herself to breathe.

Behind her, the clerk asked her if she needed anything. She mumbled a reply, then bought a soda just to keep her hands from trembling.

Fifteen minutes later, she slipped into the café. The man behind the counter had a thin face and slimy eyes that tracked all over her, as if trying to peer beneath the layers of her clothing. She paid with a folded 200 peso note.

"Receipt?" he smirked.

She didn't answer, just turned and walked away, still feeling his eyes on her.

She chose the furthest terminal. Plugged in her emergency USB. Ran the encrypted tunnel she hadn't used in six months. She opened her offshore proxy.

Blocked.

She tried a second. Then a third. Every one of her safe routes—burned.

She stared at the screen, the cold of the café's AC creeping up her arms like static. Not random. Not broad. Targeted. This wasn't just someone poking around, it was someone watching. Someone who knew how to peel back her layers.

A name appeared in one header line, a server alias she remembered all too well.

"ElS-17"

El Escriba.

Her blood turned to ice. He had found her. Not just some unidentified "they."

Him.

The one man who always understood how she worked, how she thought. The man who'd destroyed her life. The man she'd been hiding from ever since.

Lucía wiped her keystrokes and shut the system down. She pulled the drive and held it tight. A second later, she was out the door.

SEVEN

BACK IN HER APARTMENT, she repacked her go-bag. Clothes, new burner phone, USBs, cash in three currencies. Two of her IDs were still usable. One now wasn't. She'd have to head for Oaxaca by bus.

Still, though, she didn't run. Not yet.

El Escriba had found her. But she wasn't leaving empty-handed. Because there was one last thing she had to do. One final piece to move on the board before she vanished again.

She sat at the table and opened her second laptop, the air-gapped one. It had no stickers and no serial numbers. No OS beyond a hardened Linux shell, and no preloaded programs that she hadn't written herself.

She fished under the collar of her t-shirt, removing the cheap silver necklace that hung between her breasts. Uncapping the end of the pendant, she plugged the flash drive into the laptop and waited for the directory to populate.

Alpha_C3.bak

It looked harmless. A backup file. Three megabytes. Last modified: eighteen months ago. Her palms were sweating, and heat clung to her back.

She typed the decryption key by hand. No copy-paste, no saved credentials.

Tr3mbl_n0_c41g4_s0la

That line—"trembling doesn't make a leaf fall alone"—was something her father used to say when things felt off. It was his way of saying *miedo no es cobardía.*

Fear's not cowardice. Sometimes, it's a warning.

The decryption started.

Her heartbeat synced with the progress bar. When it finished, the file opened into a cold grid of data: dates, transaction codes, destination accounts, shell companies.

The cartel's darkest secrets lived inside it, wire transfers, shell corporations, silent partners, laundering trails. But it wasn't just money; there were names, too. And not just of criminal syndicates: it contained the dirty deeds of politicians and judges and bankers. If this ledger went public, the ripples wouldn't stop at the border. It would cause schisms internationally. It would shatter trust, collapse corporations, and fracture alliances.

It wasn't just a spreadsheet, it was a weapon.

She hesitated, finger poised above the trackpad. This was the second of three fragments, the middle piece. The first fragment was already in place. The third—the final piece—wasn't stored anywhere. Not on a drive, and not on paper. It lived only in her own head.

And if anything happened to her, it died with her.

She double-checked her upload path: encrypted connection to a dead-drop server, VPN chain spanning three countries, upload routed through a virtual shell in Estonia.

All green.

She clicked SEND.

Seventeen seconds later, it was gone.

Lucía leaned back in her chair, her whole body sore. Her eyes burned. Alpha_C3 was no longer in her possession. It now lived in a secure location where no one could touch it. And if anything happened to her, and the final key was lost, the entire structure of the ledger would remain locked—forever. Its truths inaccessible. Its secrets, too.

She closed the laptop and rubbed her face. Outside, a dog barked. A car crawled by too slow. She crossed to the window and nudged the curtain open with two fingers.

Just darkness.

Still, something felt wrong. The growing sense of unease that it was past time for her to have vacated this place.

While folding clothes, she opened her secure feed reader, the only one she allowed to pull headlines without alerts. She scanned the feed for anything cartel- or cyber-related. A headline stopped her.

U.S. Marshals Expand Presence in México, Appoint Senior Liaison

Her jaw tightened. She clicked.

In response to rising cross-border criminal activity, the U.S. Marshals Service confirmed a strategic increase in cooperation with Mexican authorities.

"This isn't an invasion," said Deputy U.S. Marshal Tomás Gates at a press event in Laredo. "It's coordination. Collaboration. We're here to assist, not take over."

Gates—formerly of the Two Rivers Violent Fugitive Task Force—is now embedded with Mexican federal units at an undisclosed location.

She closed the tab, her throat dry. The U.S. was moving players into place. Big ones. She shoved the laptop into the very bottom of her pack. Slipped the flash drive pendant over her head. It was empty now, Alpha_C3 was gone.

She stuffed the last of her clothes into the bag and zipped it up. Before she left, she turned off all the lights but one and left the fan running. From the outside, her apartment would look lived-in. For a few more hours, anyway.

It was borrowed time. She slipped her backpack on and exited through the rear stairwell.

On the street, she didn't look back.

———

Somewhere in México City. A darkened apartment. No windows or clocks. No way for the outside world to intrude on the work that was done here.

Somewhere in the maze of lightless code, something blinked. A trigger embedded deep in a shell corporation's subaccount.

She had surfaced.

El Escriba leaned back in his chair. The room around him was silent, but in his mind, a map ignited: networks lighting up like constellations, dead routes humming to life.

Not a full location, not yet. The signal was scrambled through three continents and bounced across defunct proxies. She was still clever.

His mouth curved up. Too clever for the dogs he kept on retainer. Sicarios were blunt instruments. She would spot them coming a mile away.

No, she didn't use traceable phones. She had no known associates. She used air-gapped machines and one-use signals. He respected that. But it wouldn't save her.

He tapped the keyboard. Another window bloomed across the screen: surveillance footage, years old. A looped recording of Lucía in a México City café. Her hair was longer then. She was laughing at something just out of frame. She looked bright and unguarded. Happy, even.

He typed a new command. Far away, someone's phone rang. Instructions followed, measured and exacting.

"Do not touch her," he said. "Not until I say."

The third fragment was still missing. It wasn't a file; it was a key. He knew she would never have written it down. Which meant it lived in only one place.

Inside her.

He glanced back at the frozen surveillance frame, her smile half-captured in a blur of movement. She had never smiled at him like that.

But she had begged. And soon, it would be for her life.

33

EIGHT

RYAN WOKE with a full body jerk. The room was dim, and for a second, he wasn't sure what had pulled him from sleep. Then he heard it.

A vibration. Low. Mechanical.

He pushed himself up, every instinct sparking. The chair under the door was still wedged in place, the bolt still drawn.

And yet, there it was again. A buzz. Then silence. Then another buzz.

He crouched beside the bed, pulling up the thin mattress. Nothing. The next vibration made him whirl around and lock his attention onto the table. He got onto his hands and knees, and then he saw it: a cheap burner phone, black plastic, taped to the underside with electrician's tape.

The screen pulsed once. A single notification: **1 New Message**.

Heart hammering, Ryan peeled it loose. He didn't touch anything else, just tapped the message.

The screen went black for a second, then flickering into a grainy video. The same angle as before. Diane's house and front yard. Noah with his soccer ball.

Ryan stared at the footage. There were some slight differences from the first video. Diane had disappeared, leaving her wash flapping in the breeze. Noah wasn't jogging across the lawn, he was standing still, his back to the camera. His posture was odd, like he was sensing something wasn't right and had frozen in fear. The camera was slowly zooming in on him. No, not zooming. *Approaching.*

The boy spun his head, looking right at the lens. At the person who was holding the lens. His face flickered from confused, to wary, to wide-eyed terror.

The camera tilted like it had been dropped, then the screen immediately went black.

A voice, flat and synthesized, layered over the video like bad AI.

"You've seen what we can do, Deputy Marshal Inglis. Now we want something from you. You will find a woman named Lucía Duarte. Confirm location. You have five days. If you do not find her, if you try to run or involve your friends, the boy dies. Further instructions to follow."

The message began to immediately repeat itself, then cut off mid-sentence, as if the clip had been severed by a knife. Ryan stared at the screen. There was no rewind; no replay or back button. After five seconds, the phone went dead. He turned it over in his hands. No power button, either.

Disposable tech. Custom firmware. This wasn't a bluff cobbled together by local cartel thugs. This was serious. Military-adjacent. If it was the cartel, they'd clearly upgraded.

Either way, they'd found him. They'd reached into his sanctuary—his shitty room, his locked door, the private space where he went to sleep, not thinking about anything but surviving another day. They'd breached his last wall.

And they had Noah.

Ryan stood very still. The room seemed to sway around him.

Noah, whose blood wasn't his, but whose mother had once laid next to Ryan in his father's hunting cabin in Tellico Plains and whispered that she would never stop loving him. Who'd gotten his name tattooed on her thigh, high enough up that every time Ryan saw it, desire had shot through his veins like liquid fire. Who'd gotten pregnant with his baby at seventeen, married him within the month, then lost the child before it could draw its first breath.

Whose life had spiraled from then, into depression, then addiction, then a life of transience and fear. Who'd died scared and dopesick, at the hands of evil men who'd used her to get to him. Then disposed of her like trash.

Now, men like that had her son. Ryan had seen the fear on his face. That instinctive, animal fear when a child senses a predator nearby.

It was the kind of fear that lived in the marrow.

———

Lucía kept walking, even after her lungs began to burn. Puerto Escondido already shimmered in the early-morning heat. Her pack dug into her back, growing heavier with every step.

She ducked into a narrow *tienda*, bought a bottle of water and a bag of plantain chips. They would have to sustain her on the last half mile to the bus station. As she walked and ate, she tried not to think about the ripple effect she'd just started. Once all three pieces had been released and the ledger reassembled, there'd be no leverage left. There'd be no more hiding out in México, switching buses and names. Nowhere would be safe, from the cartel, or from *him*.

Just the thought of his name made her pulse jump. He wasn't a plaza boss or a sicario. He didn't send death threats, he left signatures. Emptied bank accounts. Executions disguised as freak accidents.

Lucía closed her eyes, sweat gathering under her arms. He wouldn't send someone to kill her. Not first. He'd want the key. And he'd want it intact.

But more than that...he'd want *her*. Not the woman she'd

become. But the girl she'd been. The one who'd sat in his office and pretended not to flinch when he'd asked for things that sounded like commands disguised as seductions.

NINE

NINE YEARS AGO

THE RECEPTION AREA smelled faintly of lemon polish and expensive perfume. Somewhere behind the frosted glass doors, a phone rang twice, then stopped.

Lucía smoothed her skirt as she sat, crossing one leg over the other. A handful of other applicants sat in stiff silence in the waiting area, each lost in their own thoughts.

The man two seats away caught her eye. Mid-twenties, dark curls, relaxed posture. His dress shirt was rolled at the sleeves, revealing strong forearms dusted with dark hair and a faint ink mark along his wrist, like he'd been jotting notes before he came in.

He caught her staring, and offered a quick, conspiratorial smile. Leaning toward her, he asked, "Long morning?" in quiet Spanish.

She glanced at the wall clock. "Feels longer when you can hear your own heartbeat."

That earned her a soft chuckle. He tilted his head, dark eyes glinting. "First time interviewing here?"

"Isn't it everyone's?"

"Not me," he said, lowering his voice like he was letting her in on a secret. "Second try. Last time I made it to round two before Esquivel decided I wasn't…whatever it is he's looking for."

Before she could respond, the inner door opened. A sharply dressed assistant appeared. The scent of Chanel No. 5 grew stronger.

"Señorita Duarte?"

Lucía rose.

"Good luck," he murmured.

She gave a small nod, then smoothed her skirt and followed the assistant through the door.

———

The office was colder than she'd expected. Not just in temperature, but in atmosphere. It was all steel and glass and blond wood, as tasteful as it was sterile and devoid of personality. Her last job had been in a government building, which had all the charm of a used Styrofoam cup, and yet compared to this place, it had been bustling with life.

Lucía perched on the edge of the hard leather chair, her portfolio clasped in her lap. She'd spent hours choosing her outfit for this interview, finally settling on the cream satin shirt and snug pencil skirt with tan heels. But she'd not counted on how chilly the room was going to be and now—instead of focusing on rehearsing her elevator pitch—she was suddenly, and ridiculously, more worried about whether her nipples were poking through the fabric of her shirt.

It wasn't exactly the first impression she was aiming to make.

Across the vast expanse of the desk, Javier Esquivel continued to tap away at his laptop, his gaze never leaving the screen. He wore a charcoal suit with sharp lapels. No tie. His white shirt was open at the throat and glowed against his tan. His cufflinks were tiny gold skulls.

Still, he didn't look up. Lucía began to wonder if this was some kind of tactic, a test of her assertiveness, or maybe her patience. Or maybe he was just busy. Her résumé sat on top of a pile of others near his right elbow. She wondered where the curly-haired man in the waiting room was in the stack.

Finally, he cleared his throat and closed his laptop and looked up.

He was in his late-forties, his thick hair just starting to turn silver at his temples. Very good-looking, with a strong jaw and black eyes that seemed to take up more of the white around his pupils than the average person. His skin was smooth and tan, barely showing his age, and his beard was black and perfectly trimmed. He looked like he had just stepped off the set of an old Hollywood movie, playing a rogue or a pirate. Blackbeard, maybe, or Rhett Butler.

Even so, he was old enough to be her father, and she'd never had a particular thing for older men. So why did the sensation of his eyes on her suddenly make her feel like she'd stumbled over her own feet?

"I see here," he said slowly, tapping his finger on her résumé, "that you graduated top of your class. Impeccable marks." He smiled, and his face softened, though his eyes didn't. "Top percentile in economics. You also interned at the Ministry of Finance?"

Lucía nodded, pulse skimming faster now. "Yes, *señor*. For six months. Under Director Gómez's team."

"And you worked on asset mapping?"

"Yes. Primarily digital currency trails and sanctions compliance audits."

Javier tilted his head, clearly pleased. Lucía allowed a tiny bit of hope to bloom.

"So," he went on, "you understand shell structures. Beneficial ownership laws. Cross-border laundering vulnerabilities." His voice was so deep it seemed to emanate from somewhere in his chest rather than in his throat.

"I do." She straightened her spine, the hope blossoming into confidence. "And I've also studied red flag markers in corporate acquisitions, particularly in sectors that tend to invite scrutiny. Real estate, mining, logistics."

A pause. Then he hummed. "Impressive." He let the word sit between them, then looked down, flipping a page with slow fingers. "You've read the Syzmanski paper on fraud layering?"

"Of course."

"Your opinion of it?"

She blinked. No one had asked that in other interviews. "I think the conclusion undervalued the role of human behavior. Algorithms can only follow patterns. But people...people invent new ways to lie all the time."

He looked up. "And how would you rate yourself at spotting a lie?"

She paused before she answered. Was this another test? "I'm learning," she said carefully. She offered a cautious smile. "But I'm very good at patterns."

"Mmm." He leaned back in his chair now, just a little. The movement exposed more of his throat, that open collar like an invitation. His arms stretched wide across the leather chair's armrests. Relaxed. Commanding.

His gaze swept over her, not lasciviously, but intimately. As though he were dissecting her, one element at a time. Her hair. Her skirt. Her nails. Her posture.

Her nipples.

Her confidence suddenly withered and died.

"I must say," he said softly, "you present yourself well, too."

Lucía tightened her hold on the portfolio, aware of how damp her hands had become.

"Did you choose this outfit?"

"I...did."

"It's flattering," he said, his tone unreadable. "You understand appearances are a form of language, don't you?"

"Yes, *señor*."

"And you know how to speak it." He let that hang, then smiled. "That's rare. And valuable."

Lucía felt herself start to breathe again, a little warmth creeping back in. Her heart still fluttered, but maybe from something closer to anticipation than fear. She could handle this. She *was* handling it. She'd impressed him.

"Now," he said, voice dropping another octave, "why don't you do one more thing for me?"

The question was benign, but something about the way he said it made her response come out in a croak. "Um. Sure."

His smile widened, lazy and predatory all at once. "Stand up."

She blinked at him. When he continued to watch her calmly, with no hint of anything amiss in his expression, she got to her feet, trying not to lose her balance in her high heels on the thick rug. Did he…want to shake her hand or something?

Javier watched her calmly, arms still spread across his chair. He tilted his head slightly, then murmured, "Now, get on your hands and knees for me."

The words hung there, impossible.

"Then crawl. Around the desk. To me."

Lucía felt heat flood her cheeks, confusion and indignation surging.

He waited. Calm. Relaxed. Black eyes steady and utterly unreadable.

Her lips parted, ready to speak, but she couldn't even form the words. Beneath the mortification flooding her bloodstream was something else: an electric hum of danger and desire she didn't understand.

What she did understand, was that this was most definitely not the time and place for it.

Then, after what felt like a full minute, he laughed softly.

"Ah," he said, waving a hand as if brushing smoke from the air, "forgive me. That was…a joke. A poor one, I admit."

He sat forward, reaching for a pen, all business now.

"Young talent is so serious these days," he added smoothly. "I sometimes forget how intimidating I must seem."

Lucía's heart was still pounding. She gave a tight smile. Laughed a breathy, uncomfortable thing. Of course it was a joke.

Of course.

Javier signed something at the bottom of her file and closed it with a satisfying snap. "You're hired," he said simply.

He stood and extended his hand, his smile now cool and professional, as if nothing had just passed between them.

Lucía hesitated for a split second before taking it. His palm was warm, his fingers long, his grip firm.

Perfectly measured.

As she gathered her things and stepped towards the door, she felt his gaze on her back. When she glanced over her shoulder, just once, he was already reviewing the next file. All cool, polished composure.

But something about the look in his eyes when he first made that outrageous demand stayed with her. A line had been drawn between them, invisible but real.

Part of her told herself it had been fine. It had been a joke.

But another part, deep down, already knew: This was not a man who ever joked.

TEN

RYAN WENT to the window and cracked it open. Outside, the Ensenada sun bounced off the corrugated roofs of neighboring buildings, casting hard-edged shadows into the alley below. A gull cried overhead. Somewhere down the block, a car horn blared, long and irritated. Normal sounds. Life continuing, as if the world hadn't just shifted under his feet.

He leaned his forearms on the sill, feeling the heat of the frame sink into his skin. Five days. To track down a woman he'd never met.

He shoved away from the window and crossed the room, starting to pace. The tile floor was warm beneath his feet. He had to think like a marshal again.

Find Lucía Duarte.

But how? The name meant nothing. All he could deduce about her from the facts at hand was that she must have something someone wanted badly enough to snatch a kid off an American lawn to get it.

What are you going to do, Ryan? Run? Or hunt?

He sat on the edge of the bed, resting his elbows on his knees. Sweat beaded at his temples, the coastal heat making the air feel heavier than it should.

Kylie, what would you want me to do?
Silence.

He'd had hundreds of imaginary conversations with his wife over the years. Probably more than they'd had real conversations. In truth, Kylie had haunted him long before she died. Not with memories, but with guilt.

Guilt that he'd pushed her too hard after the miscarriage, when they were barely more than kids themselves. Guilt that he couldn't stop her from unraveling, from slipping into the slow spiral of depression and addiction. That he'd watched her chase danger, chase chaos, chase other men, and let his own bitterness keep him from dragging her back from the edge.

Worst of all, he'd never been able to sever the thread between them, even after she'd left town. He'd always answered her calls. Always came running. Always enabled, even when he told himself he was trying to help.

But the deepest wound, the one that wouldn't close, was this: he hadn't helped the one time it truly mattered. Maybe, just maybe, if he could help her son, he could lay a few of those demons to rest.

His jaw clenched. For a moment he didn't feel tired anymore. He felt awake in a way he hadn't in years.

Abruptly he stood, shoved the chair aside, and pulled the duffle bag from under the bed. Started packing. Clean shirt. Jeans. Extra magazines. Passport.

He hesitated before adding his badge. The chromium star still gleamed in the light. He turned it over in his hand, then slid it into the bag.

If he was going to do this—really do this—he'd need to remember who the hell he used to be.

———

The bus rocked gently with each curve in the mountain road, tires whirring against the asphalt as dusk rolled in through the scratched windows. Lucía kept her eyes trained on the murky horizon, chin tilted just enough to avoid catching her reflection in the window.

She'd been on the run for over nine years. And every time she had left a place behind, it felt like she lost a little more of herself. Not just names or bank accounts. The deeper parts. Memories. Touchstones. Voice patterns. Favorite foods. Anything that might anchor her too solidly to one life.

She reminded herself that she wasn't running without aim, not this time. She had one stop in mind: Ramiro Vargas, her father's old boss. The man who used to sneak her tamarindo candy and let her spin in the dispatch chair while her father worked on trucks in the yard. He was perhaps the last person alive who might still open a door for her without asking for an explanation first. If Ramiro said yes, she'd have a fighting chance. If he said no...

She didn't let herself finish that thought.

Shifting in the hard seat, she glanced toward the back of the bus. Just a quick scan. Old reflex.

There was no one suspicious. Just a mother dozing with a toddler splayed across her lap. A couple of students murmuring over a shared playlist. An elderly man holding a rosary and talking to himself in whispers.

And...him.

Mid-twenties, maybe. Strong jawline, thick lashes, a lean build beneath a worn denim shirt. Handsome, in a soft, non-threatening way.

He was looking at her.

Lucía's stomach tightened. She immediately dropped her gaze and shifted in her seat, casually as she could, the hairs on her arms prickling to attention. Was he watching her? Had he boarded after her, or before? She tried to replay it, tried to recall faces at the station. Nothing stood out. Had she been too distracted?

She peeked back around, just enough to confirm it.

Still looking.

But his expression wasn't cold or calculating. In fact, he was smiling. Not wide, just the barest curve of interest, the hopeful flicker of someone trying not to be obvious.

Oh. He was *flirting*.

The realization hit her like a slap. Not because of him, but because of the way her body had reacted: tense, closed off, braced for violence. Her mind had gone straight to *they've found me*, not *he's cute*. When had she last let someone look at her like that? When had she last looked back?

She turned her head again, letting the curtain of her dark hair fall into place, shielding her expression. Her heart was still thudding, but the fear had cooled into something quieter. Sadness.

The idea that someone might see her as attractive, as desirable, felt absurd. It was like being handed a ticket to a movie that had ended years ago.

There'd been a time, in another life—literally—when she'd wanted marriage. A home. Children. She'd pictured it often: messy mornings, socks on the floor, pancake batter on the counter. A husband with laughing eyes, the sounds of life filling the kitchen.

That dream was well and truly dead now. Not buried, there hadn't been time for a funeral, but long gone.

She shifted again, pulling her backpack closer between her knees. The bus was climbing now, the air thinning as Oaxaca's ridgelines came into view beyond the glass.

ELEVEN

LUCÍA ADJUSTED the lanyard around her neck, the laminated badge still too stiff and glossy to feel like it belonged to her. Her name was printed in bold: DUARTE, L.

The training floor buzzed around her, low voices, clicking keyboards, the occasional bark of a supervisor. Glass walls boxed them in like fish tanks and the morning sunlight refracted off polished floors. A few clocks showed different time zones. The one labeled "CDMX" ticked just past 8:47 a.m.

"You're sitting in the shark tank," said a voice behind her.

Lucía glanced up. It was the man from the waiting room, whose small talk had eased her nerves. He gave her a goofy smile, a half-empty coffee in one hand, his own lanyard twisted around a finger. CASTILLO, M.

"You know, where they throw the interns in to see who swims first. Or gets eaten."

Lucía let out a small laugh before she could stop herself. "So encouraging."

"I like to offer realism with a side of gallows humor," he said. "It's my specialty."

She turned slightly in her chair, studying him. He had a

relaxed, unbothered energy—sleeves rolled to the elbow, tie loose, collar just a little rumpled like he'd been running late but didn't care. His hair was still damp from the shower. It was an oddly intimate detail, and made her picture him standing naked under a stream of hot water, hands raking through his hair…

Or maybe she'd just been single for too long.

He held out a hand. "I'm Mateo."

"Lucía," she said, taking it in hers. His palm was warm, the skin rougher than she was expecting from a man who worked in front of a screen all day. "You didn't sit next to me yesterday."

"I didn't want to look too eager."

Lucía raised an eyebrow.

"Okay," he said, shrugging, "I wanted to see if you came back."

"And?"

"And here you are."

A wry smile tugged at the corner of her mouth. He didn't press it. Just sipped his coffee.

They turned back towards the projector screen where their trainer, a lanky man in a too-tight suit, was walking them through their second case of the day: shell corp unwinding protocols. Lucía's fingers hovered over the keyboard, already navigating the structure diagram like she'd seen it before.

"You're quick," Mateo murmured.

"I've done something similar."

"Where?"

"University internship. Shadowing."

He nodded. "That explains it. You're not like the others. They're still looking for the 'on' switch."

She smiled at him, or at least at his blatant attempt to flatter her abilities. No one made it into Esquivel y Asociados' Internal Data Integrity Team if they weren't already skilled analysts.

A moment later, Mateo leaned in just slightly, his voice pitched low. "See that flag on node three? It's hiding a re-routed dividend. Whoever designed this did it with their eyes closed."

Lucía paused. Then she saw it, too. He was clearly more than a pretty face himself.

"Hiding under a non-dom subsidiary," she said. "Lazy."

"Or confident. Means they've done it before and gotten away with it."

She looked up at him again. "You're not just here for the paycheck."

Mateo shrugged. He opened his mouth, but before he could respond, there was a shift in tension in the room. Heads turned, voices dropped. Lucía turned in the direction of the stares.

Javier Esquivel was walking the floor.

He moved with the same disturbing grace she remembered from her interview. Like the space rearranged to accommodate him. He wore slate grey today, the jacket tailored within an inch of its life. No tie again. The collar was open, revealing a slash of warm skin.

He wasn't looking at the trainees. He was looking at her.

Lucía's spine stiffened.

Javier paused at her desk, scanning the dual monitors. She'd flagged five nodes today.

"Lucía. I see our investment is paying off," he said.

She nodded once, sharply. "Thank you, *señor*."

His gaze slid to Mateo. "And you?"

Mateo straightened slightly. "Still learning, *señor*."

Javier's expression didn't change, but Lucía saw it, the tiniest delay in his blink. Not displeasure. Calculation.

He nodded, then moved on, the scent of expensive cologne lingering after him.

Mateo didn't speak for a moment. Then, "He already knows your name."

Lucía's eyes stayed on her screen. "He already knows all our names."

"No. He knows yours."

She didn't respond. Her fingers resumed their dance across the keyboard. But in her chest, her heart had picked up its pace. Not from Mateo, and not from fear. From the quiet, coiled certainty that she was being watched.

52

TWELVE

RYAN DROPPED his duffle on the sagging motel mattress, the springs groaning in protest, then locked the door behind him. He twisted the deadbolt, then wedged a chair under the handle.

The place was called El Rincón del Sol, though there wasn't much sun left in it. Just a rusted sign, a flickering vacancy light and a half-empty parking lot choked with dust.

He checked the window. Threadbare curtains, grime-smeared windows. No sign of surveillance. Not that it mattered, if the cartel wanted to find him, they'd already be watching.

He sat in the cracked vinyl chair and stared at the wall. His brain spun, empty. There was no plan. No trail. Lucía Duarte could be anywhere between Tijuana and Tapachula. She was a ghost, and he wasn't the kind of man who found ghosts. Not anymore.

He raked his hands through his grimy hair and let out a slow breath. "What the hell am I doing?"

His voice sounded hollow in the tiny room. The version of him that could've handled this—the deputy marshal, the hunter, the strategist—was dead and buried back in the States, alongside the life he'd torched. Now, he was just a washed-up ex-pat hiding out in a shithole town, pretending he still had something to offer the world.

His eyes landed on the duffle. There was only one option still open to him, one thread he could pull to see if it led anywhere. But it was such a long shot, he was terrified of digging it out and discovering it was nothing more than another dead end.

Don't be so pathetic. He unzipped the bag and took out his wallet. Inside, tucked in behind the only photo Kylie he hadn't destroyed, was a folded napkin. He'd kept it buried there for years. It was one of those strange relics you don't expect to carry, but can't bring yourself to throw away.

If you ever need digital eyes, I owe you one. —Lázaro.

Below was a scribbled number. Back when he was still with the USMS, working an ugly weapons-trafficking case in Sonora, Lázaro was an informant. A freelancer, who'd dipped a little too deep into the dark web and found himself with a cartel target on his back. Ryan had pulled him out of a raid gone sideways. Smuggled him through the desert in the trunk of a Toyota and dropped him off in the hills above Hermosillo with enough pesos to disappear.

He hadn't seen Lázaro since. No idea where he'd gone. If he was even still alive. But the guy had skills. Black hat stuff. If anyone could scare up a lead online, it was him.

Ryan stared at the number for a long time before he hit dial. He was using his burner phone, not the one the kidnappers had deposited in his room. Still, reaching out to anyone on any device felt like a huge risk.

But it was a risk he had to take. So he pressed the phone to his ear and waited.

One ring.

Two.

Three.

Click.

Silence.

Then a voice, low and threaded with distrust.

"*¿Quién es?*"

Ryan swallowed. "It's Ryan Inglis."

A pause, long enough for regret to creep in. Ryan was on the verge of ending the call and tossing the phone, when the voice spoke again.

"You should have let that number die."

"I didn't have a choice."

"Everyone has choices. You just ran out of good ones."

Ryan sat forward on the chair, elbow resting on his knee. "I need to find someone."

"And you're calling me? Fuck, *cabrón*. You know how many people are looking for you right now?"

"Yeah." He ran his free hand over his face. "That's why I picked up the phone."

A sigh crackled through the phone. "Give me the name."

"Lucía Duarte."

Another pause. Then the faint clatter of a keyboard. "Context?"

Ryan exhaled slowly. "Someone's looking for her. People with resources. The kind that don't post missing person flyers."

"Cartel?"

"I don't know." Another beat. "But it feels like it. Organized. Quiet. And they're willing to burn a lot to get to her. They used a kid to get to me."

A muttered curse on the other end.

"She's not a civilian," Ryan added. "At least, not anymore. If she ever was."

"So you think she stole something."

"I think she knows something," Ryan said. "Or maybe she has something. But I'm blind out here, and I've got five days to find her. Four now, actually."

Another curse. "Why you?"

Ryan shook his head, even though Lázaro couldn't see him. "No idea."

It wasn't strictly true. He'd given a lot of thought to why he'd been targeted for this job over the last twenty-four hours, and the realization he'd come to sat in his gut like a ball of lead. It was because he'd done it before. He'd tracked down a woman who'd been hiding from the cartel and delivered her up to them like a DoorDash driver. Perhaps, through dark web back channels and shady meetings between sicarios, word had gotten out. Perhaps they were passing his details around like a goddamn business card.

What a sickening thought. Hero to zero didn't begin to cover it.

He said, "All I know is, they want her. Badly."

"So do I. Now."

Ryan's jaw tightened. "I didn't call you to give you a head start."

"Relax. I'm clean these days." A hollow chuckle. "Mostly."

More typing. Then a long pause. "There's nothing on Lucía Duarte. Anywhere. You're right, she's a ghost."

Ryan exhaled and raked a hand through his hair. "Fuck."

"But," Lázaro went on, "there's been a name come up a few times on private boards. Some traffic a day ago—encrypted nodes, Latin America subnet. Someone asking about Alpha_C3. Ring a bell?"

Ryan stood, pacing the cramped room. "What is it?"

"Ledger fragment. Financial. Think Panama Papers meets snuff film money."

"Okay. Is it her?"

"No one's using the name Lucía Duarte. She's way smarter than that. But the Alpha_C3 drop? Same encryption signature I saw on a leak a few years back. Sinaloa-linked shell companies." Lázaro's tone shifted, quieter. "Whoever did it then, and whoever did this now, they hide in the exact same way."

Ryan frowned. This hacker shit was not his lane. But he understood patterns of concealment. They were as distinct as fingerprints. And once you learned someone's pattern, you could find them again. "Can you trace the Alpha upload?"

There was a long pause, and Ryan wondered if he'd pushed his luck too far.

Finally, Lázaro said, "Not over the phone. Not for this. You want this kind of help, you come to me in person."

"Where?"

"South of Mulegé. Boat launch at Punta Prieta. Midnight tomorrow. Come alone. Come quiet. You bring any heat, I vanish."

"I'll be there."

"Don't be late, Marshal." The line went dead.

Ryan lowered the phone and stared at the blank screen.

Marshal. No one had called him that in years.

———

The sun had just started to drop when Ryan pulled the battered Toyota pickup onto the shoulder. A rusted sign half-swallowed by desert brush read "San Ignacio: 52km." He leaned back in the seat and let the engine idle, his spine aching from hours behind the wheel.

The truck was borrowed—stolen, technically—from a guy he used to bounce out of Club Persephone on weekends. Julio had owed him a favor, and Ryan hadn't asked too many questions about the keys. It ran, mostly. That was all that mattered.

He cracked the door open and stepped out, stretching until his shoulders popped. For a moment, the silence felt oppressive. Ryan looked up at the sky—wide, and blisteringly blue. All around him, the Baja desert pulsed with heat. Nothing but scrub, dust and endless road ahead.

He climbed back in the truck and kept driving.

THIRTEEN

OLD SHIPPING CONTAINERS sat cracked open like giant metal tombs, half unloaded or filled with forgotten palettes of moldy textiles. Trucks dozed under sun-bleached tarps. And there, in the back corner of the freight yard, was the office—barely more than an aluminum box propped up on cinderblocks.

Lucía hesitated at the gate, sweat rolling down her spine. She adjusted her cap lower and tucked her hands into the sleeves of her top.

She wasn't here for nostalgia. She was here because she needed one thing: a roof over her head, where no one would think to look for her. Just a few days of shelter. Time to figure out how to get ahead of El Escriba's men, what to do about the third fragment, and maybe—if luck decided to stop spitting in her face—how to find a way to vanish for good.

Ramiro had been her father's friend, back before her father's death had been written off as "accidental." Back when this place still ran as a functioning freight yard. Before the cartel moved into town and did what it did everywhere in México: sucked businesses and livelihoods and people dry, like a vampiric plague.

If there was one person left who might open the door without asking too many questions, it was Ramiro.

She pushed through the chain-link and crossed the lot, gravel crunching beneath her boots. The office door creaked open before she could knock.

She hadn't seen Ramiro in more than fifteen years. She expected him to have aged, but not this much. His face was bony, the skin around his jaw gone slack. His once-thick mustache had surrendered to white stubble. He glanced at her, recognition flaring in his eyes. He immediately looked away, as if even holding her gaze was a dangerous thing to do.

"*Estamos cerrados.*"

She forced herself not to slump with disappointment at his less-than-welcoming reception. "I'm not here for a quote."

He wiped his hands on a rag, still refusing to look at her. "Lucía Duarte, *sí?*"

She nodded.

"You shouldn't be here."

"I didn't have a choice."

Ramiro spat in the dirt and jerked his head toward the office. She followed him inside. The place was dark, cooler than outside, and smelled like dust and brake fluid.

"Your father," he said, pouring two glasses of water from a plastic jug, "was the only man I ever knew who tried to stay honest in this business. That made him noble. And an idiot."

She accepted the glass and took a drink. The water was warm and slightly metallic, but it steadied her. "I need help," she said. "Just a place. Off the grid. A few days. I'll be gone before you even remember I was here."

"You think I don't know what's going on?" Ramiro set his glass down harder than was necessary. "You've kicked a hornet's nest, *niña*. People are asking questions in dark places. Bad people. You bring that here, you burn what's left of my peace."

"I didn't come here to burn anything." Her voice was steadier than she felt. "I just need somewhere no one will find me."

His laugh was low and humorless. "Then you are about ten years too late."

She said nothing. The silence stretched. Ramiro sighed, irritable, and folded his arms. "I can't shelter you, *mija*. Not this time. I have a grandson in high school. I won't put a bullet through his bedroom wall because I feel sorry for the girl who used to curl up in my dispatch seat and fall asleep."

Lucía stood, shouldering her backpack. Disappointment sunk into her stomach with the weight of a bowling ball, but beneath it was something worse—a hollow, cold emptiness that made it hard to breathe. For a moment, she'd let herself believe he might say yes. That some thread from her past hadn't frayed completely.

Her mind was already racing. If not here, then where? She had no friends she could trust. No relatives. Every road she could think of ended the same way: with her being caught. And being caught by the kind of men hunting her was a fate worse than death, and one that would certainly end in it.

Her throat was tight, but she forced herself not to sound as fragile as she felt. "I understand."

She turned for the door and had nearly reached it when Ramiro spoke again.

"There's a trail station, up near Santiago Apoala." His voice caught slightly on the name, as if saying it out loud might put him on the hook for something he'd been trying to avoid. "Old smugglers used it during the union crackdowns. No road in, not anymore. Just goat paths. It's still standing, last I heard."

Lucía froze, the air rushing back into her lungs so fast it made her dizzy. She turned slowly, searching his face, making sure she hadn't imagined it.

Ramiro still wouldn't look at her. The rag in his hand was twisted tight, his knuckles white. His gaze flicked instead to the window, to the empty freight yard beyond, like he was checking for someone who might see him doing this.

For a moment she didn't move. Part of her was afraid that if she stepped closer, if she spoke too quickly, he'd change his mind and the door would slam shut on her. So she stayed still, her voice measured. "How do I find it?"

Only when he opened a drawer and pulled out a grease-stained map did she let herself believe he might actually mean it.

He unfolded it on the desk and traced a finger north. "Here. You'll need to hike the rest. Watch for the switchback. It's easy to miss."

"Anyone else know it's there?"

"If they do, they haven't used it in years. No cell towers. No neighbors. Just wind."

Lucía folded the map. When she spoke, the words felt like they emanated from somewhere lower down in her body than her throat. "Thank you."

"You're your father's daughter, Lucía. Just try not to die like him."

She stepped back out into the heat, slipping the paper into her pocket. Her jaw set hard.

She wasn't planning to die at all.

———

Lucía's thighs were on fire. The air had thinned somewhere near the last switchback, and every breath now felt like inhaling through fabric. The trail—if it even could be called that—was little more than a fading animal track, threading through weeping pines. Mercifully, though, the heat had fallen away as soon as the road climbed.

She paused to catch her breath, hands on her knees, the sound of blood rushing in her ears louder than the wind in the trees. Above her, the pines stretched in jagged silhouettes against the sky. Below, a sheer drop vanished into mist and shadows.

"This is insane," she muttered.

She had a compass. She had Ramiro's map, which she was grasping like it was the last page in a holy book. But what she didn't have was balance, or trail sense, or boots that didn't feel like they were trying to eat her toes. The pack on her shoulders was too heavy, the ghost laptop inside thudding against her back with every step.

She started moving again, slower now, scanning the rocks for anything that slithered. The last village was miles behind her, and she hadn't seen another person since leaving the narrow dirt road where she'd stashed her motorbike under a fallen tree. It hadn't been much, just a battered red Italika with one good brake. She'd paid a teenager in the village a few hundred pesos for a "test ride" he didn't expect her to return from. But when the trail got too steep, she'd had to abandon the bike and tackle the rest of the way on foot.

She stumbled. Her foot caught on a root, pitching her forward. She twisted just in time to avoid face-planting into a patch of thorns and slammed her hip into the dirt instead. Pain flared. She hissed through her teeth and stayed there for a moment, heart hammering.

Then she saw it.

Not a meter away, in the dappled light: a snake. Curled at the base of a rock. Copper-brown, thick-bodied, motionless, but very, very awake.

Lucía froze. She wasn't an expert, but she knew enough. Not bright-colored. No rattling. Silent, serious. Maybe a pit viper. Maybe just a local species sunning itself. But she wasn't about to take a vote.

Slowly, inch by inch, she shifted her weight back, using her elbows to push herself upright.

The snake never moved.

Neither did she, until it finally slipped, silently, back into the underbrush, as if dismissing her.

Lucía stood, shaking now for a different reason. Her legs itched with sweat and nerves. Her hands were dirty. A pine needle was stuck to her cheek.

"Tech support, my ass," she muttered. "I'm not built for this."

She kept going. Cicadas pulsed somewhere high in the

branches, a constant metallic hum that rose and fell with the wind.

Another half-hour passed before she saw the roof. It peeked through the trees like a mirage, corrugated metal, rusted in patches, sagging slightly to one side. The cabin was half-hidden in a natural crease in the hillside, a blessing from the terrain. She approached slowly, watching for signs of recent activity. There were none.

The door creaked when she pushed it open. Inside: one room, musty and dark. A wood stove. A rickety table. A cot with a mildewed mattress. Spiderwebs in the corners. No light, no running water. But it was a shelter.

She shut the door and slid the bolt. Dropped her pack. Sank onto the cot. The ache in her legs had gone bone-deep. Her palms were scraped. Her ankles swollen.

But she'd made it.

FOURTEEN

LUCÍA PEELED OFF HER BOOTS, wincing at the raw skin on her heels. Blisters were already forming across both feet. The price of hiking in cheap, too-new boots over uneven terrain. Her socks were damp with sweat, and her toes ached.

She didn't have much to treat them, just a travel-size bottle of iodine, a strip of gauze and a roll of tape. She dabbed the iodine on, wrapped her toes as best she could and muttered under her breath when the sting made her eyes water.

Despite the cool air up here in the mountains, her shirt was soaked through with sweat, her hair sticking to the back of her neck. She stripped down to her tank top and jeans.

She hadn't eaten since before sunrise. From the main pocket of her pack, she pulled out a Ziploc bag of tortillas, dried mango, and two small cans of tuna packed in oil. She peeled one open and dipped the tortilla in. The salt and fat were welcome.

She ate quickly, still standing. Then, digging into her bag, she retrieved her ghost laptop. Dropping it onto the mattress, she got down on all fours and peered underneath the cot. Using the light on her phone, she illuminated the far corners. There was dirt, dead leaves and the carcass of something long-dead. But no snakes.

The floorboards were ancient. It wasn't hard to pry her finger-tips beneath one and ease it up. With the phone light, she checked the space beneath. It was dry and dusty, with no signs of rodent nests. It would do for hiding equipment if she had to bail quickly.

She got up, dusted off her hands, then set up her laptop on the table by the window.

Out came the signal-booster antenna. It was handmade, cobbled together from radio junk and a salvaged solar array. She set it outside the window and angled it toward the southern ridge where the last usable cell tower stood. Barely half a bar, but that was enough. She unrolled the thin solar mat, its cells catching the last of the light, and plugged it into the battery pack humming on the floor. She waited as the machine booted up, the screen casting soft light in the gloom. Then she began to hunt. Not for anyone in particular, but for anyone looking for her.

She started with her digital tripwires. Each alias, burner account, and crypto transaction she'd ever abandoned had been embedded with trace triggers—harmless-looking scripts that, if activated, would ping her ghost laptop and tell her someone was poking around in places they didn't belong.

Nothing. Yet.

She leaned back in the hard chair and stretched her sore shoulders. Her legs still ached from the climb. She hesitated, then opened the final tool: a cloaked identity packet meant as bait. Just a username, tied to an innocuous-looking account buried in a low-traffic data pool. She'd never used it for anything real, but the breadcrumbs linked it, indirectly to the last known alias she'd used in México City.

If someone was digging for her, they'd find this.

She clicked "Deploy."

It was like sending a flare into the dark. Anyone watching the sky would see it. But only someone who knew what they were looking for would chase it.

Her fingers hovered over the keyboard. Maybe this was a mistake. Maybe she should've kept hiding. Waited them out.

But that was the thing about shadows. They didn't always pass. Sometimes, you had to step into the light and see what came running.

She encrypted the net, logged the ping trail, then closed the laptop.

The trap was set.

———

She pumped water from the rusted pipe outside the cabin and filled a battered kettle. The water was brownish at first, then cleared. She boiled it on the stove, poured half into a tin cup, and sat outside on the cabin step as dusk rolled in like smoke.

Night fell fast, all at once, as it did in the mountains. The horizon went from gold to indigo in minutes, and with it came the sounds. Insects hummed. Something with claws scrambled across the tin roof. In the trees beyond, something howled, high-pitched and wild. A coyote, maybe. Or a fox. But there were jaguars in these parts, too. The forest whispered all around her: crickets and creaking branches and something larger, slower, crashing through the brush in the distance. Maybe a boar. Maybe a big cat. Maybe nothing.

She wasn't good with fear. Not the primal kind. Out here, it wasn't the cartel that scared her the most. It was nature.

She drank, cradling the cup between her hands, and looked out over the trees. The scent of smoke from her wood stove drifted through the air. Then she got up and locked the door behind her. She stared at the darkened window for a moment, then shoved a wooden bench against the door, just in case.

She turned off the light and waited for the world to notice she was back.

FIFTEEN

LUCÍA LEANED against the low concrete wall, her blouse sticking to her back in the heat. The air tasted like sun-warmed asphalt and smog, but at least up here it was quiet.

She hadn't meant to come here. She'd just kept climbing stairs, past the top floor, through an unlocked maintenance door, until she'd found the sky.

Her badge hung around her neck, twisted and caught in the neckline of her shirt. Her head still buzzed with numbers, shell corporations, and off-shore trusts, like the code had crawled in behind her eyes and refused to leave.

She heard the door open behind her and didn't turn.

"You're not going to jump, are you?" came Mateo's voice. "Because if you are, I call dibs on your monitor."

Lucía let out a breath that was half a laugh, half exhaustion.

"Is this where you follow all the interns?"

"Only the ones who correct the trainers mid-presentation," he said, joining her at the ledge. "That was savage, by the way. You made Calderón visibly sweat."

"He was wrong."

"Absolutely. But most of us just pretend not to notice."

Lucía didn't smile. "Pretending isn't one of my skillsets."

Mateo studied her, then pulled a pack of mints from his pocket and offered one. She took it.

He leaned forward, elbows on the ledge. "You know, I was sure you were going to laugh in my face when I tried talking to you in the waiting room."

"You didn't try," she said. "You did."

"True. And you didn't laugh. That was encouraging."

Lucía glanced sideways at him. "You talk to everyone like this?"

"No. Just the intimidating ones."

She smiled despite herself. A small breeze lifted the edge of her blouse. The city stretched out before them, thousands of windows blinking in the sun.

"I've never worked somewhere like this," she said. "Everything's sharp. Cold. Perfectly curated."

Mateo nodded. "Feels like a place built to break people."

"That's comforting."

"I said 'feels like.' Not 'is.'"

She didn't reply.

Then he added, voice lower now, "Look, I don't know how long I'll last here. But you? You're going to eat this place alive."

Lucía dropped her gaze and gave a quick shake of her head. "You don't know me."

"I don't," he agreed. "But I know what it looks like when someone walks in and already has a bigger game in mind."

"What does it look like?"

His eyes roamed all over her face. There was something tender in his expression, something that made her think he was about to cross an invisible line between them. Her stomach clenched, and she groped blindly for a response to have ready, something that would put him off...or maybe encourage him. She hadn't made up her mind yet. She felt suddenly unprepared for this moment, like she was about to be asked a question by a teacher when she hadn't done the reading yet.

But just as he opened his mouth, the door behind them opened and Javier stepped onto the rooftop. He didn't look surprised to see them.

Lucía froze.

"Castillo," Javier said coolly, his eyes barely flicking to Mateo. "Back to your station."

Mateo stiffened. "Yes, *señor*."

He threw Lucía a glance—brief, but cautious—then left without another word.

When the door closed behind him, Javier crossed the roof in slow steps, hands in his pockets. "I didn't realize the break schedule included off-grid locations," he said.

Lucía swallowed. "I needed air."

"This isn't the air you want to breathe in this city," he said. "Too full of exhaust."

She said nothing.

Javier moved to the ledge beside her, close enough for her to feel the presence of him. Not touching. Just...close.

"You're settling in well," he said. "Your numbers are already outperforming second-years."

"Thank you."

"Castillo's clever, but distracted. He lacks discipline. You don't."

Lucía's throat was dry. "He's kind."

"Kindness has its uses. So does ruthlessness. You'll learn the difference soon enough."

She didn't look at him, but she could feel his gaze. It seemed to touch her skin like a hand. It wasn't appraisal. And it wasn't desire, not exactly.

It was possession.

"I should go back in," she said quietly.

He stepped aside, just enough for her to pass.

She did. But as she reached the door, he said softly behind her, "Watch the company you keep, Lucía. Not everyone is who they pretend to be."

She turned. He wasn't looking at her anymore, just at the skyline.

The moment hung there like smog. Then she stepped through the door and let it close behind her.

SIXTEEN

THE ROAD to Punta Prieta had crumbled in places, eaten away by years of salt wind. Ryan drove the borrowed pickup with the headlights off for the last mile, navigating by moonlight. The Pacific stretched black and immensely vast to the west, nothing but water and shadow all the way to the horizon.

He pulled off onto a gravel turnout and killed the engine. The wind came off the sea in gusts, thick with brine. Surf pounded the rocks below the cliff like a slow, angry heartbeat.

He checked his mirrors. No lights behind him. No sign he'd been followed. Still, he kept his hand near the pistol at his side as he got out and shut the door.

The path to the boat launch curved downward in loose gravel and coastal scrub. Crickets chirped in the underbrush, but otherwise, the night was still. The kind of stillness that pressed against your ribs. That made you feel like you were being watched.

He rounded a bend and saw the glow.

A single LED lantern lit up the small concrete dock that jutted like a broken finger over the cliff's edge. A battered skiff bobbed in the swell below, tied to a steel ring half-swallowed by moss. On the dock, a man sat cross-legged, his laptop open on a folded military blanket, a cigarette burning between his fingers.

Lázaro hadn't changed much. Skinny, black-eyed, wiry in a way that suggested coiled tension more than fragility. His beard was longer, peppered with grey now. He wore a ratty soccer jersey, faded jeans, and canvas shoes held together with duct tape.

He looked up as Ryan approached.

"You look like shit, Marshal," Lázaro said in heavily-accented English.

"I'm not a marshal anymore."

Lázaro's eyes flicked over him, boots worn down to nothing, road dust on his jeans, the tension in his shoulders that said he hadn't slept right in days. He took a drag, then exhaled. "Maybe not by title. But you've still got the look. The posture."

Ryan didn't answer. He crouched beside him, eyes scanning the screen. Lázaro's interface was minimal—lines of code, ping logs, node trees branching like veins.

"What are we looking at?"

"A ghost net echo. Something crawled out of the dark." He tapped a line. "Alias tied to a defunct crypto wallet. Dead for two years. Then it lit up. A ping from the Oaxaca subnet. Rural node. Hill country."

Ryan frowned. "Could be anyone."

"Sure. Could be a fluke. But the metadata signature matches a packet I saw back in the Sinaloa dumps. And the routing obfuscation is…elegant. Not cartel. Not amateur either. This is a woman who doesn't just hide. She vanishes and makes you forget she was ever real."

"So it's her."

"It's someone like her. And she wants people to find her." He raised an eyebrow. "Or she wants them to try."

"Can you trace the node?"

"Best I can do is region. It's dirty, rural. No direct coordinates. But she slipped. Just enough. Might've been on purpose. That's the thing about bait—you gotta leave it bleeding a little."

Lázaro typed something and the map zoomed in on a band of mountains east of Oaxaca City. Remote. Sparse.

"She's up there?"

"I'd bet money. Which I don't have, so you know I'm serious."

Ryan stood, the sea wind tugging at his clothes. The waves below crashed with that same hypnotic rhythm, relentless, patient. "How long do I have before someone else finds that breadcrumb?"

"Could be days. Could be hours. Depends on how many people are watching."

Ryan turned toward the path, already picturing the mountain terrain, the kinds of places someone like Lucía might hide. Remote trailheads. Abandoned logging cabins. Places with no signal and no exit strategy.

"Send me everything."

Lázaro didn't move.

"You're sure you want to chase this? You said yourself, you're not the guy who hunts bad guys anymore, Inglis. You're just another one of us now."

"I don't have time to question it."

Lázaro ground out the cigarette. Then he pulled a flash drive from his pocket. "Here. One-time loadout. Burn it after."

"Thanks."

"Don't thank me. If she's as smart as I think she is, you're walking into a trap."

Ryan looked down the path again, heart ticking faster now.

"Maybe," he said. "But at least it's one I can see coming."

SEVENTEEN

HUMMING. There was a humming sound coming from… somewhere. It was soft and low but growing louder.

Lucía woke with a start. The cot creaked beneath her as she bolted upright, breath catching in her throat. Her tank top was damp with sweat. The cabin was still dark, the faintest sliver of blue at the window marking the hour before dawn.

The sound was a low buzz coming from her laptop.

She flung off the covers and dropped into the chair, bare feet hitting floor. The screen flared to life.

Tripwire triggered.

Her stomach dropped. One of her cloaked identities—one she'd left dangling as bait—had been pinged.

She pulled up the data trail. The access signature was layered, stacked with enough VPNs and route bounces to make most analysts give up.

But she wasn't most analysts.

She parsed the signature again. It wasn't cartel. Too careful. She scrubbed deeper, looking for code patterns. The metadata was precise. Calculated. Like a field op running tech support. Fast, clean, professional, but not the kind of chaotic aggression cartel traffickers used when probing for targets.

Government?

No. Not directly. Too freelance. But good.

Her breath slowed. Her fingers hovered over the trackpad. "They sent someone," she whispered. She stared at the screen, her own reflection ghosted in the black background.

It wasn't the cartel coming in with guns blazing. Not yet. Whoever this was had taken the bait, and now they were moving. Which meant she wasn't safe. Not even here.

But she knew the trail now. And this time, she wouldn't wait to be caught.

EIGHTEEN

FROM THE MOMENT Lázaro handed him the flash drive, Ryan had been moving. He drove south to Guerrero Negro, then from there he paid cash to a man with a skiff to cross the narrow sea at dawn. They docked at Santa Rosalía, a dust-coated town clinging to the coast.

From there, a night bus inland. Three hours of bouncing over half-paved roads beside a family of goats and a drunk who sang *corridos* in his sleep. At first light, he hit the Guaymas airport and bribed his way onto a cargo flight heading toward Oaxaca. The plane touched down just after four p.m.

Then came the final leg.

A rusted Nissan 4x4 rented under a false name took him most of the way up into the Sierra Norte. The last ten kilometers were too rough for the truck's suspension, so he parked at a forgotten trailhead and went the rest of the way on foot.

Now, after nearly a full day of nonstop movement, he was deep in the Oaxacan highlands, somewhere in the misty folds of the Sierra Norte. The daylight was fading. His margin was closing.

The sun had disappeared behind the jagged peaks, leaving the forest in deep cobalt shadow. Ryan moved fast, but was careful to avoid a twisted ankle or burning through too much of his water supply. The GPS on his burner phone had cut out an hour ago, and there was no cell signal. But he had Lázaro's instructions from the flash drive he'd given him, and his own hand-sketched map gave him a rough heading.

He adjusted the strap of his pack. Inside: water, protein bars, a compact med kit, backup ammo and his Walther PPK.

His breath came even. His boots crunched pine needles. Somewhere far off, an owl called.

Ryan crouched by a narrow bend in the trail and studied the terrain ahead.

The trees thinned here. There was smoke on the wind, thin and faint, like someone had let a cooking fire die down slowly. Not enough to be careless. But just enough to mark the presence of life.

He checked the wind. South-to-north. Good. He'd stay downwind.

He moved forward, slower now. On either side of the trail, the underbrush was disturbed in places—unnaturally symmetrical gaps, the kind made by a human hand. Ryan's eyes caught the faint glint of a wire strung knee-height between two branches. He froze, followed the line, and saw the small metal canister tucked under a rotted stump.

Nonlethal. Flashbang, maybe. He disarmed it with a stick, careful not to shift his weight too far off the trail.

She was expecting company.

Another thirty meters forward, he stepped over what looked like an innocuous pile of leaves. Beneath it, a shallow pit lined with broken bottles and thorns. Crude, but effective. Ryan felt the smallest curl of admiration. This wasn't just paranoia. This was strategy. She'd been busy up here.

At the tree line, he pulled the pistol from his pack and chambered a round with quiet, practiced hands. He didn't like carrying it drawn. But walking into an unknown perimeter, alone and outgunned, meant bending rules he used to live by. He kept it low and close as he advanced, every step tested before committing.

There were signs of passage here: a broken branch, the faint indent of a boot print in the loam. Recent.

The forest fell away to reveal a gulch in the hillside. The cabin sat in its hollow, almost perfectly camouflaged. A sloped metal roof with a small solar panel patched on one side. No light was visible from within.

But she was in there. He could feel it.

Ryan eased behind a boulder and pulled a monocular from his side pouch. Through the lens, he scanned the perimeter. One entrance. No motion. The trail leading to the door had been brushed recently, but not well enough to hide the signs from someone who knew what to look for.

He holstered the scope and backed off three steps, deciding on an approach. That's when he felt it. The chill up his spine. The sense of being watched.

He turned, too late.

A sharp voice behind him: "Don't move."

Then the pressure of a gun barrel between his shoulder blades.

"Drop the weapon. Slowly."

Ryan didn't argue.

He let the PPK fall to the mossy ground. Raised his hands.

Behind him, a woman stepped into view, shadows clinging to her like a second skin. Her dark hair was tied back, her expression unreadable. The gun in her hand didn't waver.

"You have three seconds to tell me who you are," she said, in softly-accented English, "or I paint the trees with your skull."

Ryan's mouth twisted into a wry smile.

"Nice to meet you, too, Lucía."

NINETEEN

THE MUZZLE OF the gun never shook. Ryan kept his eyes glued to it. In her small hands, the thing looked like a cannon. The recoil alone would probably set her on her ass. But her voice had been calm, measured, and there was no mistaking the threat in it. Ryan had spent a good amount of time staring down killers, and he knew the most dangerous ones weren't loud. They were quiet. Certain.

He raised his hands slowly, palms open.

"Back toward the cabin," she said.

Ryan obeyed. The slope was uneven beneath his boots, the trail loose with pine needles and small stones, but she tracked him with precision.

Up close, she was smaller than he'd expected. Five foot five, maybe. But there was no mistaking the intent in her stance. Eyes sharp, mouth tense. Her shoulders moved like someone used to being hunted.

He reached the cabin door.

"Open it. Slowly."

He did.

The interior was dim, lit only by the glow from a solar lantern on the table. Sparse setup—cot, table, laptop. Survival gear, stacked and clean.

Lucía stepped in behind him and kicked the door shut. Then she gestured to the chair at the table.

"Sit."

Ryan moved slowly. She didn't flinch.

The zip-ties came next. She grabbed them from a bag on the table, near the lantern, and he noted how quickly she tied him off. Not pro-level, but practiced. One looped around his wrists, another cinching them to the back of the chair, then two more securing his ankles to the legs.

"You tie everyone up before asking their name first?" he muttered.

She said nothing. But she came closer. Close enough that he could smell the trace of sweat on her skin. Her hands were steady as she checked each tie.

Ryan sat still, letting her work. Letting her feel in control. He wasn't sure how trigger-happy she was, but he was sure of this: one wrong word and she'd put a bullet in him and vanish by morning.

She stepped back and finally spoke. "You're tracking me."

"I didn't say that."

"You didn't have to."

She circled him slowly, like she was inspecting a bomb. Or deciding where to place the first hole.

"Who sent you?"

"No one sent me."

"Then who are you?" she demanded.

Ryan hesitated. He considered giving her one of the many aliases he'd used since crossing the border two years ago. Then it occurred to him that his cover had already been blown to fuck, so it hardly mattered anymore what she called him. So, it may as well be the truth. "Ryan Inglis."

"Should I know that name?"

"Not unless you've been watching U.S. Marshals' Most

Wanted lists."

She stared at him. No flicker of recognition.

"Why are you here, Ryan Inglis?"

Good question. He wasn't exactly sure what he'd expected to happen when he found her. He'd imagined confronting her, maybe scaring her into talking. He'd hoped she'd be innocent— just a name on a list, someone swept into something she didn't understand. And if she wasn't?

Then he'd do what he had to. Buy time. Stall. Figure out why she mattered so much. Maybe contact the people who sent the burner phone. Maybe not. The plan had never been clear.

But now, tied to a chair in a stranger's cabin, with a gun in his face and no backup coming, the fog around that plan felt a whole lot thicker.

"Because someone's coming after both of us," he said. "And they're not going to knock."

Her jaw flexed. She pressed the barrel of the gun to the side of his neck. The sensation was ice.

"You work for them?"

"Who?"

"The ones coming for me."

Ryan swallowed. "No."

"Then who the fuck are you working for?"

"No one. Not anymore."

For a second, she looked almost disappointed.

He stared at her, blood pounding. She was close now. He could see the curve of her neck, the rapid rise and fall of her chest, the sweat at her temple. Close enough that he could smell the heat coming off her skin.

She studied his face like she was trying to decide what kind of man he was. Whether he would break easy. Whether he deserved mercy.

Her finger twitched against the trigger. Her jaw pulsed, but her expression didn't change.

He tensed, ready to twist, to kick, anything—

Then: *buzz.*

A vibration.

Lucía flinched.

The second burner phone. The one the kidnappers had left him.

Buzz. Buzz. Then silence.

She stepped back and looked down.

It was in his jacket pocket. Keeping her body as far from his as she could, she reached in carefully and pulled it free. The screen lit with a single new message.

Her eyes flicked up to his. "Who gave you this?"

Ryan stared at the phone. Then back at her. "That's what I came to find out."

———

Lucía turned the burner phone in her hand, her pulse throbbing behind her ears.

1 new message.

She tapped the screen. A line of text appeared in blocky white letters against a black background: "Clock's ticking. Find Lucía Duarte or the boy dies."

The message dissolved after three seconds, replaced by the blank home screen.

Her breath snagged. She stared at the screen as it went black. "Who gave you this?" she demanded, turning back to the man in the chair.

But he wasn't in the chair. The zip ties lay on the floor. Snapped in half.

Her stomach plummeted. Then a hand caught her wrist, spun her. The phone hit the floor.

She twisted, fast, but not fast enough. His body pressed into hers, one arm braced across her chest, the other wrapping her gun hand. Her Colt clattered to the floorboards.

She sucked in a sharp breath.

"Easy," he said, voice low, urgent. "I'm not here to hurt you."

His grip wasn't crushing, but it was firm. Unrelenting.

She pushed back, but his body was like a wall. Tall, hard-muscled through his shirt.

"Take your hands off me."

"Only if you stop pointing guns at me."

His breath was at her ear. His heartbeat, steady. Unshaken.

The cabin was too small. Too quiet. She could smell the sweat on him, the faint trace of something under it, gun oil, maybe. Her body was responding in ways she hadn't prepared for. Not here. Not now.

"How?" she hissed. "The zip ties—"

"Plastic weakens in heat. It gets brittle. A little leverage, it pops."

Damn it.

Her pulse thudded. She was breathing too fast.

"Are you going to kill me?"

He didn't answer immediately. His grip loosened just enough to let her turn.

They were face to face now. Inches apart. His eyes were bright blue, guarded but not cold.

"No," he said. "I came here to talk."

She could strike. Knee to the groin. Elbow to the jaw. But she didn't.

He released her slowly. She didn't move.

He bent and retrieved her gun but didn't raise it. They stood in silence, tension snapping between them like electricity.

Lucía stepped back, reclaiming the space. Her hand brushed the edge of the table, grounding her. "Then talk."

His eyes flicked to the burner phone on the floor, still dark. "They sent me to find you. I didn't know why. Not at first. But now I think we have the same enemy."

Her hands trembled slightly. Not from fear. From adrenaline. From proximity.

"You think I'm just going to believe that?"

"No," he said. "But you don't have a lot of options left."

She stared at him. He was right. She hated that. "Sit down. Over there."

He did.

She dropped into the opposite chair, the air between them still humming.

"You have five minutes," she said.

"That's all I need."

TWENTY

LUCÍA SAT STIFFLY in the wooden chair, painfully aware that her gun was now in Ryan Inglis's possession. He held it calmly at his side, not pointed at her, but its absence from her own lap left her feeling exposed in a way that had nothing to do with weapons.

Across from her, he leaned forward, forearms braced on his knees. Still as stone. Watching her like a man waiting for a verdict. The burner phone sat between them, screen black now, as if the message had never existed.

Clock's ticking. Find Lucía Duarte or the boy dies.

She ran the words again in her head. They hadn't said it to her. They'd said it about her. To him.

"Start from the beginning," she said.

Ryan nodded once. Then he started to talk.

He told her about the first video. The surveillance footage. The boy playing soccer in a Tennessee yard. The woman—his ex-wife's mother—in the background.

Lucía didn't interrupt. But she watched him closely. The tight line of his jaw. The way he said the name *Noah* like it hurt.

"He's your son?" she asked quietly.

Ryan shook his head. "Not mine. I barely know him. Kylie and

I, we had a complicated relationship. We were kids when we got married. Things went sideways fast. After she died… I thought he was safe. With her mother."

"And now he's not."

He exhaled through his nose. "No."

Lucía leaned back. The chair creaked beneath her. "So they want me. And they're using the boy as leverage."

"Looks that way."

"Why not just come for me directly?"

He shrugged. "Maybe they couldn't find you. Maybe they want something from you and they don't want to risk killing you by accident."

She stared at him. "They want the ledger."

"What ledger?"

She hesitated. Then shook her head. "Doesn't matter. Point is, they want it. And they think I still have it."

"Do you?"

She looked away. "I had pieces. The last of them was uploaded yesterday. There's nothing left." The lie rolled off her tongue with surprising ease.

He leaned back now too, letting the silence stretch. "They think you're still valuable. That makes you bait."

She nodded slowly. "And you're the hook."

"More like the line," he said dryly. "I don't think they care what happens to me once I've done my job."

Lucía laced her fingers together and rested her hands on the table. For a long moment, she didn't speak. But her mind raced. He was waiting for instructions from kidnappers, men she could only assume were cartel. And she was the package to be delivered. The leverage was obvious: if he turned her over, he might get the boy back.

So she had to make herself more useful than the ransom.

"You said they'll contact you again," she said, voice careful. "But you don't know what they'll say. What if they want proof? What if they want you to bring me in?"

He didn't flinch. But his silence told her enough.

"I might be able to find the boy," she added quickly. "Faster than they can."

His eyes narrowed. "How?"

"I don't know yet. But I can trace financial pings, encrypted messaging, network activity—anything. If they're moving him, there'll be a footprint. No matter how careful they are."

It wasn't just survival. It was the boy. His name—Noah—had stuck in her head like a splinter. If there was a way to help him and not die trying, she'd take it.

It hung between them, a lifeline hastily braided, already fraying.

He said nothing, just scrolled his eyes over her face. She didn't like being looked at, and the way he was doing it was deeply unsettling.

"Well?" she prompted.

———

Ryan hadn't moved. Not since she made the offer.

Lucía sat across from him, hands still folded on the table. Her eyes tracked him, waiting. She wasn't fidgeting. She didn't look scared. But he could tell she knew she was vulnerable.

He had her gun. Not pointed at her. But it was there, clasped lightly in his hands. The ball was very much in his court.

He got the sense that she wasn't used to that. Wasn't used to not being in control, of not being the smartest, most capable person in the room. He gathered from the way she spoke there hadn't been many occasions when she wasn't. He studied her face, reading her: calm exterior, looking for possible signs of internal damage.

You have five days. Two, at most, left now.

And Lucía's voice echoed: *I can find him faster than they can.*

Could she?

He didn't know her from a hole in the wall. He sure as shit

didn't trust her. But she hadn't begged. She hadn't bargained. She'd laid out a plan, sharp and fast.

And she'd flinched when he mentioned the boy. Not the way someone flinches when their own life is in danger. The way someone flinches when they recognize a life that shouldn't be wasted.

He looked down at her gun, turning it over in his hands. "Colt 1911. Doesn't seem like…you."

Her gaze sharpened. "How on earth would you know what seems like me?"

He shrugged. When it came to weapons, he just knew. She seemed like the kind of person who'd favor something efficient and unremarkable. Sleek. Modern. A Glock, maybe. Not this—an old slab-sided relic from a bygone era.

Her eyes dropped to the weapon. "It was my grandfather's. Then my dad's. I've had it with me since…"

She trailed off, but he caught the words she hadn't said, or some variation of them anyway. *Since I had to leave. In a hurry.*

A relic, maybe. But people didn't carry their past for nothing. Especially not when it weighed this much. He knew, because he'd had to do the same. More than once. And he'd watched others do it, too.

"You don't trust me," she said.

"No."

"I don't trust you either."

"Good."

They sat in silence again.

"If you double-cross me," he said quietly, "there won't be a second warning."

Lucía didn't blink. "Noted."

He nodded once. Lifted her gun and slid it across the table.

She took it with one hand. Didn't aim it at him. Didn't thank him, either. But something passed between them in that moment. Not trust.

Something else.

He said, "They're holding a kid. They need somewhere secure. Low visibility, but accessible. Somewhere they already control."

She nodded. "If that upload rattled the right cages, I might be able to see who's moving money or scrambling to cover their tracks. That might give us a location, or at least a chain of names." She got to her feet. "If I can get us to a connection point, somewhere quiet, I can try to trace who moved after the upload."

He stood up too. "Then let's move before they beat us to it."

The air was heavy with adrenaline. He could feel her heat as she brushed past him, walking toward the bed where her pack was laying.

They didn't have a plan yet. Not really.

But they had a pact. And sometimes, that was enough to start a war.

TWENTY-ONE
NINE YEARS AGO

"TELL me that line doesn't look off," Mateo muttered, pointing at the screen. "Right there. That transfer loop."

Lucía leaned closer, squinting. "It's a recursive shell."

He nodded. "Exactly."

"It's not an error. It's a masking sequence."

"Yeah. But why would a customs brokerage in Veracruz need that much masking?"

Lucía didn't answer. Her fingers hovered over the keyboard, then withdrew.

Mateo sat back and folded his arms. "I don't like it."

"Then don't poke at it."

"Seriously?"

Lucía finally met his eyes. "You want to stay employed?"

"I want to know what the hell we're actually working on."

"This isn't new, Mateo. Every intern here knows the game. We tidy the fronts. We make things pretty on paper."

"Pretty's not the word I'd use for this."

Lucía looked away.

He softened his tone. "I know you see it, too."

"It's none of our business," she said quietly. "We have contracts."

Mateo leaned in. "You think contracts matter to people like Esquivel?"

That caught her attention.

He tilted his head. "You really think he doesn't know what we've seen in those logs? The redundancies? The offshore payouts? Come on. It's a washing machine. Just a fancy one."

Lucía's silence said enough.

Mateo reached out and gently closed the laptop. "You're scared."

"I'm cautious."

"No," he said. "You're smart. There's a difference."

She stood, pacing toward the windows. Below them, the city glittered like a mirage. Somewhere out there was the version of her that hadn't taken this job. She wondered what she would have been doing. Maybe she was out on a date with a hot guy, which was something this version of her hadn't done in forever.

Mateo's voice was quiet behind her. "He watches you, you know. Esquivel."

Lucía turned slowly.

"Everyone sees it," he went on. "You think it's subtle, but it's not. He looks at you like you belong to him."

Her face didn't change, but something in her shoulders tightened.

"He's never touched me," she said.

"That doesn't mean he hasn't made a claim."

She didn't respond. Only crossed her arms, holding herself in the silence.

Mateo stood now too, closing the distance between them, but not invading it.

"Lucía," he said softly. "I know it's not my place. But if you ever need out, if something happens, I want you to know I'd help you."

She met his eyes.

The affection there was quiet, steady. Not obsessive. Not *possessive*. Just...real.

And she wanted to believe in it. She wanted to believe in someone. So she stepped closer, close enough to smell the cologne on his collar, faint and clean. For one moment, it felt like she might reach for him. Let herself fall toward the safer gravity.

But then, down the hall, the elevator chimed.

She tensed. A long pause followed. No footsteps. Mateo looked toward the corridor. When he turned back, Lucía was already gathering her things.

He didn't press. He just watched her go.

TWENTY-TWO

LUCÍA PACKED her things in silence. She hadn't spoken since they agreed to work together. Ryan sat a few feet away by the door, silent, checking over his gear but never fully taking his eyes off her. He wasn't hovering, but he wasn't leaving her alone either. Maybe he was giving her space. Or maybe he just didn't trust her enough to let her out of his sight.

She zipped the bag, then sat heavily on the edge of the cot. She'd spent nine years vanishing. Building walls between herself and the world. Moving like a shadow through digital corridors and dusty roads. And now she was choosing to surface. To act.

With a man she didn't know, let alone trust.

She snuck a glance at him while pretending to focus on rechecking that her pistol was still loaded. Annoyingly, his handsomeness was still the first thing her brain decided to flag every time she looked at him. Annoying, *and* stupid. *Okay, so he's attractive,* she chided herself. *He looks like a cowboy off the cover of one of my mom's old Mills and Boons. Complete with the baby blues and the jawline that could chisel ice.*

She focused instead on his less superficial traits. To build a character profile of him. He had the look of someone who'd buried more than one body for the badge. But there was something behind his eyes when he talked about the boy. Not desperation exactly. Not guilt. Something harder. More enduring. Like he'd carried a thousand regrets and was trying not to add this one to the pile.

She shoved her Colt into a side compartment of her backpack, then leaned forward and rubbed her hands over her face. Her stomach churned.

She wasn't supposed to care. Not about strangers. Not about kids she'd never met. But the thought of that boy—frightened, alone, used as leverage by monsters like El Escriba—made her sick. Mateo had always been the bleeding heart. The one who'd pushed her to see there was a human cost behind the misplaced numbers, the false invoices and fake payrolls. The one who'd convinced her that flagging those wire transfers was as good a way as taking out the cartel's stranglehold on their city as going in all guns blazing.

The memory of him hit her like a bruise. Her throat tightened. She pushed the thought away, then returned her focus to her packing.

———

Ryan crouched by the door, checking his gear for the third time. The mag of his weapon was full. The safety clicked cleanly. His pack was well stocked with all the bare essentials for disappearing again if this all went to hell.

Which it probably would.

Behind him, Lucía moved quietly, zipping compartments and coiling cables. He didn't watch her directly, but he could almost feel her movements. She wore anonymity like armor: hair tied tight, no makeup, clothes that were clearly designed to make her look anonymous. Forgettable. She needed to try harder in that regard. The thin black turtleneck sweater and low-slung cargo pants she was wearing did nothing to make her anything but immediately memorable to anyone who appreciated the female form. And her lack of makeup just highlighted how her attractiveness was natural.

He forced his attention back on checking his kit, which didn't need checking. He didn't trust her. But he'd agreed to her plan, and now he was betting everything on a woman he'd known for less than an hour.

The thought almost made him snort out loud. He bit back a smile at the irony. He had known Jessica Meeks for a grand total of three days before he'd nearly thrown everything away for her. He was going to beat his own record.

But the alternative was handing her over to people who'd kidnapped a child. Or maybe being forced to kill her himself.

Lucía thought she could trace the boy. She'd sounded confident, maybe even sincere. But confidence didn't mean shit in the real world. The cartel had deeper pockets and more bodies. They could buy time. They could buy blood. He'd seen what they left behind.

What worried him wasn't just the cartel. It was what would happen if the two of them succeeded. Because if they found the boy and saved him, what then?

He was still a fugitive. Still a man with a burn notice from his own government. If he handed Noah over to the authorities, he'd be arrested on the spot. And if he tried to run again, with a kid in tow—one that wasn't even his—he'd be hunted harder than ever.

His freedom was already a fiction. This plan—Lucía's plan— just chained him tighter to the consequences. He didn't want to think about what would happen if they failed.

He scrubbed a hand over his jaw, the rasp of stubble grounding him. Then he straightened, reached into the side pocket of his pack and pulled out the kidnapper's burner phone. He'd done what they'd asked, he'd found Lucía Duarte. But whatever their further instructions were, he didn't want to hear them.

Crossing to the table, he set it down. Lucía didn't say anything, but when he looked up, her gaze had shifted briefly to the phone. Then to him. Her expression seemed to relax, if only for a second. She gave a tiny nod.

He straightened, rolled his shoulders, and checked the time. Not long until first light.

Lucía moved to join him, boots quiet on the floor.

He opened the cabin door and led the way outside. The mountain air bit at his skin, sharp and cold. The first sliver of dawn split the horizon, painting the treetops in pale light.

Ryan paused, turning to look at her. "You ready?"

Lucía nodded. "As I'll ever be."

TWENTY-THREE

THE CLEANING STAFF had come and gone. The outer offices were dark, their glass walls reflecting fragments of city light. Even the servers had quieted, their usual humming softened to a low murmur beneath the raised flooring.

Lucía sat curled in her chair, knees drawn up under her, eyes rimmed with exhaustion. Her screen glowed softly against her face, lines of code blinking like a living organism. Every few seconds, a simulation refreshed. Each time, it ran cleaner than the last.

Her final bug—a recursive routing loop that buried six entities deep in a shell structure—was dead. She'd killed it an hour ago, and still she couldn't make herself stop watching the data flow like water down a mountain.

This was it. The system model was complete. A full-spectrum simulation that could predict, flag, and trace movement through offshore holdings across multiple jurisdictions with minimal noise.

It shouldn't have been possible. But she'd done it.

She leaned back, dragging her fingers through her hair, still twisted into a loose bun at the nape of her neck. Her blouse was wrinkled. Her mascara had long since worn off. She didn't care.

She'd never felt more alive.

A soft voice came from behind her.

"You solved it."

She startled, turning in her chair.

Javier Esquivel stood just inside the doorway. His suit jacket was gone, sleeves rolled to the elbow. The top buttons of his shirt were undone. He looked as he always did: controlled, elegant, utterly unreadable. And painfully good-looking.

Lucía scrambled to sit properly, brushing invisible lint from her skirt. "I didn't realize anyone else was still here."

"I wasn't," he said. "But Espinoza flagged the server activity. He said someone was pushing your simulations past the cap. I assumed it was you."

She flushed. "I didn't mean to overrun the limit. I'll throttle back the—"

He held up a hand, stopping her. "No need. If the cap couldn't handle your work, the cap was wrong."

Lucía blinked.

He crossed the room slowly, folding his arms as he stopped beside her desk. His black eyes flicked across her screen.

"This is the deep-structure model," he said, more statement than question.

Lucía nodded. "I got the blind routing fix to work. It replicates how the shell accounts use intentional misalignment with tax jurisdictions, like you suggested. I nested it inside a parallel index that breaks anytime an observer tries to reverse-engineer it in real time. That was the trick."

He was silent for a beat. Then: "Show me."

Her throat tightened. "Now?"

He smiled, and it almost reached his eyes. "Unless you've got dinner plans."

She definitely didn't. And even if she had, she would have canceled them.

He nodded once toward the glass hallway. "Come. Let's look at it properly."

Lucía hesitated for only a moment. Then she grabbed her laptop and followed him. The click of her heels echoed softly in the dark.

———

Lucía set her laptop down on the conference table and tried not to notice her own reflection in its polished glass.

Javier moved around the table slowly, adjusting the angle of the nearest chair so it faced her more directly. Then he sat, long limbs relaxed, one ankle casually hooked over his knee.

"Begin," he said.

She opened the simulation, voice steady despite the rapid thud of her heart. "So the issue with the previous trace models was always the noise. Too many false positives, especially when dealing with multi-jurisdictional flows. But if you—"

"Where did you get the idea for the nesting failsafe?"

She hesitated, then gave a half-shrug. "I was thinking about shell games. Street hustlers. How they keep their mark guessing but also give them just enough pattern to follow…just enough to feel confident they're winning."

His eyes sparked with amusement. "You've been watching street hustlers?"

"I grew up near street markets," she said. "They're unavoidable."

Javier chuckled low in his throat. "I always said good engineering begins with good crime."

She smiled involuntarily.

They continued for another five minutes, Lucía walking him through the layers. He never looked away from her. Not even to glance at the code. It was like he was watching her explain herself, not just her work.

When she finished, she realized she'd been leaning forward, breathless. She closed the lid of the laptop, cheeks warm.

He didn't move. He only said, "Brilliant."

Lucía's mouth opened, then closed again. The word hung in the air like a trick of acoustics.

"Do you know how rare it is," he said quietly, "to meet someone who can not only build something elegant...but understand what it truly is? What it means?"

Lucía swallowed. "I think so."

"No," he said, his voice dropping, "you don't."

He reached out and, with two fingers, gently lifted a lock of hair that had fallen loose near her temple.

Lucía froze.

He didn't tuck it behind her ear. He simply held it. Studied it. Studied her.

Then, after a heartbeat that stretched too long: "You should go home."

Lucía nodded, throat dry. "Yes."

He released the strand of hair.

She gathered her things with hands that didn't tremble until she was facing away from him. As she stepped into the hallway, he didn't follow. He didn't need to.

He'd already made sure she would never forget this night.

TWENTY-FOUR

LUCÍA AND RYAN left the cabin before sunrise, hiking down the narrow trail in silence, neither quite ready to break the fragile agreement they'd made. The sun had been nothing more than a dull glow behind the trees then, but by the time they reached the bottom of the ridge and hitched a ride with a produce truck heading west, the heat was already building. The ride was slow, bumpy, and smelled like onions. The truck hit the outskirts of a town with a leaning sign and a single cellphone tower.

Civilization, Lucía thought.

"Food," Ryan said, nodding at a roadside café.

He hailed the driver to stop and they got out, lugging their packs in tow, which doubled as a disguise: to a casual observer, they looked like backpackers. A couple, maybe. Him American, her a local. As much as Lucía wanted a shower and to wash her hair, she knew better than to draw attention to herself by trying to look clean, rested, or soft. As much as it grossed her out, dirt and fatigue were a kind of disguise.

The café had peeling turquoise walls and plastic tables, and the only thing worse than the Wi-Fi was the coffee. But Lucía had made do with less.

She sat at the far end of the open-air patio, one foot hooked around the leg of her chair, her back to the wall. The laptop was open on the table in front of her, antenna angled to steal whatever signal she could. The screen glowed with her improvised data trap: a digital fishing hook cast into cartel waters. Her hands moved quickly, shoulders tight.

Across the table from her, Ryan chewed the last bite of his *torta al pastor* and pushed aside the empty plate. He hadn't said much during the meal, too busy inhaling it like a man who hadn't eaten properly in days. She couldn't blame him. Her own plate was scraped clean.

He watched her without a word now. She could feel him more than see him, elbows resting on the table. He hadn't touched his coffee. Or blinked much, for that matter.

"You're staring again," she said without looking up.

"Just trying to figure out if you're actually doing something or pretending real hard."

She arched an eyebrow. "You want to do this part?"

"I'd rather have a root canal."

"Then hush."

A flicker of movement on the screen caught her eye in a darknet node she'd been monitoring since the Alpha_C3 drop. The timing was right. The encryption pattern too close to be coincidence.

Her pulse kicked. She tapped into the stream, fingers flying.

"What is it?" Ryan asked, sitting forward.

"Something just moved. A dummy account. Only it's not dummy anymore. Someone logged in."

"Who?"

"Too soon to tell. But it's cartel-connected. Could be someone involved with moving money related to the kid."

"Can you trace it?"

"Not fully. But I can isolate the access route and see what city the signal passed through before hitting the chain."

She paused. Zoomed in.

Salina Cruz.

"There we go," she murmured.

Ryan leaned in. "That's something, right?" he said.

She nodded slowly. "It's a lead."

She glanced up and their eyes connected in a way that almost felt physical. She suddenly felt hyperaware of him. Of the way he smelled like dust and sweat and soap. Of how close his hand was to hers.

There was a time and a place for such observations, and this sure as hell wasn't one of them.

She cleared her throat. "We'll need to access public records next. Trace the ownership of that shell company."

"And you think that'll lead us to the boy?"

She exhaled. "It might. And if not, it'll lead us to whoever's moving money to keep this operation afloat."

Ryan leaned back, nodding slowly. "I guess you are pretty good at this."

She sat back in her chair. "My father used to say numbers never lie. People always did."

One of his eyebrows spiked and his lips curved up in a smirk. "And I thought I had trust issues."

She tore her eyes away from his mouth. "Then I guess we go to Salina Cruz."

Lucía saved the logs and disconnected. As she packed up the laptop, she felt his eyes on her again, not hard this time. Not suspicious. Just watching.

She didn't like how aware she was of it.

TWENTY-FIVE

NINE YEARS AGO

THE OFFICE WAS ALMOST unrecognizable after hours. Gone was the whirr of printers, the dry shuffle of paper, the low clatter of keys. The air felt thicker, stiller. Only a few lights remained on, strategic pools of glow that made the hallways seem longer and the shadows deeper.

Lucía stood outside Javier's office door, smoothing her blouse. She wore black tonight, a high-neck silk shell tucked into fitted slacks, and no jewelry but the slim silver watch she never took off. Her hair was pulled back sharply, as if the right hairstyle could armor her against the undercurrent of whatever this was.

The meeting had been scheduled that morning. A calendar invite. No details. Just:

7:30PM – Esquivel. Mandatory.

She knocked once.

"Enter."

Javier sat behind his desk in a dark shirt—the cuffs rolled neatly to mid-forearm, no jacket, the top button undone.

She stepped in. The door clicked shut behind her.

He didn't rise.

"Sit," he said, gesturing to the chair across from him. His tone was easy. Even…casual. But the air felt wrong.

Lucía sat and crossed her legs, trying to appear composed.

Javier picked up a pen and gestured to the portfolio. The desk was mostly clear except for one thick, bound portfolio. "You've been working on this case, yes? The restructuring of the Biomarx shell network?"

"Yes. I updated the compliance map last week. And flagged the three accounts that didn't reconcile against the Costa Rica filings."

A small smile touched the corner of his mouth. "I saw. No one else caught that."

"I know," she said, before she could stop herself. Then flushed.

Javier leaned back slightly in his chair. "You're aware the entire Lima division botched the offshore filings. Not just the transfers, but the timestamping. That error could've cost us twelve million in retroactive penalties."

"I was just—" Lucía started.

"Looking," he interrupted, but not unkindly. "You look deeper than most." His eyes met hers. "And you understand what you're looking at."

Lucía felt the skin along her forearms ripple. She swallowed. "I try to."

"No. You do." He tapped the pen once on the desk. "It's rare. Rarer than beauty. And your beauty, Ms. Duarte, is already rare enough."

There it was again. That slow, disarming cadence. The way he said her name like he enjoyed the feel of it in his mouth.

Lucía's pulse picked up speed. She tried to hide it by shifting in her chair. "Is there something wrong with the portfolio?"

"No. You did well."

Lucía's throat felt suddenly dry.

He didn't look at the documents. He looked at her. "You know what I admire most about you?" he asked.

She said nothing.

"You're not impressed by power. Not in the way most people are. You're intrigued by it. You want to understand how it works.

You want to reverse-engineer it." He tilted his head. "You want to build your own."

Lucía's mouth parted, but no answer came.

He rose to his feet and walked slowly around the desk toward her. Had he always been this tall? This imposing? Her head dropped back to take him all in.

"You thought I didn't notice?" he asked, softly. "The way you study everything. Everyone. Even me."

Lucía's gaze dropped for half a second.

He noticed. Of course he did. "Good," he said.

Then he looked down at her and said, quietly: "But you're still a little afraid of me."

He wasn't touching her—he wasn't even that close to her— and yet she felt glued to her seat. She lifted her eyes to meet his. "Maybe."

"Good," he said again, and then he leaned down over her, placing both hands over her wrists on the armrests. His touch was light, but he was still pinning her in place.

The silence stretched. Heavy. Charged. Lucía's breath came shallow now.

He leaned closer. "You like this," he whispered. His mouth hovered over her throat. His knee pressed against hers, separating them.

Lucía froze, unsure. Torn between fear and thrill.

He laughed softly. "Such a serious expression," he murmured. "Relax, *mi cielo*. You know I would never hurt you."

His mouth found hers and the kiss was immediately all-consuming. There was no slow build-up, no tentative exploration, just his tongue sliding against hers, his lips crushing hers, his teeth nipped her bottom lip. Desire pumped into her veins, but it was mixed with something else, something that burned almost as much.

He broke off the kiss, breathing heavily, then stepped back releasing her. But only for a second, it seemed. Because, with a flick of his hand, he said, "Get up."

She did, her legs shaking so much she had to grip the edge of the desk.

"Take those fucking clothes off."

It was the way he said it, the demand laced with absolute certainty that it would be obeyed, that made her fingers go to the buttons on her blouse. She was so turned on, she could feel the dampness between her legs. Her body was operating on desire and adrenaline alone and it was happy to take the lead. She had nearly reached the last ones, when suddenly the burning turned to ice in her stomach.

He had undone his belt, the gold buckle clinking as his erection strained against the expensive fabric of his trousers. His hand moved to the zipper—and stopped. His eyes snapped back up to her face, noticing that she wasn't moving.

"I..." she began, voice thin and frayed. "I can't." Her fingers started retracing their steps, fumbling over each of the buttons. "This isn't what I want."

The heat in his eyes flickered, then vanished. In its place: rage. Cold, sharp, and immediate. It was like a switch had been flipped.

She took one step back—then another—her movement clumsy and hurried. But he didn't go after her, and he didn't speak. He just stood there, belt hanging open, watching her with that same blank fury, like he was already recalculating her value.

Lucía reached the door and opened it with trembling fingers.

Then, with as much control as she could summon, she closed it behind her. Firmly. Deliberately. And with a calmness that seemed to come from somewhere outside her body, she kept walking.

Her heels echoed down the empty hallway. She reached the elevator, hand trembling slightly as she hit the call button.

It was then she saw him.

Mateo. Leaning against the wall near the elevators, a folder under one arm, his eyes dark and unreadable.

Lucía stopped. "Mateo."

He nodded once. "Hey." His voice was soft. But something inside it was wrong.

She stepped forward. "What are you—"

"Working late," he said. His eyes went to her blouse, buttoned wrong. "Like you."

There was a pause. The elevator arrived. She hesitated, then stepped inside.

He didn't follow. As the doors slid shut, their eyes held for just one moment too long. And Lucía knew: Something had changed.

And it would never change back.

———

In the days that followed, Lucía had expected something to happen. A message. A signal. A shift in behavior. But Javier remained precisely as he had always been: cool, sharp, unreadable. He didn't treat her differently. He didn't treat her at all.

In the morning meetings, he addressed her like everyone else. In emails, he cc'd her as needed. If anything, he seemed to take greater pains to remain impersonal. And that—somehow—was worse.

It made her feel like a secret even to herself.

Mateo had noticed. Of that, she was sure.

His jokes at her desk had stopped. No more long walks to the break room. No more shared coffees or quiet sarcasm in the elevator. He answered her questions with nods and clipped phrases. Smiled, but without his eyes.

Lucía could feel the change like humidity in the air, dense and invisible.

Late on a Tuesday, she found him alone in the print room. He was feeding documents into the heavy black-and-white copier, the green light dragging slowly across each page.

Lucía stepped in and shut the door behind her. "Hey."

Mateo didn't look up. "Hey."

She stood awkwardly beside the paper bin. "You've been scarce."

"Busy." The machine whirred. "I'm on the Roji-Fuentes account now. They've got a three-day audit window."

"You didn't say anything."

He glanced over. "You didn't ask."

The copier beeped.

Lucía's fingers curled against her hip. "Mateo—"

He pulled the fresh stack of papers off the tray and turned to her, suddenly. "I liked you, you know." The words hit like a physical shove.

"I know," she said quietly.

He nodded. "And I knew I didn't stand a chance."

Lucía's jaw tightened. "It's not like that."

"No?" His voice was soft, but not kind. "You don't have to explain, Lucía. You're brilliant. And he sees that. Maybe that's enough."

"Nothing happened. I walked out."

Silence fell again, thick as dust.

Mateo handed her a single sheet from the stack. "This is for your review. Tomorrow." He brushed past her and opened the door. Paused. "You're better than him. You know that, right?"

He didn't wait for her answer. He left her in the small fluorescent-lit room, alone with a sinking weight in her chest.

———

She worked late that night. Or tried to. The office was quiet again, the open floor dim except for her pool of light and the humming blue screen.

She stepped away for coffee. No more than five minutes, but when she returned to her desk, her browser was closed. Her keyboard was crooked.

Lucía stared. She hadn't closed her browser. She never angled the keyboard like that.

She sat down slowly. Logged in. There was nothing missing or changed. But something was off. She checked the access logs on the internal terminal. Someone had pinged her machine. Briefly. A local IP. No login attempt. Just…ping.

Lucía shut off the monitor. Her reflection looked back at her in the black glass. Blank-eyed. Tight-lipped.

It wasn't a mistake. It wasn't curiosity.

It was a message.

Someone had been at her desk. She looked across the open office floor, rows of cubicles now ghostly in the dark.

Lucía reached for her bag, packed her things slowly, and left.

She didn't look back. But the sensation followed her out, across the marble foyer, into the night, and down every empty block.

Someone was watching. Someone had always been watching.

TWENTY-SIX

THE CAFÉ'S shade offered a brief reprieve from the heat, but now the sun was back in full force, weighing down on Lucía's back as she stepped outside. She let the screen door click shut behind her and moved toward the edge of the lot where a sliver of shade was cast by a dying jacaranda tree.

Ryan was still inside, paying the bill. She sat down on her pack and closed her eyes. They had a plan now. A lead. A city. It felt like something tangible, a thread they could pull, one that might —just might—have Noah on the other end. But that feeling came wrapped in a strange kind of stillness. Almost a hush. Like the lull before a storm breaks.

She opened her eyes and scanned the road, the lot, the tree line. A breeze kicked dust across the asphalt. No one lingered or stared.

And yet. There it was again. That feeling.

Not danger, not exactly.

Attention.

It wasn't a threat you could see, it was one you could feel. A presence that knew too much about you. Knew your tells. Your silences. The things you never said.

Javier.

She breathed in through her nose, slow and controlled, forcing her pulse rate down to something she could control. This wasn't a new fear. It was a remembered one.

The café door swung open. Ryan stepped out, adjusting the strap of his duffel. He looked at her for a second, just long enough to read the way she wasn't moving. "You good?"

Lucía gave a short nod. "Just the heat."

He squinted at her. "You were staring at nothing."

"I was thinking," she said. "That's allowed, isn't it?"

Ryan didn't answer right away. Just shifted his weight and handed her a bottle of water. "Drink something. We've got about a mile to that hostel, and no one's offering rides."

Lucía took the bottle but didn't twist the cap. "We'll be fine."

"Didn't say we wouldn't be," he muttered, stepping off the curb. The sun caught the line of sweat darkening his collar.

She followed, keeping pace beside him, her fingers clenched too tightly around the bottle.

He didn't ask again. But she could feel his eyes flick toward her every few steps, like he was trying to read something in her body language.

Lucía kept her gaze forward, but her thoughts stayed behind.

In the dust. In the shadow. In the shape of a man she hadn't seen in years, but who never really left.

TWENTY-SEVEN

NINE YEARS AGO

THE CALL CAME in just after lunch. "*Señor* Esquivel would like to see you in his office," said the receptionist.

Lucía blinked at the phone, heart skipping. "Now?"

"Yes, *señorita*. Right away."

She stood too fast, nearly knocking her chair off balance. Her blouse clung at the back from hours of stress-sweat. She hadn't touched her lunch.

Across the room, Mateo looked up from his screen. Their eyes met for the first time in days. She couldn't read his expression.

She smoothed her skirt and walked to the elevator.

The top floor was always too cold. A calculated chill designed to discourage lingering. Lucía's heels echoed down the corridor. She could hear her own breathing.

This was it. This was the moment she was going to get fired from the only job she'd ever wanted. The only job that had ever challenged her or had felt like it was going to lead to the life she wanted. The life she'd worked so hard for. All because she'd refused to sleep with her boss, a man whom she'd both fantasized about and was attracted to, but who had asked for something she just wasn't prepared to give.

When had her life become so fucking complicated? So out of her own control? And how on earth could she gain it back?

Javier's door was open. He was standing by the window, facing out over México City. The skyline shimmered with late sunlight, steel and glass humming with distance.

"Come in," he said, without turning.

Lucía obeyed.

"You've been working late," he said.

She didn't answer.

He turned. Dressed, as always, in casual authority. He gestured to the chair opposite his desk.

She sat.

He tapped a file on his screen and rotated the monitor slightly so she could see it. "There's an account here. Layered beneath a defunct logistics firm. It was recently flagged for inconsistencies."

Lucía stared blankly at him for a long moment. This wasn't about the other night. This was about work. Actual work.

He shook his head irritably, as if she were being deliberately stupid and he had no time for it. So she leaned forward, scanning the spreadsheet.

"In this firm, there are three sets of books," Javier said. "Two of them are lies."

She frowned. "And the third?"

He smiled. "The one we don't show the authorities."

Her eyes darted up to meet his. His tone was level. Neutral. But she felt the warning behind the words.

He continued, "This is off-roster work. Not billable. No paper trail. I need you to reconcile these files. You'll report only to me."

Lucía's mouth went dry. "Is this…internal?"

"Let's call it sensitive."

He tapped a key. A secondary folder opened. It was encrypted. But she saw the name in the metadata: **SinalData Holdings.**

The name struck a bell she didn't like. She forced her expression flat. "I thought you trusted only senior staff with discretionary accounts," she said.

"I do."

Silence. Lucía sat back slowly, spine straight. Again, all she could do was stare at him. This meeting had gone nothing like she'd imagined. She wasn't being fired, she was being promoted. She was being invited into a secret upper echelon within the firm, where the real clients lived. The real money, too. And the real power.

SinalData. Sinaloa.

Cartel.

Javier's smile never shifted. "You'll work from home. Air-gapped. No backups. No questions."

She said nothing, just looked at the screen. The folder blinked, waiting.

He slid a USB drive across the desk toward her. "Still want the job?"

Lucía took the drive. The plastic felt heavier than it should have. Then she heard herself say, "Yes."

———

Downstairs, the elevator doors slid open. Lucía stepped into the lobby, pulse still drumming from the conversation upstairs. She adjusted her grip on the USB drive in her palm, fingers clenched so tightly the edges were biting into her skin.

Ahead, Mateo stood by the front desk, flipping through a file. He glanced up as she approached.

Their eyes met. She couldn't read his expression. Couldn't afford to try.

She kept walking.

If he spoke, she didn't hear it. If he moved, she didn't see it. She passed him like smoke sliding past a closed window.

If she turned around now—if she met his eyes, if she let him see what she was holding—he'd know what she'd agreed to.

And she wasn't sure she'd survive the look on his face when he realized how far she'd gone.

TWENTY-EIGHT

NINE YEARS AGO

THE ELEVATOR LIGHTS above Lucía hummed softly. Somewhere below, the firm was settling into its nightly silence, screensavers blooming across empty monitors, the hum of expensive machinery whispering through the bones of the building.

Lucía gripped her satchel with both hands. Her pulse felt loud. She wasn't late. Not technically. But Mateo had texted her twice. Just the letter: **L?**

She'd replied: **On my way.**

The elevator chimed. The doors opened onto the 9th floor, Legal Records and Archives.

He was already there. Waiting. He didn't turn when he heard her steps, just kept scanning a large screen, his arms folded across his chest.

The overhead lights were too bright. Rows of filing cabinets and locked shelves gleamed dully around them.

"Mateo?" she asked.

His voice was flat. "When were you going to tell me?"

Lucía blinked. "Tell you what?"

He turned now. His eyes were tired. Angry. Hurt. "That you're working on something, something Javier hasn't cleared through audit or legal."

Her mouth opened, but no words came.

"I know you," he said. "You don't miss steps. You don't forget protocols. So if you're hiding something—"

"I'm not hiding it."

"You've encrypted it off-grid."

She exhaled slowly. "It's a side project. Confidential. He trusts me."

Mateo barked out a short, mirthless laugh. "He owns you."

"Don't," she said, and the word came out harsher than she intended.

He stared at her. "Lucía, you know what this is. I found the shell company he used in Panama. It connects back to a holding firm in Jalisco. And that connects to—"

"Stop," she said again. Her hand was trembling. "You don't understand."

"Then explain it to me."

She didn't speak. She couldn't. Maybe because she'd only vetted this in a dark corner of her own mind. Only given it the green light because it fed into her own ambition, but which she knew she could never justify out loud. Could never explain the logic behind continuing to work with a man who'd abused his own position of power over her to try and get up her skirt. And then let him pull her even deeper into a very dangerous world.

Mateo stepped closer. He lowered his voice. "Look, I'm not accusing you. I'm trying to help. But I need to know what he's making you do. Are you helping him launder money? Cartel money?"

She flinched.

He saw it. That was all the answer he needed.

A long silence passed between them, cold and breathless. Finally, Lucía said, "He'll kill you, Mateo."

"If that's a threat—"

"It's not. It's a fact. You don't cross him. Not out loud. Not even in your head."

"I'm not afraid of him."

"Well, I am."

Another silence. But softer now.

He reached out and took her hand. "You don't have to do this alone. We can fix it. Together."

She looked at his fingers curled around hers. They were warm and steady. She remembered how his hands had been one of the first things she'd noticed about him. She'd never had a dirty thought about him; never fantasized about those hands gripping her hair or her ass, but that might have come, if she'd let him in. If she hadn't been hypnotized, like a snake dancing to Javier's tune.

And it wasn't too late, right?

She squeezed Mateo's hands, and he squeezed back. For the first time in weeks, she let herself breathe. "You'd really help me?"

He nodded.

"I don't know how," she whispered.

"We'll figure it out. We just need time."

She nodded. Slowly.

"Tomorrow," he said. "Meet me at my place. We'll plan everything then."

"Okay."

He squeezed her hand again. "I missed you," he said.

She didn't answer, but she didn't let go either. And for the first time since she set foot in this place, she began to feel the tension drain from her body, and a petal of hope begin to bloom.

Lucía stood outside Mateo's apartment, her heart beating fast. She'd walked here, carrying nothing but the USB in her jacket pocket and her phone. Every step she'd taken had felt lighter than the last.

They had a plan. Mateo had said they'd fix it. Together.

She knocked again. Firmer this time.

Nothing.

The hallway was quiet. No neighbors coming or going. Just

the ticking fluorescent overhead and the low buzz of a dying fly near the window.

She tried the handle. It wasn't locked. Her stomach dropped. She stood on the threshold, the handle still in her hand, ice creeping up her spine.

It took all her mental strength to convince herself to step inside.

"Mateo?"

No answer.

The place was dim. Curtains still drawn. Coffee mug half-full on the table. Seeing them gave her a flare of hope. Maybe he'd overslept. Maybe he was in the shower. Maybe—

She turned toward the bedroom. And stopped.

The smell hit her first, metallic and musky. The light from the hallway fell across the floorboards. His hand was visible just past the edge of the bed. Palm-up. Still. Fingers half-curled like they'd tried, and failed, to grasp something in the final seconds.

There was blood on the walls. And the floor. Not a pool. *A spill.* It had soaked into the grain of the wood like ink into paper.

She didn't scream, she just stood there. Panic and horror were crawling up her windpipe, clutching at her throat, preventing any sound from escaping. The USB in her coat pocket suddenly felt like it weighed a hundred pounds.

This was the consequence. This was what happened when you said *yes* to someone else.

Then she heard a sound. A soft *click* in the hallway.

Lucía froze. The door to the stairwell creaked shut, echoing down the corridor.

Her pulse climbed into her throat. Whoever did this wasn't just gone, they'd only left minutes ago.

There was a buzz in her pocket. She pulled her phone out with trembling fingers. No number. Just a message.

Are you coming in today? —J

The letters blurred as her vision swam. Javier. He wasn't really asking her to come in. He was giving her a destination—one he controlled, one she wouldn't walk out of.

She stared at the body one last time. The weight of guilt and grief pressed against her ribs, but survival screamed louder. She backed out of the apartment, slowly, silently. Yanked the door closed behind her.

In the hallway, she didn't breathe until she'd made it to the stairwell. She pressed her hand to her chest. Counted to ten. Then again.

She could fall apart later. Right now, she had to disappear.

———

The bus terminal was loud with engines and shouting. A baby screamed somewhere near the long-distance kiosk. A man smoked beside the restroom sign, his eyes half-shut in the fluorescent light.

Lucía stood at the automated ticket machine, entering a fake name she'd memorized. She paid in cash. The bills were damp with her palm sweat.

Her stomach ached with hunger. She ignored it.

Javier's USB was zipped into the lining of her coat. She hadn't let it out of her sight since she left the apartment. Somehow, it still felt heavier than it should. Like it carried Mateo's body inside it.

The screen blinked. Her ticket printed.

Puebla. Then south. Then gone.

She took the slip and moved like a sleepwalker into the crowd. No calls. No luggage except for her backpack. No goodbyes.

She'd destroyed her old phone in the sink of a public restroom, then flushed the SIM card. Her email was wiped. Her financial trail stopped cold the moment she withdrew the last of her pesos and converted it to anonymous cryptocurrency at a bitcoin ATM.

At the bottom of her pack, wrapped in an old dish towel, was her grandfather's Colt 1911. It hadn't been fired in decades, but it was clean, oiled, and loaded, her father had made sure of that. She hadn't planned on taking it. But when she'd seen it in the drawer while she was hastily packing a few clothes into her backpack, she'd known she'd feel safer with it.

By the time they found Mateo's body, if they even bothered reporting it, she would be a phantom.

But the hardest part wasn't vanishing. It was staying vanished.

Over the next month, she moved like smoke. Veracruz. Tabasco. Campeche. Each place left behind as quickly as she arrived. She cut her hair. Learned to walk differently. She didn't keep receipts. She didn't ask questions. She didn't look anyone in the eye longer than two seconds.

She used burner laptops for everything. Air-gapped, always wiped. She never stayed anywhere more than five nights. Never visited the same café twice. Never let herself be photographed. She'd learned from the best. Javier had trained her to be precise and fastidious, in his way.

And now she was using every ounce of that education to disappear from him.

In one of her first safehouses, she stood before a cracked mirror, inspecting the lines around her eyes. The dark circles beneath them.

Her old self had died with Mateo. The woman staring back was someone else entirely.

Not Lucía Duarte. Not anyone. Just a shadow wearing human skin.

She lifted the drive to eye level. It was no longer a key, it was a curse. Proof. Power. And vengeance waiting to be unlocked.

One day, she would finish what Mateo had wanted to start. But not yet. Not until she was safe, and ready. Not until she could strike in a way that Javier would feel in the marrow of his bones. She slipped the drive back over her neck. Pulled the curtain closed.

And vanished.

TWENTY-NINE

RYAN CLOCKED the shadow within a few minutes of leaving the café. A man. Muscular build. Sunglasses, scruffy mustache, short sleeves. Walking slow. He didn't look local: too pale and too polished. And he wasn't sipping coffee or checking his phone. He was watching them.

Ryan adjusted his pace, letting Lucía move a step ahead. She hadn't noticed; she was distracted, muttering something about offshore routing patterns.

They turned down a narrow side street lined with faded signs. The heat had pooled there, thick and slow. Laundry flapped from upper balconies.

The man turned too.

Ryan stopped at a rusted iron gate and bent as if to tie his boot. Lucía slowed, glanced back.

"What?" she murmured.

"Keep walking," Ryan said under his breath. "Don't look. We've picked up a tail."

She stiffened but obeyed.

The man passed, trying to look bored. Then Ryan moved.

He stepped in fast, caught the man by the collar and shoved him into the wall. Not hard. Just enough to jolt the nerves.

"Why're you tailing us?" Ryan hissed.

The man blinked, startled. Then his expression reset, like a soldier falling into protocol.

"I don't know what you—"

Accent: American. Low-level Fed? Contract work? Hard to tell.

"Wrong answer." Ryan pressed him harder. "Try again."

The man winced. "I'm just a tourist. You're out of your mind, man. This is assault."

Ryan slammed him into the wall again, harder this time. "You've got a new watch tan, military cut, and boots that cost more than this whole street. Try again."

The man gritted his teeth, eyes darting once past Ryan toward the open street. "I was told to observe only. No contact. Just eyes."

Ryan narrowed his. "Not good enough."

The man flinched but held his ground. "I'm not cleared to say more."

Ryan's voice dropped to something colder. "You're not cleared to lie either."

The man hesitated, too long. Ryan drove his fist into his ribs. The guy gasped, sagging under the blow.

"Who the fuck sent you?"

A pause. Then finally, through gritted teeth: "Gates. Tomás Gates."

Ryan froze. Of course it was him.

That half-second of distraction was all the man needed. He surged forward, shoving Ryan off balance and driving a shoulder into his ribs. Ryan stumbled, pain flaring through his side where he'd thrown the punch.

The man twisted, landed a quick elbow to Ryan's jaw, and broke free.

Ryan lunged, but the man was already bolting down the street, weaving between the laundry lines and startled pedestrians.

He didn't look back.

Ryan swore under his breath and turned toward Lucía, who had just rounded the corner.

"What was that?"

He exhaled. "Not cartel. Worse."

"Worse?"

"Government." He winced, rubbing his knuckles. "Tomás Gates is in México. And he's watching us."

"I saw his name in a news brief," she said, her voice tight. "Gates. He gave a statement about cross-border coordination. I didn't think he'd be here, though."

Ryan grabbed her elbow. "Come on. We're not sleeping outside tonight."

Ten minutes later, they ducked into a crumbling hostel off another side street, past a rusted bell and a bored girl at the front desk who didn't ask for ID. Cash only. Room 12.

Lucía threw the bolt and dropped her bag on the bed. Ryan slumped into the only chair.

His ribs ached. His jaw throbbed. His nerves were screaming. It was too early in this run for surveillance teams and federal tails.

He looked up to find Lucía watching him. Her expression had changed. There was a small frown etched between her eyebrows. She looked almost…worried.

She stepped closer, eyes narrowing on the cut at the corner of his mouth. "You're bleeding," she said, voice lower now, more focused.

Ryan touched his lip with two fingers and looked at the smear of red. "It's nothing."

She didn't move away. "Let me see."

He hesitated, but didn't stop her as she leaned in, brushing her thumb gently against his cheek to angle his face toward the light. Her fingers were steady and warm.

It was the closest they'd been since the cabin, and it felt different now. Her breath grazed his skin. His heart picked up speed.

Then she stepped back, clearing her throat.

Ryan shifted in his chair, trying to shake off the moment.

"What the fuck's in this ledger, Lucía?" he asked, voice rough. "Why's it so damn important?"

She turned her head away and crossed her arms. "It's hard to explain to…" she trailed off, but it was clear what she was going to say. *To someone like you.*

He gave her his best *don't fuck with me* look. "I'm not an idiot. Try me."

She sighed. "Think of it as a diary."

He raised his eyebrows. "A diary?"

She nodded. "Except, instead of feelings, it's full of blood money, false invoices, and ghost companies." She looked back at him, meeting his eyes, but with a guarded expression. "My job was to make it look clean. Now, it's a loaded gun."

He exhaled, propping both his hands on the armrest. "Great. And it's pointed right at us."

———

The SUV idled in a patch of shade just off the main road, heat shimmering over the hood. Deputy U.S. Marshal Tomás Gates sat in the driver's seat, field tablet resting on his knee, the screen flashing red:

Agent: SIGNAL LOST.

He didn't swear. Just stared at the blinking alert for a moment, jaw flexing. Then he let out a slow breath through his nose.

"Inglis made him," he muttered.

Carlos Reyes, his local tech liaison guy, was in the passenger seat. He gave a low grunt of agreement. "He's ex-marshal. Instinct like that doesn't retire, right?"

Gates didn't answer. He was staring at a still image from earlier surveillance. It was grainy and sun-washed, but clear enough to make out a man and a woman, walking fast out of a gas station. One was Ryan. And the woman beside him…

Lucía Duarte.

She was angled away from the camera, but Gates knew. The

way she carried herself—alert, precise, like someone who'd spent years waiting for the world to catch up with her—was unmistakable.

Reyes leaned closer. "So it's really her."

Gates nodded once. "She's been off the map for years. Everyone assumed she was dead. Or protected. Or both."

"What changed?"

"She left a trail."

Reyes raised an eyebrow. "The ledger leak?"

"Not the first time," Gates said. "There was something a couple years back. People called it the 'Sinaloa Dumps' Quiet leak, full of cartel financials. Disguised just well enough to be missed by the casual eye, but someone wanted it found."

"Her?"

"No doubt in my mind," Gates said. "She used to work for Javier Esquivel. She knew things. Things she tried to make public. The Sinaloa leak didn't go far. Not enough proof, not enough eyes on it. It almost felt like a test run."

"And now?"

"Now she's doing it again. Smarter this time. And I think Inglis is helping her."

Reyes looked sideways at him. "I thought you were just here for the kid. Noah."

Gates didn't answer right away. He just stared through the windshield at the dusty road ahead.

"I am," he said finally. "But Lucía Duarte...she's something bigger."

Reyes studied him. "You really think she still has the full ledger?"

He closed the tablet. "I think she's carried it with her every day since she ran."

THIRTY

LUCÍA WAITED until the door was locked, the curtains drawn. Only then did she open her laptop.

Ryan was still in the bathroom, tending to his bruises. She heard him rustling around in his first aid kit, uncapping of a bottle of painkillers or antiseptic. The kind of noises that sounded normal in a place like this.

She sat cross-legged on the bed, the laptop balanced in front of her. He came out a few minutes later, shirt off, jaw darkened with stubble and bruises. The blood was gone from his bottom lip, but it was still swollen and red. She had to force herself not to stare at it. Problem was, the only other place to stare was at his bare chest, which was heavily muscled and dusted with golden hair. It spread across his pecs, then trailed down his flat stomach, before heading south and disappearing beneath the waistband on his jeans—

"That the ledger?" he asked.

Lucía's eyes flew back up to his eyes, which were cooly surveying her, giving no indication they'd just caught her perving. Her cheeks heated, matching the warmth that was spreading low in her stomach.

She forced her attention back to her screen. "Most of it."

"You said you'd already leaked parts."

"I did." She paused. "It's the last part they want back."

Ryan stepped closer. "Why?"

Lucía clenched her jaw. He was only a few feet away, and she swore she could feel the heat radiating off him. Was he one of those men who ran hot? Who, when you lay in bed with him naked, almost burned you when his skin touched yours?

Her cheeks were now so hot they probably glowed. "Because it's the key," she said, glad that her voice came out steady and business-like. "Not just to the money, but to the names."

"You mean, like, cartel leadership?"

"Cartel, yes. And bankers. Politicians. Two cabinet-level officials in the Mexican government. A guy who used to work at Langley."

She let that settle, then went on: "This isn't just criminal evidence. It's leverage. It's blackmail. And it's an insurance policy…one I wasn't supposed to survive long enough to cash."

She paused, then added, "It's encrypted at 256 bits with a triple-split key. Military-grade encryption. Unbreakable unless you're God or a quantum computer. I used it to protect the ledger."

Ryan folded his arms. "And that key is the final fragment?"

She nodded. "It's a sequence only I know. Without it, the other two fragments are just noise. They can't decrypt it, they can't stitch it back together." She tapped the side of her head. "And I've never written it down." She smiled, but there was no humor motivating it. "That's why they haven't killed me. Why they can't."

She leaned forward, speaking slower now. "They need me to open the vault. Only then can they destroy its contents."

Ryan stared at the screen. He didn't move, didn't speak. But something shifted behind his eyes. "That's a hell of a target," he said quietly.

Lucía closed the laptop. "No. It's a hell of a weapon."

Lucía lay on her side, staring at the faded water stain spreading across the wall. The laptop was back in its case.

Ryan sat on the floor by the window, leaning back against the peeling wall, shirt still off, knees drawn up loosely. He hadn't asked more questions. Not about the ledger, not about the key. But the silence between them was thick enough to hold shape.

He cleared his throat. "How?"

She glanced at him. "How what?"

He took a moment to answer, as if he'd forgotten the question he was asking. "…did you get involved in all this?"

Lucía rolled onto her back, staring up at the cracked ceiling. "My dad worked in logistics in Oaxaca City. Freight shipments. Containers. The kind of job that meant he knew what moved where, and when. He never said much, but I think he saw more than he let on."

Ryan didn't speak, so she went on.

"I was good at math. Got a scholarship. First in my family to go to university. Graduated in finance. I used to dream about IPOs and ethical investment portfolios." She gave a faint, self-mocking smile. "I thought I'd end up in one of those sleek skyscrapers in México City, pushing numbers around. And I did. For a little while."

"And that's where you met him," Ryan said.

She hesitated. Then nodded. "I interviewed with Javier Esquivel when I was twenty-five. He ran a boutique investment firm with impossible connections. It felt like a fantasy job, exclusive and powerful. And he…" She hesitated again, then offered a small shrug. "He was very persuasive."

Ryan said nothing.

Lucía sat up on the bed, elbows on her knees. "It wasn't legal. Not all of it. I figured that out quickly. Offshore routing. Fake donors. Shells inside shells. But it was genius, like watching a chess match played in eight dimensions."

She looked down at her hands. "At first, I told myself I'd learn what I could, then leave. But then he asked me to help with something bigger. Said it would only be temporary. Private. A special ledger system, for a 'client of significance.'"

Ryan frowned. "The cartel."

She nodded once. The memory of that name on the encrypted ledger when he'd first shown it to her jumped into her mind. *SinalData Holdings.* "Sinaloa. I saw what the ledger was tracking: port fees, ghost shipments, smuggling channels through Chiapas. And not just money. Names. Bribes. Political protection. I was building a financial nervous system for a hydra, and I was in too deep to pull out."

"And you stayed?"

"For a little while. Because I was scared. And because I was under his spell. I wish I could say it was all fear. But part of me still wanted his approval. Still believed I mattered to him."

She stared out the window for a long moment. "Eventually, I couldn't ignore it anymore. I told my colleague Mateo. We were going to make a plan. I don't even know what we were intending to do with it. Expose it, maybe. Leak it to the press, or to someone in the government who hadn't already been bought." She shook her head. "It all sounds so naïve, now."

She paused, but Ryan didn't respond, so she kept going, even though these were things she'd never said out loud before. "We were supposed to meet that morning at his apartment." She hesitated. Her jaw clenched, and she had to force the next words out. "The door wasn't locked. I remember thinking that was strange. And the lights were off, but the windows were open. Like someone wanted the neighbors to hear if I screamed." She swallowed. "He was on the floor by the bed. Face down. One arm bent behind him like it had been broken. There was blood on the wall. On the ceiling. They'd made it messy, on purpose. His eyes were open."

Her fingers curled against her leg.

"Officially, it was ruled a break-in. Wrong place, wrong time. But nothing was taken. Not his wallet. Not his laptop. Not even his watch." A pause. "Just him."

Ryan didn't interrupt.

"I ran," she said softly. "I took the ledger and vanished. I've been moving ever since."

She folded her arms across her knees. Her voice went flat. "So. That's how I got involved."

Lucía's eyes drifted to him again. He was watching her. Not like she was a threat. Just with that same steady gaze he'd had since day one.

His bare chest rose and fell, slow and even. The bruise along his ribs was darkening.

Her gaze dropped, then flicked back to the ceiling. *Dios mío, contrólate.* "We should get some sleep," she said, her voice a little too crisp.

Ryan pushed off the wall. "Yeah."

He didn't look back as he crossed to the other bed and lay down. But the air between them stayed heated.

THIRTY-ONE

RYAN LAY ON HIS BACK, one arm under his head, staring up at the ceiling. He hadn't moved in hours, but he hadn't slept either.

Lucia's voice still echoed in his head. Her story. Her past. Mateo. Her boss, too. Ryan had clocked the waver in her voice when she'd gotten to that part of her story. And it told him that there was a hell of a lot more to that chapter than she'd been prepared to divulge.

Persuasive. She'd said it like it tasted bitter in her mouth. Like it still lingered. He'd heard women use that word before. Usually when they didn't want to say *manipulative*. Or worse. It wasn't the ledger that stuck in his mind now. Not the theft, not the fleeing. It was that one word. *Persuasive.*

Javier Esquivel.

Ryan had worked with predators before. Some wore suits instead of tattoos, but the wiring was the same.

She wasn't who he thought she was. Not just a fugitive with a stolen flash drive and a shady backstory. She was someone who could have disappeared forever and didn't. Who could have sold that flash drive to the highest bidder and be living on a private island somewhere.

He turned his head slightly. She was curled on her side, facing the wall, her breathing slow and steady.

There was something fierce about her. But fragile, too. Not weak, but worn thin, like she'd been shouldering this burden for a long time and it was taking its toll.

He exhaled slowly and shut his eyes.

They had a long way to go. And God help him, he was starting to care whether she made it to the other side.

———

The image on the monitor was grainy, pulled from a second-rate CCTV camera mounted above a roadside tienda. Javier Esquivel studied the image without blinking.

Lucía was seated in the passenger seat of a battered pickup truck, face half-turned in profile. Her hair was wind-blown, pulled into a knot at the base of her neck. She wore no makeup. Her hands were folded in her lap. She looked alert. Next to her sat a man.

He was angular and broad-shouldered. Mid-thirties, possibly forty. American, by the set of his jaw and the cut of his T-shirt. One hand on the wheel. The other resting on the seat between them. Close. Too close.

"Where was this taken?" he asked, voice smooth.

His aide—a smartly-dressed man, hands clasped behind his back—said, "Tiny village in the Sierra Norte mountains. Twelve hours ago. They stopped for fuel. Paid cash. Cameras were wiped within the hour."

Javier nodded. "But you salvaged this."

"Yes, sir."

He kept staring.

There was something about the curve of her posture that struck him: not defensive, but no longer afraid. She wasn't shrinking from the man beside her. She wasn't keeping her guard high.

That was new.

He zoomed in slowly, until her face came into focus. Even now, after all these years, her image still sent something sharp through his bloodstream. She looked older, of course. Harder around the edges. But that only made her more interesting. There was a real fight in her now, something that hadn't existed before she ran.

Javier clicked once, saving the image to a private folder. Then he switched to the next screen—a different feed, a different room.

A child paced in a corner, kicking a deflated soccer ball. The shot didn't show much of his face, just a spray of freckles and a mop of unmistakable red hair.

Still safe. For now.

Javier leaned back in his chair.

He had underestimated Inglis. That much was clear. The plan had been simple: dangle a ghost of Kylie Inglis in front of the man, give him a whiff of cartel activity, and point him toward Lucía. Let him do the hunting for them. Let his grief and guilt drive him into her orbit, then tear them both apart.

But now…they were working together. Not adversaries. Allies.

His jaw flexed. He didn't like variables. And Ryan Inglis was now a very large variable. Worse: Lucía clearly trusted him. That was dangerous.

He tapped a knuckle against the edge of the desk.

Killing Inglis would be easy. But that wouldn't solve the larger issue. He didn't want Lucía dead. Not yet. Not like that. He wanted her cornered. Bent, not broken. There was a difference.

And now she'd given him something useful: she'd shown her weakness.

Connection.

That was something he could use.

Javier closed the surveillance feed and opened a blank message window. He began to type, slow and measured, each keystroke deliberate. A command for his contact embedded in the Salina Cruz municipal offices. A new file was being prepared. A new trail. One that would seem plausible, even urgent.

He would let them find it. He would let them believe they were still winning.

And when they were exactly where he wanted them—desperate and divided—then he would pull the thread.

Lucía would come back to him and bring his stolen property back with her. One way or another.

THIRTY-TWO

THEY HIT the coast just after sunrise. Salina Cruz was a port city perched on the edge of the Isthmus of Tehuantepec. Port cranes lined the horizon like skeletal giants. The main road ran downhill toward the port, lined with mechanic shops, taco stands, and boarded-up storefronts. The bus station café where they got off had no real walls, just a cracked tile floor and a faded Coca-Cola awning that flapped like a sad flag.

Ryan stood by the open frame, trying not to lean on the sticky counter. Gulls circled the nearby dumpsters, their cries high and shrill, wings casting shadows over the road.

He tried not to look at Lucía. She was in the booth behind him, hunched over her laptop, hair pulled into a low bun. The morning light caught the soft shadows under her eyes and the curve of her jaw. She wore a faded gray tee and jeans dusted with road grime, but somehow she still looked…incredible.

"Do you ever blink when you're in data mode?" he asked.

"Do you ever shut up when you're bored?" she shot back, still typing.

He smiled. "Touché."

Lucía exhaled through her nose, eyes flicking over the screen. "I followed the Salina Cruz signal to a shell company," she said.

"They filed a storage lease, the address is behind a dead shipping yard. And a power meter there just came online."

Ryan frowned. "So someone's using a fake address."

"Or hiding in one," Lucía said. "Could be nothing. Could be everything."

A gust of wind pushed through the café, bringing with it the sharp, greasy tang of fish guts and engine oil.

Ryan nodded, rolling his shoulder against the weight of his gear. He was still half-distracted by her. "Either way, we check it."

———

The place looked like it had been abandoned mid-apocalypse. Rusted corrugated siding. A chained-up gate. Concrete walls mottled with salt bloom.

Ryan knelt by the gate, checking the padlock. "It's been opened recently," he murmured.

"Footprints, too," Lucía said. "Somebody's been through here."

They scaled the fence two minutes later, boots crunching on gravel as they crossed into the yard. A squat building sat at the back, windowless and square. Ryan moved first, sweeping the perimeter, weapon drawn.

"Stay behind me," he said, not looking back. She muttered something, but he heard her soft footfalls trailing him as he rounded the side of the building.

They slipped inside through a broken door. The interior was hollow: concrete floor, old crates stacked along one wall.

Ryan moved through each room, clearing it fast. Empty.

He lowered his weapon. "Nothing."

Lucía exhaled hard. "Damn."

She moved to one of the crates and pried it open with a piece of rusted metal. Inside: rotted packing foam, a rusted electrical coil, and a torn receipt.

Ryan leaned against the wall. "Dead end."

Lucía didn't move. "It doesn't make sense. The money moved from this company. The signature matches. It should've led somewhere."

"Well, it didn't," Ryan snapped. He regretted the sharpness even as it came out, but the frustration was rising in his throat like bile. He was hot, and hungry and so tired he could barely think straight. "We're running out of time, and every one of these leads is colder than the last."

Lucía turned, her expression sharp. "Don't put this on me. You think I'm not aware of the stakes? That I don't know what happens if we don't find that boy?"

He crossed his arms. "You're the one with the map. So far, it's gotten us nowhere."

Her eyes blazed. "*I'm* the one with the map? You mean the one I built while running for my life? While hiding in shit motels and stealing Wi-Fi from corner stores?"

Ryan opened his mouth, then shut it.

Lucía stepped closer, close enough he could smell the sharp citrus of her shampoo, or maybe just the heat rolling off her skin. "I know what I'm doing. I don't need you second-guessing me every time something doesn't explode into answers."

Ryan didn't back down. "I'm not second-guessing. I'm just tired of chasing shadows."

The silence that fell between them was too tight, too close. Her eyes flicked over his mouth before she looked away.

Ryan's voice was low. "You said it yourself. Could be nothing, could be everything."

She looked at him, anger flashing. "Yeah, well, I was hoping for the second one."

He forced himself to soften. "We'll find the right lead."

Lucía shook her head, then started walking toward the exit. "You know," she said over her shoulder, "for someone who hates chasing shadows, you sure do spend a lot of time standing in them."

He followed, lips twitching into something that almost resembled a smile.

———

Gates leaned over the table, elbows planted between cables and monitors. The feed from drone B-17 flickered, then stabilized. A grainy image resolved: Ryan and Lucía emerging from the shipping yard's back entrance, their expressions tight, body language guarded, but aligned.

Behind him, the surveillance team murmured updates. A local handler tapped in the next grid overlay. The thermal signature of their vehicle flared, then dimmed as they turned south along the coastal road.

Reyes picked up his tablet and scrolled through the latest field notes. "We've got a clean intercept window. If you want them stopped, this is it."

Gates watched the screen in silence, arms crossed. "Let them go."

Reyes blinked in surprise.

Gates looked back at the screen, re-watching Ryan guide Lucía into the vehicle like she was something fragile. His jaw tightened. "Log their route. Keep the drones high. No close pings. I want eyes, not footprints."

Reyes hesitated. "So we're not engaging?"

"Not yet. Let them believe they're in control." Gates stepped away from the monitors, his voice low. "When the time comes," he said, "we'll be ready."

THIRTY-THREE

OUTSIDE THE MOTEL WINDOW, the neon "Vacancy" sign buzzed, half the letters burnt out. The place looked like it had been forgotten by time and remembered only by desperate travelers.

Lucía sat on the edge of one of the twin beds, still dressed, eyes fixed on the soft blue light of her laptop. She wasn't working anymore, she was just staring at the code she'd already run, willing it to yield something new. The cursor blinked like a heartbeat, steady and mocking. She scrolled through familiar commands, but her thoughts refused to settle.

Her mind wasn't on the screen.

It was on Ryan, in the shower.

She could hear the water running behind the closed door, the rhythmic hiss and splash of it unnervingly intimate. Every time she caught the rhythm, she imagined steam curling around his shoulders, tracing the bruises across his ribs. She'd seen them earlier, when he peeled off his shirt with a wince. Her eyes had lingered too long. Again.

She closed the laptop gently and stood, pacing the cramped length of the room. The window showed nothing but the glowing edge of the sign and a parking lot slick with oil stains. Somewhere nearby, a motorcycle revved and faded into the night.

A buzzing itch of tension had settled into her skin. Restless. Uneasy.

The bathroom door creaked open. Her pulse jumped.

Ryan stepped out, towel around his neck, shirtless and scrubbed clean. His jeans hung low on his hips, revealing the V-cut in his abs that pointed southwards like a goddamn arrow. His hair was damp, curling slightly at the edges. He looked younger. Softer. But no less dangerous.

Lucía tried not to react. She failed.

He caught her eye, then looked away just as fast.

"Your turn," he said, voice low and rough.

She nodded, edging past him, careful not to touch. Inside the bathroom, she let the door click closed and exhaled slowly. Her reflection in the mirror looked like someone she didn't quite recognize. Her cheeks were flushed, her eyes a little too wide. She splashed water on her face, as if cold would burn off the distraction.

When she came out, towel in hand, Ryan was lying on top of the blanket, one arm behind his head, the other draped across his chest. His pistol was on the bed beside him. He was flipping a cartridge in the air, catching it, flipping it again. The motion was hypnotic.

"Everything okay?" he asked.

She squeezed the water out of the ends of her hair with the towel. "You still mad at me?"

He stopped flipping the cartridge. "No." A pause. "Maybe."

She crossed to the second bed and sat, elbows on her knees. "I didn't mean to snap earlier."

"I know," he said. "You're under pressure. So am I."

A long beat.

"You think we'll make it out of this?" she asked.

Ryan's mouth quirked. "I used to. Not so sure anymore."

She paused for a long beat. "Why are you really on the run?"

He was quiet for a moment, then said, "Surely you must have Googled me by now."

Lucía gave a faint smile. "Actually, no. Some things I prefer not to turn to the internet for."

He let out a dry chuckle. "Well, that's new."

She waited.

"I was a deputy U.S. marshal," he said. "Served on a fugitive task force out of Tennessee. I did good work. But I made a mistake. I got compromised, and I put a protected witness in danger. Crossed lines I shouldn't have."

Lucía said nothing.

"I let her down. In more ways than one." There was a long pause. "So I ran."

"Do you regret it?"

He was quiet again, then said, "Every day."

"If you could go back," she said, "would you?"

"To the Marshals?" He snorted. "There's no going back. Once you cross a line with them, you don't return."

She said nothing, letting his words sink in. It was clear he didn't just mean that the Marshals Service had turned their backs on him. Whatever he had done had caused his whole country to paint him as an enemy.

"You just get better at pretending you were always meant to be here," he said.

She looked over at him, something flickering in her gaze. "Yeah," she murmured. "I know that feeling."

The silence shifted. The air between them seemed to crackle, as if the broken neon sign outside the window was electrifying the air. It felt harder to breathe than usual, and she felt a slow burn ignite low in her belly.

He sat up slightly, wincing as the movement pulled on his ribs.

"You need anything?" she asked quietly.

"Other than a time machine?"

She forced herself to break whatever spell this situation, and his shirtlessness, had cast on her. Walking to the mini fridge, she pulled out a water bottle and tossed it to him. "Hydration, actually. Revolutionary concept."

He grinned and twisted the cap off, taking a long drink. She watched the movement of his throat as he swallowed, the bob of his Adams apple.

He caught her looking. "You know," he said, "you don't have to keep your guard up all the time."

She arched a brow. "I'm not sure that's true."

"You let it down with me. Back in the cabin."

Her face went still. "That was strategy."

"Sure," he said, but his voice was softer now. "And this?" He gestured to the space between them, so narrow now it could be crossed in a breath.

Lucía's heart pounded. "This is logistics."

Ryan laughed, a real one this time, warm and weary. He stood and crossed the room, stopping just short of touching her. "You're a terrible liar."

She looked up at him, the motel light catching in her eyes. She felt her chest rising and falling, but she couldn't seem to get oxygen into her lungs. The burn in her belly had become a full-on inferno. "Goodnight," she whispered.

Ryan didn't move for a beat. His face was as impassive as ever, but she could swear his eyes had dulled with desire. Then they cleared, and he stepped back. "Night."

She turned and dimmed the light. The shadows between them stretched like tension cables.

Lucía lay down, eyes open to the dark. She told herself to breathe, to rest, to let it go, but her body wouldn't listen. Her blood hummed with a nervous electricity, as if something in her had been reawakened after years of quiet.

It scared her, this feeling. This pull toward something she couldn't control, couldn't logic her way out of. Wanting someone was dangerous. Trusting someone was even worse. She had spent so long building walls, learning to live without this quiver in her belly. And now here it was, curling beneath her ribs like a live wire.

From the sound of Ryan turning restlessly in the other bed, she wasn't the only one chasing sleep and failing.

THIRTY-FOUR

THE MOTEL ROOM was still and heavy with warmth, the filtered light creeping through the slats of the broken blinds. Outside, Salina Cruz was waking up. Lucía heard the clatter of a street vendor's cart, the low whine of a scooter weaving through traffic on the coastal road.

She stood at the sink in the bathroom, toothbrush dangling from her fingers. Her hair was still wet from the shower and stuck to her back. The ceramic tiles were cold beneath her bare feet.

She stared at her reflection. Not at the dark circles or the lines of fatigue around her mouth. Not at the fading bruise on her shoulder or the scratch on her collarbone she didn't remember getting. But at her eyes.

They looked too awake. Too alive.

She rinsed her mouth, turned off the tap, and leaned on the counter. Ryan was still asleep in the other room or pretending to be.

Her mind went back to Mateo, as it so often did in these quiet moments when she had nothing to distract her mind.

He'd been brilliant. Witty. Endlessly curious. And he'd cared about her in a way that no one ever had. Why, oh why hadn't she chosen him? Why hadn't she let him cross that invisible line on the rooftop that time?

And why had she let Javier do it instead?

Or maybe it wasn't a case of her *letting*. Maybe it was a case of him *taking*.

Or worse, her letting him take.

Lucía sat on the edge of the tub. A lump rose in her throat. She swallowed it down.

The cartel didn't just kill people. They erased them. They rewrote timelines and histories, altered official records, made it so you never existed. Mateo hadn't just been murdered. He'd been wiped from the world. And every time she got closer to someone, she felt the echo of that threat inside her chest.

She hadn't let anyone in since.

She thought of the way Ryan had looked last night, half in shadow, half in that lurid neon glow. The sound of his voice in the dark. The rawness in it when he spoke about regret.

She wanted to keep her distance. She'd planned to. But something about him made her forget how. He was dangerous in a way she hadn't prepared for. Not because he carried a gun. But because he *saw* her, even when she didn't want to be seen.

She hadn't told him the whole truth about Javier Esquivel. *El Escriba*. She hadn't told him that he was the first man who'd ever made her feel seen. And the first man who made her doubt herself for it. His control had been so subtle at first. So polished. So charming. By the time she realized how carefully he had shaped her…

It was too late.

Lucía closed her eyes and let the memory drain from her, but it clung stubbornly, leaving a sour taste on her tongue and a hollow ache in her chest.

Even now, after everything—after Mateo's death, after years on the run—she could still feel the ghost of Javier's grip at the nape of her neck. The weight of his gaze. The way he had made her question not just what she was doing but who she was.

Her fingers brushed the tile wall beside her, grounding her in its cool roughness.

She inhaled deeply through her nose, counted to five, then exhaled slowly. Then she rose from the edge of the tub.

She wasn't the same girl Javier Esquivel had molded all those years ago. Not anymore.

She was someone else now. Someone who would finish what Mateo started.

———

Ryan sat on the edge of his mattress, elbows on his knees, listening to the shower hiss shut. A few minutes later, the bathroom door clicked and steam spilled out. Lucía stepped into the doorway, toweling water from the ends of her hair. She caught his eyes for half a second, then moved past, set her towel on the chair, and reached for the laptop.

"Morning," he said.

She lifted a hand in answer, already flipping the lid, the screen lighting her face. He stood, went to the tiny kitchenette, and poured boiling water into two paper cups with instant coffee. It tasted like burned cardboard, but it was better than nothing.

When he handed her one, she barely glanced up in thanks. "I take it you've found something?"

"The shipping warehouse was definitely a front," she said, fingers flying. "Money flowed through it and promptly vanished."

He eased onto the bed opposite, watching the muscles in her jaw work as she focused. It was like seeing a storm gather. Controlled energy. Nothing wasted.

"So what are you looking for?" he asked.

"Something sloppy," she said. She scrolled, stopped, scrolled back. "The shell company is registered in Chihuahua. Transactions cross-check to a seafood supplier west of Puerto Cortés." She trailed off, eyes narrowing.

"Got something?" Ryan asked.

Lucía nodded slowly. "Altamar Seafood. On paper, it's shuttered. But there's activity in the subsidiary accounts. Tiny movements. Cleaning crews. Furniture rental. And one invoice for child-sized clothing."

Ryan's stomach flipped. "You think that's where they're holding the kid?"

"Could be."

"Any way we can make sure this time before we go in all-guns-blazing?"

She nodded. "Whoever filed this line will know. It's a little local tax office."

He ran it over in his mind. It sounded like a lead, a real one this time. The marshal in him started parsing the options, building the plan. "Okay. We start at the tax office. Find the clerk who keyed this. Or the person who gives them orders." He stood, checked the angle of the sun through the blinds. "How far is it?"

"A fair way. It's out past the industrial strip," she said. "Too remote for a bus and too far for a taxi. And if we're right about it, we might need a fast exit." She stood, zipping her laptop into her backpack. "So we're gonna need some wheels."

———

They left the motel before dawn, sticking to side streets and alleys. Ryan hung back, letting Lucía lead the way down a crumbling back street near the freight yard, weaving through shadows and shuttered storefronts until they reached a mechanic's lot with a hand-painted sign and a chain-link fence. Inside: a graveyard of sun-blistered sedans and salt-rusted pickups.

Lucía didn't hesitate. She headed straight for the oldest Nissan pickup on the lot: a squat, four-door Hardbody with bald tires, a busted headlight, and peeling paint that might've once been red. Then she rapped on the side of the trailer that served as an office. A teenager opened the door, shirtless, and reeking of last night's *mota.* Ryan kept his hand near his pistol, ready to step in if things turned bad.

But he didn't have to. Lucía didn't raise her voice, she spoke just loud enough to make the kid nervous. And whatever she said in Spanish, it worked. Five minutes later, she tossed Ryan the keys like she'd just borrowed them from a friend.

"No papers," she said as they climbed in. "No air con. And second gear's a gamble."

By the time the sun began to claw its way up over the docks, they were on the road.

———

The sun had just begun to burn through the haze when Ryan eased the battered truck onto the coastal road that skirted the edge of Salina Cruz. The pavement shimmered ahead, warped by heat. Glimpses of the Pacific flashed between crooked palms and low, tin-roofed shops just opening for the day.

He adjusted the mirror. Lucía was silent beside him, her face turned to the window, sunglasses hiding her eyes. Her hair was pulled back and exposed the clean line of her jaw and throat, and he had to drag his gaze away more than once. The collar of her shirt was damp with sweat already, clinging to her skin where it met the seatbelt.

They hadn't said much since they'd left the mechanic's yard. It didn't matter at first; the silence gave him a chance to think about the task ahead of them and ready his mind.

But after a while, the silence began to stretch so thin it almost hummed.

Ryan cleared his throat. "You always this quiet on road trips?"

Lucía didn't look over. "Depends on the company."

The corner of her mouth twitched. Not a smile, exactly. But close enough to send a slow spread of warmth through his stomach. He filed the moment away, something small and private he could replay later.

He tapped the steering wheel, letting the rhythm fill the silence. He wasn't used to this kind of company. Most of the time, in his old life, the person riding shotgun was either a fellow marshal or a prisoner. Lucía was neither. Truth be told, he had no idea what she was. She was a complete mystery. And every hour he spent with her, he found himself wanting to ask questions he had no business asking.

"You ever think about what you'd do if none of this had happened?" he asked.

She tilted her head slightly. She turned her face toward the window. Outside, the sea blurred past in glints of silver and turquoise. "I used to think I'd get married," she said eventually. "Have a kid. Maybe two. Keep one of those…" she trailed off, searching for the words, her mouth quirking up in a self-deprecating way, "whiteboard calendars on the fridge. Learn how to cook something other than eggs."

Ryan glanced at her, surprised.

She gave a faint smile. "I know. Doesn't quite fit the profile."

"It's not that. I just…" He shrugged. "I guess I figured you were more career-first."

"I was." Her smile faded, eyes tracing the horizon. "I mean, I wanted both. The family. And the corner office. I thought I could have it if I worked hard enough. If I played it right."

"And did you?"

"I got the office," she said. "Glass walls. Expensive coffee. A mentor who saw something in me." She paused, voice cooling. "Or maybe he just saw something he could use."

Ryan didn't answer.

Lucía shifted in her seat, gaze still fixed outside. "I didn't plan to fall for that world. But I did. The elegance. The power. It felt like belonging. For the first time."

Ryan pondered her words, trying to decipher what she meant by *fall for*. "And now?"

"Now? I want to burn it all down." A long pause. "And figure out what's left of me when it's over."

He glanced at her. Her eyes were still on the window, the sunglasses hiding whatever look she didn't want him to see. But her fingers were curled tight in her lap, and it was clear to him those words cost her a lot to say out loud.

"And you?" she asked, turning to him and catching him off-guard. "If you weren't running?"

He exhaled. "I was never much good at the whole dreaming thing." He glanced across at her. "But maybe a quiet place. Some land. Preferably in the mountains."

She digested that. "For me, it would have to be by the sea. I get anxious when I'm too far inland."

He glanced across at her. "Easier to escape?"

She didn't respond, but he guessed he'd hit the jackpot. Maybe a nerve, too.

They drove a few more miles in silence. The air grew thicker, the temperature rising inside the car. Sweat gathered under his arms, and he rolled the window down another inch.

Eventually, Lucía pulled out her laptop, resting it on her knees. Ryan kept stealing glances. Her brow furrowed in concentration, her fingers tapping in rapid bursts. He liked watching her work. She was so relentless. Precise. A far cry from the chaotic mess he often felt inside his own head.

Her leg brushed his gearshift hand once, accidentally, and she didn't move it right away. His pulse jumped. She didn't seem to notice, or maybe she did. She shifted a little in her seat, subtly, but he caught the flick of her glance.

The road curved. A slow, winding bend that gave them a glimpse of something other than the ocean in the distance. Ryan shifted in his seat, muscles tight from the long ride.

"We should stop soon," he said. "Stretch our legs. Maybe get something that passes for food."

Lucía nodded without looking up.

He spotted a roadside stand a few miles on and turned the truck into its lot. It was just a few plastic tables, a grill, and a hand-painted sign promising tacos and *cerveza*. They ordered bottled water and chorizo tortas, sitting at a table shaded by a torn umbrella. Flies buzzed lazily in the heat.

Lucía peeled the paper off her sandwich, took a bite, and moaned softly. "God, I forgot what real food tastes like."

They ate in a slow, companionable silence. Ryan leaned back and closed his eyes, letting the warmth soak into his bones. For a moment, it almost felt normal.

They lingered just long enough to finish their food, then headed back to the car. The sun was high now, baking the road. The air shimmered like a mirage, heat rolling off the pavement.

Back inside the truck, Ryan noticed the way she pushed her sunglasses up onto her head. A bead of sweat rolled down her neck. He looked away quickly, but not before she'd caught him.

"Something on your mind, Marshal?"

He kept his eyes on the road. "Plenty."

Lucía turned the radio on and flipped through until she found a scratchy station playing old Spanish love songs. She didn't change it.

Ryan let the music drift between them, slow and sentimental.

She looked out the window, resting her chin on her hand. Her voice was soft when she finally spoke. "You think we'll actually find him? The boy."

He didn't answer right away. Then, "I have to believe we will. If I didn't…"

He trailed off. She didn't push him.

They drove in silence for a while longer, the sky widening above them, the road stretching out ahead, hazy with heat fumes. The air between them buzzed, like the static before a storm.

THIRTY-FIVE

THE ROAD to the tax office had turned from cracked asphalt to gravel, then to something that barely resembled a road at all. Sun glared down on the hood of the vehicle, and dust curled in waves behind them as Lucía studied the location pin glowing on her screen. Her fingers tapped out patterns on her thigh, nerves wound tight.

"You sure about this?" Ryan asked from behind the wheel.

Lucía threw him a side-eye. "You mean, surer than I was last time?"

He kept his face carefully impassive. "That's not what I said."

They pulled up in front of a squat concrete building that looked like it hadn't seen a fresh coat of paint since the early 2000s. One security camera hung limp over the front door, its lens cracked. A half-torn sign read OFICINA REGIONAL DE IMPUESTOS. A stray dog lay sprawled in the shade of the entry-way, too lazy or heat-stricken to react.

Ryan grunted. "Hell of a place to hide a money trail."

Lucía tucked the laptop into her backpack and slid out of the truck. The air outside felt like a hair dryer against her face. The only sounds were the ticking engine and a cicada chorus from the dry scrubland behind them.

"How do you want to play it?" Ryan asked.

"Soft entry first. If it's locked, I have contingencies."

He raised a brow but said nothing. He was letting her lead, like he had with the car purchase. She couldn't work out if it was refreshing or patronizing, and now was hardly the time to analyze it.

The front door creaked open with surprising ease. Inside, the place was even more depressing: a patchwork of flickering fluorescents, dead ceiling fans, and dust motes in the slats of sunlight coming through the blinds. A single receptionist desk stood empty, the chair tucked in, unused. A fake snake plant in a plastic pot tried but failed to add some life.

"Charming," Ryan muttered.

Lucía found a terminal behind the counter and booted it up. It wheezed to life. While she waited, she took a bottle of water from her pack and drank deeply, passing another silently to Ryan. He accepted it with a nod and glanced toward the hallway.

"Anyone here?"

"Place is on the books but barely functional," she said. "They keep it open for paperwork that hasn't been digitized yet. It's basically a dead site."

Ryan prowled the room like a caged animal while she worked. The desktop OS was a decade out of date. She inserted a USB patch loaded with custom scrapers and her fingers darted across the keys.

A few minutes later, she found the transactions she was looking for. Altamar Seafood. Her stomach flipped.

"Got something?" Ryan asked.

"Hold on." She kept scrolling. A transaction was tagged "verified," timestamped two days ago, but it was filed under an archive last accessed four months prior. That shouldn't be possible.

She clicked into the metadata.

And froze.

Ryan noticed immediately. "What is it?"

Lucía swallowed hard. "These files were altered recently. But it's hidden beneath layers that look old. Like someone scrubbed it and then put it back."

Ryan moved closer, peering at the screen.

"That a problem?"

Lucía's fingers moved quickly, pulling up a string of embedded markers. There. In the last line of obfuscated code, a digital signature. Not obvious. But she knew it.

Someone had known they would come. Someone had built the breadcrumb trail deliberately. The shell company, the tax filings, the child-size clothing invoice—it was too perfect. Like it had been designed to drag them to this very place at this very time.

Her heart stuttered. "Ryan, we need to go. Now."

He blinked. "What—?"

"It's a trap."

The words had barely left her mouth when the first shot cracked through the window. Glass shattered. Ryan shoved her to the ground. "Down!"

THIRTY-SIX

RYAN'S SHOULDER slammed against the floor with a jolt that knocked the air from his lungs. The first gunshot still echoed in his ears. He didn't wait; he dragged Lucía with him behind the desk as shards of glass rained down in vicious arcs. They hit the tiles like sleet, skittering and sharp.

"Stay low," he barked. His hand went to his hip and his PPK cleared leather with a snap.

Another shot cracked overhead. A fluorescent bulb exploded in a burst of sparks. One bullet sliced clean through the countertop, burying itself in the drywall inches from Lucía's head.

She flinched, covering her ears. "They're flanking," she said, breath ragged. "Two shooters at least. Maybe more."

He swore under his breath. He could see the shadows now—flickering movements outside the broken window, gliding like wraiths. Too disciplined for street muscle. Whoever they were, they were trained, armed, and not fucking around.

Blood trickled from a shallow cut on Lucía's cheek. "We have to get out of here. There must be a back exit."

Ryan nodded, angling his body toward the narrow hallway behind them. He stood, helping Lucía to her feet.

Then the front door exploded inward.

Wood splintered, hinges ripped. A tall man entered, all tactical black and purpose—no mask, just dead eyes. He raised an assault rifle with the calm precision of someone not expecting to miss.

Ryan fired. Two quick shots.

The man moved like water, ducking into cover behind a filing cabinet and firing.

Bullets tore into the wall behind him. Whoever this bastard was, he wasn't just a trigger-happy thug, he was methodical.

Lucía cried out. A round caught her shoulder and spun her into the desk with a thud.

"Lucía!"

"Fuck! I'm hit."

Ryan felt his heart stop, then restarted beating at twice the rate. "Where?"

"Shoulder. I'm okay."

The shooter was still behind the filing cabinets, repositioning. Ryan could hear the scuff of boots on linoleum. He surged forward, grabbing her under the uninjured arm. Another spray of gunfire ripped through the air, shredding papers, punching through furniture. He ducked low, shielding her with his body.

Her face was pale, lips drawn tight in pain, but she was still conscious. "You good to move?"

"Better than staying here."

He nodded. "Alright. Go!"

They bolted down the hallway, Ryan firing blindly behind them to suppress the shooter. He kicked open the back door. Blinding sunlight, heat, and the dry rasp of cicadas hit them. A cracked lot stretched behind the building: chain-link fence, weeds, a rusted water tank.

Movement at the fence line—a muzzle flash.

"Down!"

They dropped behind an ancient dumpster as bullets stitched the wall. Ryan leaned out, squeezed off two rounds; one ricocheted, the second made the shooter duck.

The PPK clicked empty. Ryan hit the release, yanked the spent mag clear, and shoved in another. The slide stayed forward, so he racked it once, the action snapping loud in the still air. "Truck's around the front," he said.

"That's where they are."

"Yeah. But it's still our only ride."

They ran, low and fast, hugging the wall. Lucía stumbled once, caught herself, pushed on. Her right shoulder was slick with blood.

They reached the corner. Ryan risked a glance and saw the truck was still there, baking in the heat. Two men were standing near the front steps of the tax office, scanning the road. "On my mark, you run for the passenger side."

Lucía's face was pale but set. "Okay."

He stepped out, fired three quick shots. The attackers flinched and scattered for cover.

"Go!"

Lucía bolted.

Blood trailed behind her as she sprinted for the car. She dropped beside the front fender and yanked the passenger door open, using it as a shield. Her back hit the metal, breath coming hard.

Bullets punched into the gravel nearby.

She raised the Colt with one hand and fired—once, twice—forcing the shooters to duck again.

Ryan moved, sprinting low across open ground. A round skipped off the dirt just behind his boots. He vaulted the hood and slid into the driver's seat in one fluid motion, ducking low below the dash.

His hand went straight to the ignition. Nothing. No keys.

"What are you waiting for?" Lucía shouted, braced behind the open door, gun up again.

"They took the fucking keys," Ryan hissed, crouched in the footwell. He slammed a fist against the steering column.

He drew the folding knife from his boot, snapped it open, and stabbed it up into the plastic under the wheel. It cracked. Wires spilled loose. His hands shook, but he stripped two wires with the blade, twisted them.

Sparks jumped. The engine coughed, sputtered.

Died.

Another shot punched through the rear window. Shards exploded across the seat. Lucía ducked instinctively but stayed in place.

Ryan cursed under his breath, found another wire, twisted it tight. "You're not dying here," he muttered. He wasn't sure if it was to her or himself.

He found the starter line, crossed it with the others. Another spark. The truck gave a choking roar and caught.

"Move!" he shouted.

Lucía scrambled into the seat, gun still clutched in her hand and slammed the door. Ryan swung his pistol up and fired two shots through the half-shattered windshield. The return fire cut off.

He jammed the truck into gear and hit the gas. The tires screamed. A final round shattered the side mirror as they tore down the road, dust boiling behind them.

"Hang on."

Lucía slumped against the seat, lips pale, hands wet with blood. "That was no coincidence."

"No," Ryan said. His knuckles whitened on the wheel. "That lead was planted."

"And we took the bait."

THIRTY-SEVEN

RYAN DROVE like the devil was on his heels, which, judging by the bullet holes riddling the truck and the woman bleeding out beside him, wasn't far from the truth. The rearview mirror showed nothing but empty road and swirling dust behind. No one was tailing them, at least for now.

Lucía was slumped against the passenger seat, her face ghost-pale, lips bloodless. Her fingers clutched a balled-up T-shirt she'd taken from her backpack against her shoulder, blood soaking through the fabric in sticky waves. Her breath came in shallow, rasping gasps, each one more labored than the last.

"You still with me?" he asked, knuckles white on the steering wheel as he took a sharp curve too fast.

"Yeah," she whispered, voice thin and shredded with pain. "Bullet's still in, I think. Burns like hell."

"Don't talk. Just hold pressure. We'll stop soon. I'll get a look at it."

They hit a patch of uneven road, and the whole truck jolted. Lucía let out a strangled sound, curling further into herself. Ryan's gut clenched. He needed to get her off the road, now.

He scanned the roadside and spotted a narrow dirt turnoff veiled behind scrubby trees. Without warning, he yanked the wheel and veered off. Gravel spat up under the tires as the truck rumbled to a stop beneath a cluster of mesquite.

He killed the engine then jumped out and sprinted around to her side. The door stuck, then gave. Lucía tried to move but slumped sideways, the blood loss catching up to her. He caught her just in time, bracing her against his chest.

"Shit," he muttered. "Come on, Lucía. Stay with me."

He laid her out carefully on his jacket, spread across the dirt and gravel. Her skin felt clammy beneath his fingers, breath fluttering like a baby bird. She winced as he peeled back the blood-soaked T-shirt, revealing a wound high in her shoulder—angry, swollen, still seeping red.

"This is gonna hurt like fuck," he said, pulling out his pocket knife and lighter.

Lucía gave him a faint, wry smile. "That your version of bedside manner?"

"Don't get used to it."

He sterilized the blade and carefully widened the tear in the skin, hoping to spot the bullet. Nothing visible. It was lodged too deep. Her body jerked under his hands, a cry catching in her throat.

"Damn it," he swore under his breath. "It's too far in. I can't get it."

"Don't stop," she panted. "We can't go to a hospital. We can't."

"Then what the hell do you suggest, huh? You bleed out in the dirt?"

Her hand found his wrist. Weak, but steady. "Just…stop the bleeding. Buy us some time."

He wrapped the wound as best he could with gauze and tied it off with a torn strip of his own shirt. It wasn't enough. Her pulse was too fast. Her skin was losing its color.

A low groan escaped her lips. She was fading.

And then he heard the crunch of tires on gravel. Faint, but growing louder.

Ryan's head snapped up. He was on his feet, pistol out, finger on the trigger. There was a plume of dust in the distance, rising off the road they'd just come down.

A vehicle, approaching fast.

Ryan stepped in front of Lucía, shielding her with his body. There were no trees. No cover. Nowhere left to run. If it was the mercs again, this was it.

He squared his stance and raised his pistol.

The SUV crested the slope and began to slow. Its shape came into focus—big, boxy, government-issue. Tires crunched over gravel as it rolled to a stop ten yards away.

The driver's door opened. A tall man stepped out slowly, both hands raised in plain view. He was broad-shouldered, olive-skinned, maybe mid-forties. Wearing tactical pants, boots, a soft-shell jacket zipped halfway up. A U.S. Marshals badge swung from a lanyard around his neck, catching the light.

His face was unmistakable.

Deputy U.S. Marshal Tomás Gates.

"Easy, Ryan," Gates said, calm as ever.

Disbelief slammed through Ryan like a punch. The gun didn't waver. "How the hell did you find us?"

"We've been following cartel signals. This area lit up like Christmas when that tax office got hit."

Lucía stirred weakly behind him. Ryan's glance flicked to her, then back to Gates.

"She needs a doctor."

"Yeah," Gates said. "And she's not gonna make it much longer unless we move now."

"Why should I trust you?"

"Because you don't have a choice."

Ryan's jaw clenched. The silence stretched taut.

Finally, he lowered the gun. Not all the way, but enough.

He turned, crouched down beside Lucía. Her eyelids fluttered. Her lips were cracked, whispering something he couldn't make out. He lifted her again, slower this time. Her head fell against his chest.

Gates opened the back door of his vehicle. "Put her in. I know a place we can take her."

Ryan hesitated just a breath longer. Then he nodded.

He eased Lucía into the SUV. Gates moved around to the front and slid behind the wheel.

Ryan got into the back seat, never taking his eyes off him.

Trust would come later. Right now, he had to keep her breathing.

———

Ryan crouched in the back of the SUV, knees braced against the seat in front. Lucía lay across the bench seat, her head in his lap, skin slick with sweat and grit. Blood stained the collar of her shirt and had soaked through the bandage he'd hastily wrapped around her shoulder. The fabric clung damp to her side, and her breath came shallow and fast.

The bullet was still inside.

"You got a med kit?"

Gates's eyes met his in the rearview mirror. Keeping one hand on the wheel, he reached across and opened the glove box. Pulled out a white plastic box.

Ryan grabbed the box, resting it on the front seat console. He opened it and did a quick stocktake: bandages, gauze pads, alcohol wipes, a sheet of ibuprofen, an instant cold pack, some scissors, gloves and a bottle of iodine. Better than nothing. But nothing that would treat a bullet wound.

He ripped open a couple of gauze pads and held them against the wound, applying pressure with both hands. "Sorry," he muttered.

Lucía blinked up at him, dazed. "Not your fault."

She was trying to be brave, but he could see the strain in her clenched jaw, the sweat gathered in her hairline. She'd lost too much blood. Her skin was clammy and pale.

Gates was speaking again, but Ryan had drowned him out.

His focus was on Lucía's face. It was drawn and sweat-slicked. Every time the SUV hit a bump, her lashes fluttered like she was caught between dreams and pain. Her hand twitched against his thigh.

He couldn't stop replaying the moment he'd heard her say *I'm hit*. The words had landed like a gunshot to his own gut. That instant, sickening jolt, as if the ground had been yanked out from beneath him.

It wasn't just adrenaline or shock. It was something deeper: the creeping realization that he might lose her. Not just a partner, or a source of intel.

Her.

The thought scraped at something raw and vulnerable he hadn't let himself examine—not in years. He'd watched too many people vanish behind the veil of violence and bad timing already. He couldn't do it again. Not with her.

He tightened his grip on her hand. She didn't stir. *Please*, he thought, and didn't know who he was asking.

He glanced up to find Gates watching him from the front seat.

Ryan looked up, voice rough. "Why the hell have you been tailing us?"

Gates didn't look away from the road. "Watching," he said. "There's a difference."

"Why?"

Gates exhaled. "Because I'm hunting the same thing you are. Noah Carmichael."

The name landed hard.

Lucía was barely conscious now, blood soaking the seat beneath her. "You're not after Ryan?" she said, voice hoarse.

"No," Gates said. "And right now I think we've all got more urgent problems."

"Can you take us somewhere safe?" Ryan asked.

Gates nodded once. "I know just the place."

THIRTY-EIGHT

THE HOUSE WAS TUCKED behind a rusted metal gate, half-eaten by the wild brush of the coastline hills. There were no exterior lights, no clear driveway, just a gravel track that vanished into the growing dusk. Gates maneuvered the SUV down it, the headlights cutting a narrow path through the undergrowth.

"This place secure?" Ryan asked, breaking the silence as they bounced to a stop in front of the darkened house.

Gates killed the engine and leaned forward on the wheel. "As secure as anything gets out here."

Ryan opened the door, gravel crunching under his boots. Lucía was barely conscious, her weight limp as he gathered her in his arms.

Gates moved fast, unlocking the door with a key from around his neck. He led the way through a sparsely furnished front room to the nearest bedroom.

Ryan laid Lucía on a narrow bed with taut white sheets and a folded blanket. She let out a soft moan, her face twisted in pain. Her tank top stuck to her side where blood had soaked through the bandages.

"She's crashing," Ryan muttered, brushing damp strands of hair from her forehead.

Gates disappeared into a hallway and returned moments later with a trauma kit, a portable vitals monitor, and a small cooler marked with medical tape. "Got lidocaine, forceps, sterile gauze, and sutures. Bullet's still inside. You're gonna have to take it out."

Ryan stared at him. "It's deep."

Gates raised a brow. "You trust me to do it?"

Ryan didn't answer. He just pulled on the nitrile gloves Gates handed him.

Lucía stirred, mumbling something unintelligible. Her body twitched against the mattress.

"Get me a bowl of clean water and some towels," Ryan said, already tearing open gauze packets.

Gates moved through to the kitchen, and Ryan got to work. He cut away the bloodstained fabric of her top, swabbed the wound, and injected the lidocaine. Her skin flinched under the needle, but she didn't wake.

The tools gleamed under the low light of the bedside lamp. Ryan found the entry wound, shallow but bleeding steadily. He eased the forceps into the torn flesh. A quiet metallic scrape, then resistance. He shifted his angle.

Lucía twitched, a strangled sound escaping her lips. Her fingers locked onto the edge of the mattress.

"Almost there," Ryan murmured, sweat beading along his temple.

Finally, the bullet came free. He dropped it into a metal tray with a dull clink.

Lucía's body slackened. She'd passed out.

Gates returned with the water and towels. Ryan worked fast, flushing the wound, dressing it tight, and checking her vitals. The monitor beeped softly—steady, but weak.

He washed his hands at the kitchen sink. Blood swirled pink down the drain. Gates leaned against the doorframe, arms crossed.

"You did good," Gates said.

Ryan dried his hands with a rag. "Why are you helping us, Gates? Really?"

There was a long beat before Gates replied. "Because I still believe in what we swore to do. And because there's a seven-year-old boy in danger who didn't choose any of this."

Ryan looked away. Gates didn't sound like he was lying. In fact, from his memory of his time working with the man, this kind of *swoop in and save the day* bullshit was exactly his MO.

And hadn't he done exactly that? If he hadn't shown up when he did, Lucía would almost certainly have bled out on the side of that road in Salina Cruz. Another woman he wasn't able to save.

"Ryan, believe it or not, you used to be one of the best fugitive hunters I ever worked with. So maybe we stop stepping on each other's toes. Especially when we want the same thing."

"And after?" Ryan asked. "What happens when this is over?"

Gates didn't blink. "One thing at a time."

He tossed the rag in the sink and faced Gates. "What do you know about Noah?"

Gates rubbed a hand over his jaw. "Came across my desk a week ago. Missing persons report, filed out of Tennessee. Grandmother named Diane Carmichael. Said her daughter had died and the boy was all she had left. Claimed he up and vanished without warning."

Ryan exhaled but said nothing.

Gates continued. "When the name *Kylie Inglis* showed up on the maternal records, that flagged the whole damn system. Her death, the circumstances, and who she used to be married to." He gave Ryan a pointed look.

Ryan didn't flinch. "So they handed it to you."

"Pulled me off a cartel smuggling case in Laredo. Gave me the file. Told me to follow the smoke." He paused, tilting his head slightly. "Everyone in the Marshal's Service knows the Inglis story. But I still ran the trace myself. Did my own digging."

Ryan said nothing. A silence opened up between them.

Then Gates added, more softly, "I met Kylie once, you know."

Ryan looked up, surprised.

Gates gave a half-shrug. "Years ago. You were stationed in Memphis, I think. Some fugitive hand-off brought me through town. She came to the field office. Sat in your car for two hours while we finished up the paperwork."

Ryan glanced away, jaw tight.

"She looked tired," Gates said. "Thin. Nervous. But she smiled when you came out. I remember that."

Ryan said nothing, but his knuckles were white where they gripped the counter. Then he asked, "You believe he's still alive?"

Gates exhaled before he answered. "I wouldn't be here if I didn't."

Ryan could feel Gates watching him, but he said nothing. Just nodded once. Then he added quietly, "If you know all about me, you know I'm still on the Marshals' Most Wanted list, right?"

Gates gave him a long look.

"And you're not planning to haul me in?"

"Not unless you give me a reason to."

Ryan arched a brow. "That easy, huh?"

"Look, I'm not here to score points. The mission is the boy. If bringing you in was my priority, we wouldn't be having this conversation."

Ryan let that sit. He didn't fully believe it, not yet. But for now, they had a shared goal, and that was enough.

He returned to Lucía's bedside. Her breathing was slower now, less ragged. Her skin was still pale, but no longer ghost-white. He adjusted the blanket over her, letting his hand linger near her shoulder.

She'd made it through—barely.

Gates appeared in the doorway and tossed him a bottle of water. "Get some rest. I'll take first watch."

Ryan didn't reply. He took the water and sat in the chair beside her, eyes fixed on the rhythm of her chest rising and falling. Outside, the wind rustled through dry brush, and the hush of distant waves pulsed against the rocks below.

THIRTY-NINE

LUCÍA WOKE SLOWLY, surfacing from a dreamless dark that left her limbs heavy and her mouth dry. The ceiling above her was unfamiliar: bare, wood-paneled, a ceiling fan spinning on the lowest setting. The light in the room was golden, the kind that meant the sun was either rising or setting. Her body ached like it had been filled with lead. Even blinking took effort.

Pain pulsed through her shoulder as she tried to shift. Not sharp, but deep, the kind that made her stomach clench and her teeth grit. Bandages. Stiff fabric. A tug beneath her skin that told her something foreign had recently been removed.

She wasn't dead. She hadn't been taken. That much she could piece together.

A soft rustle drew her gaze. Ryan sat in a chair nearby, head bowed, one hand resting on his knee, the other wrapped around a water bottle. He looked like he hadn't slept. His shirt was bloodied—her blood, she guessed—and his jaw was shadowed with stubble. There was a tenseness in his shoulders that hadn't eased, even in rest. When he saw her stir, he leaned forward.

"Hey," he said, voice low and rough. "You're awake."

She nodded slightly, wincing at the movement. Her throat was raw. "How long?"

"Few hours," he said. "We got you stabilized. Bullet's out. Fever's breaking."

Lucía let her eyes close for a moment, absorbing that. She wasn't safe, not really. But she wasn't dying anymore either. Her skin was clammy, but the pressure behind her eyes had lessened.

"Where are we?"

"Safehouse somewhere north of Salina Cruz. Gates knew a spot."

At the mention of that name, her eyes snapped open again. A flare of alarm burned through the fog.

"You trust him?" she asked, voice barely above a whisper.

Ryan hesitated. That told her enough.

"I trust him to want the boy safe," he said finally. "Beyond that… I'm watching."

Lucía exhaled through her nose. Her body felt like paper—thin, fragile, dangerously close to tearing. She hated this part: the weakness. The dependence. The vulnerability of needing help, of having no choice but to accept it.

"He had med kits, a trauma cooler," Ryan added. "Everything I needed to patch you up."

"Convenient," she murmured.

Ryan didn't argue. Instead, he stood and crossed the room to the table where a glass of water waited. He brought it back, bracing her gently with one hand as he helped her drink. His touch was surprisingly careful, reverent even, like he understood exactly how close she'd come to vanishing.

Lucía sipped slowly, the coolness hitting her tongue like a shock. "*Gracias*," she said when she finished.

"*De nada.*"

He didn't move away right away. His hand lingered for a moment on her arm before he stepped back.

"You scared the hell out of me," he said.

Lucía swallowed, letting that sit between them. His voice carried something she wasn't ready to deal with. Something almost like…feelings.

"It wasn't your fault," she said quietly.

"Doesn't change the fact I was standing right there."

They lapsed into silence. Outside, a bird cried once and went quiet.

Lucía looked at the ceiling fan. "You ever feel like you keep surviving, but only in smaller and smaller pieces?"

He didn't answer right away. Then, "Yeah. More than I'd like to admit."

She closed her eyes again. "I don't know if I can trust him," she said after a while. "Gates."

"You don't have to. Just long enough to get the kid out."

She nodded. It was the best they could do.

"But if he so much as flinches wrong," Ryan added, "we walk. Deal?"

Lucía met his eyes. "Are you sure we'll still be able to?"

He raised his chin and inhaled. "Trust me, between the two of us, we can outrun Tomás Gates."

Between the two of us.

She felt sleep tugging at her again, softer this time. It no longer felt like surrender, just rest. And that was what truly unsettled her. Not the pain. Not the bullet wound. Not even Gates in the other room. But the quiet certainty that if Ryan stayed by her side, she might actually begin to feel safe.

And that was truly terrifying.

As she drifted into sleep, her last thought wasn't of missing boys or encrypted threats. It was of a calloused hand against her arm. And the unbearable ache of wanting to believe it might stay there.

FORTY

PALE MORNING LIGHT seeped through the cracked blinds, painting thin stripes across the safehouse walls. The room smelled of salt air, and the faint antiseptic tang from the night before. Ryan sat at the edge of the kitchen table, a printed satellite photo spread between him and Gates. The map was creased from travel, its edges frayed. Gates had already circled their target in red ink.

Lucía perched nearby on the couch, a blanket wrapped around her shoulders, a thermal mug cradled in her hands. Her face was pale but sharper than last night. Awake. Alert. Listening. The collar of a clean shirt tugged awkwardly against the bandage at her shoulder.

Gates tapped the compound, a walled property nestled just inland from Puerto Cortés, a tiny settlement a few miles up the coast. "The Altamar Complex," he said. "Technically a seafood distribution facility, but it's been dry for years. Now it's a fortified stash house with docks out back. Water access. Boat routes to the mainland."

Ryan leaned forward. "How many guards?"

"I've had my tech guy Reyes do a full recon. Five we can confirm on shift at any given time. Maybe more inside. Thermal scans show vehicles coming and going irregularly. No fixed schedule. Whoever runs it doesn't want patterns."

Lucía cleared her throat. "If Noah's there, he won't be visible. They'll keep him in the interior block. Minimal windows, heavy surveillance."

Gates nodded. "Exactly. We go in fast, hit the comms relay first, then the perimeter cameras."

Ryan stepped closer, eyeing the red markings on the paper. "What's the ingress plan?"

"Boat drop. Quiet outboard, approach from the reef. We'll beach two hundred yards from the fence line and hike the rest.

"We go in fast and hard. Split once we breach. Ryan, you and I sweep the south wing. Lucía hits the control room, pulls any data she can on recent shipments, lockdown overrides, or movement logs."

Ryan frowned. "She's not cleared for fieldwork. She took a bullet less than a day ago."

Lucía didn't blink. "I'm not sitting this out."

"No one's asking you to sit it out," Ryan said, tone sharper than he intended. "But that compound won't go easy. And if they see your face—"

"Then they know I'm still a threat," she cut in, calm but steely.

Gates studied her, then nodded, almost approving. "She's right. If anyone can crack their internal files, it's her. Besides, we need her eyes on the network. Whoever's running this place didn't build it for fish."

Ryan hesitated. His jaw tightened, hand flexing against the back of a nearby chair. "Fine. But she stays on comms."

Lucía gave him a look that was pure fire. "Don't give me orders."

"She operates from the boat," Gates said. "It's stable, has power, and it keeps her mobile. We'll set her up with secure comms and a digital tap into the compound. If anything goes sideways, she'll see it before we do."

Ryan crossed his arms, his gaze dropping back to the satellite printout. It all sounded too clean. Too rehearsed. He didn't trust it, and he didn't trust Gates. Not fully. Maybe not even partially.

Lucía caught his eye. She gave a near-imperceptible shake of her head—*don't voice it. Not yet.*

Ryan stood and moved to the window. Outside, the hills dropped off sharply toward the sea. A cluster of gulls circled in lazy arcs overhead. A small boat bobbed near the rocky inlet, distant and slow.

Gates went on, "We hit them at midnight. Lights out. No vehicles. All battery-powered gear. I've got NV scopes and suppressed weapons if we need them."

"You bringing anyone else?" Ryan asked.

Gates hesitated. "Just us and Reyes. A bigger team draws attention. We can't afford that."

Lucía asked, "What happens if the intel's wrong? If he's not there?"

Gates's answer was immediate. "Then we get out fast."

Ryan turned to Gates, jaw tight. "And what's your play when this is done? You handing me over to the USMS? To spend the rest of my life in a federal prison?"

"No," Gates said. "You get this boy out, you walk. That's my word."

Ryan exhaled sharply, dragging a hand through his hair. The plan sat between them, full of holes they couldn't afford to face.

But they were going anyway.

Ryan sat at the table, his PPK stripped and scattered in neat rows across a dishtowel. His hands moved with practiced calm: clean, oil, reassemble. The ritual of it settled his nerves.

Gates leaned in the doorway, arms crossed, watching. "What were they calling you back in Ensenada? El...Muro?"

Ryan fitted the barrel back into the slide. Smooth, mechanical. "You've been keeping tabs on me for a while, then."

He stepped into the room, picked up a chipped mug, and poured himself coffee from the stovetop pot. "It fits," he said, ignoring Ryan's comment.

Ryan locked the slide back into place with a sharp metallic click and finally looked up. "You here to help, or to talk shit?"

Gates shrugged, taking a sip. "Just trying to see if the guy I knew is still in there somewhere. Because if he's gone? Might be I'm working with a statue."

Ryan exhaled through his nose and began threading his belt holster. "You think I wanted to walk away? You think I liked what happened in that hurricane?"

Gates didn't flinch. "I think you couldn't live with it. And instead of facing the wreckage, you bolted south. Hiding in hovels, behind fake IDs and aliases."

Ryan stood abruptly, the chair scraping back.

Then Gates added, quieter now, "You were a damn good marshal. One of the best I knew. I hated that you flamed out like that. I still do."

Ryan looked away, fingers tightening around the back of the chair. After a beat, he said, "You ever wonder why we never really got along?"

Gates's grin was faint, but not cruel. "Because I followed the rules. And you followed your gut."

Ryan nodded slowly. "And look where that's gotten both of us."

————

Lucía sat on the bed with her legs curled under her, the scratchy blanket bunched around her waist. Her shoulder throbbed beneath the gauze.

Outside the half-closed door, she heard low voices. Ryan and Gates. Their tones were muted but not undecipherable. Clearly, there was a thread of history between them, something old and unfinished, and she could feel it through the walls.

Every instinct screamed. It was too clean. A federal marshal arriving with medical supplies, real-time surveillance data, and an escape plan? Minutes after she took a bullet?

No. She didn't believe in coincidence. She especially didn't believe in coincidence when it showed up with a badge and a strong jaw.

Lucía slid to the edge of the bed, her bare feet brushing the cold floor. Her breath hitched as she pushed to stand. The room tilted. She gritted her teeth and let the wave pass. Her shoulder burned like it had its own pulse. She sat back down.

Her head ached, but her thoughts were clearer than they'd been in days. Her fear had crystallized into focus. It wasn't the look Gates had given Ryan that bothered her. That had been all surface—friendly tension, something old and personal and half-buried. Something to do with pride, or maybe betrayal. Men like them wore past wounds like old medals.

No. It was the look he'd given her when he thought she wasn't watching. Calculating. Measuring. Like he was appraising a locked vault.

Light-headed, she scooted back and leaned against the wall, her breath slow and shallow.

He knows too much. He has too much. And he asked too few questions.

The door creaked. Ryan stepped inside, his silhouette cutting across the floor. He held two mugs, one steaming.

"You should be resting," he said.

She gave him a tired smile. "So should you."

He crossed to her, handed her the mug. Coffee. Warm. Bitter. She curled her fingers around it, grateful for the heat.

He took a full step back, like he was putting a designated amount of distance between them. He did that a lot: came close, then retreated. Like a tide. She wondered idly what it would feel like if—when—he enveloped her completely. He wouldn't be like water. He would be hot and hard and thick—

She deleted the rest of that thought from her mind like she was clearing a line of code she didn't need.

She rested the mug on her thigh. "Gates is risking a lot for us. You believe that?"

Ryan said nothing for a long time. Then, "No, I don't. But I do know we can't get into that compound without his help." He placed his mug on the table beside her bed, then turned to look at her, voice softer now. "And I also know he helped save your life."

A beat. Her voice held no warmth. "Maybe." She looked at the wall, not at him. "Or maybe he's saving something else."

Ryan didn't push. But he didn't look away either.

The silence between them stretched, taut as wire. She felt his eyes on her. With it came a sensation of self-consciousness, something she'd hadn't felt in a long time. Normally, when she sensed someone was watching her, it triggered only panic. She'd have to go back many years in her memory to find a time when it set off a feeling like this. A feeling like every centimeter of her skin was suddenly on display. Like she was exposed.

In an attempt to tamp the feeling down, she took a sip of coffee, then looked up at him over the rim of the mug. "El Muro, huh?" she said dryly.

His brow furrowed.

"I heard it through the wall," she added. Her smile was faint but real. "Ironically enough."

Ryan gave her a look.

She shrugged one shoulder, careful of the bandage. "But walls don't just keep things out, you know. They also keep things in."

Ryan didn't speak, but something flickered across his face.

"So what happens," she said quietly, "when the wall comes down?"

He didn't answer. Instead, he stepped forward.

Her heart toppled over itself. The atmosphere in the room changed instantly. It was like he'd rolled a live grenade onto the floor between them. This wasn't joking and innuendo anymore: This was real and they both knew it.

The heat from his body met hers before his hands did—one hovering just beside her jaw, hesitant, the other brushing lightly against her wrist.

Her pulse thundered.

He leaned in. Just enough…but not quite enough. And waited.

Lucía lifted her chin. Her free hand came up, fingers catching the front of his shirt.

She whispered, "You gonna move, cowboy, or do I have to push the damn thing down myself?"

That made him smile. Then his mouth found hers.

It was gentle. Introductory. Either one of them could pull away and end it and no harm would be done. They could laugh about it awkwardly later and blame it on a heady combination of adrenaline, blood loss and the weird situation they both found themselves in.

His lips melded with hers, warm and wet, his mouth opening to glide his tongue against hers. Her heartbeat filled her whole head, and it pulsed between her legs.

She didn't pull back. She pulled him closer.

———

The kiss scorched through Ryan like a match to dry tinder. For one fleeting, breathless second, all his caution, all his edges, melted. Her mouth was warm, insistent. A tremor went through her hand as she gripped his shirt, and he shifted immediately, mindful of her wound.

His hand cupped the uninjured side of her jaw with a reverence he hadn't known he possessed. His other hovered just beneath her elbow, steady but feather-light, as if any pressure might unravel her entirely. The smell of her skin—clean sweat, blood, coffee, and something warm he'd started to think of as hers —seeped into his senses.

He drew her closer by instinct, only to feel her flinch, barely, as the motion tugged her shoulder. That broke through the haze. He exhaled a breath that was nearly a groan and leaned back just enough to search her face.

"You okay?" he murmured.

Lucía blinked at him, dazed. Her lips were parted, slightly swollen, her hair sticking to her temple. "Yeah," she said, voice a little hoarse. "Just...don't stop."

He gave a half-smile. "Not planning to."

He leaned back in, slower this time. More deliberate. Their mouths met again, and this time the kiss deepened. It wasn't hurried now, but molten, layered with everything they hadn't been able to say aloud. Her hands slid up his chest, fingers curling into the soft cotton of his shirt. His own hands traced down her spine and settled at her waist, careful not to aggravate her injury. Every part of him was straining to stay gentle, when every part of him wanted more.

Her breath hitched as his lips moved to her jawline, then lower, skimming the curve of her neck. Her pulse thudded against his mouth, fast and shallow. She tilted her head back, eyes fluttering shut.

Then—

The door creaked open.

Gates.

Ryan froze. Lucía stiffened in his arms.

"Well, hell," Gates said, voice bone-dry. "If I'd known you two needed a moment, I'd've brought candles."

Lucía ducked her head, drawing back, cheeks flushed and breathing ragged. Ryan stepped between her and the door almost automatically, tension locking into his spine.

Gates raised his hands, mock-surrender. "Relax. I'm not here to cockblock. Just figured you'd want to know, we've got a window." His tone turned crisp. "Boat's ready. Weapons staged. We move before midnight. You've got an hour to gear up."

He lingered a beat longer than necessary, gaze flicking between them. There was no grin on his face. Just a flicker of something Ryan couldn't quite place. Amusement, maybe. Or warning.

Then he was gone.

The door clicked shut behind him. The air he left behind felt colder.

Ryan turned back to Lucía, who was still flushed but composed. Her lips were parted, her breathing just beginning to steady. She sat back on the bed, brushing her fingers over her mouth like she was trying to ground herself.

"That man," she muttered, brushing a hand through her hair, "has the worst timing on the planet."

Ryan gave a soft, reluctant laugh. "Yeah. Always did."

He sat beside her. Neither of them reached for the other again, but they didn't pull apart, either. A beat passed. Then another.

"We're really doing this?" she said.

He nodded slowly. "Yeah. We are."

FORTY-ONE

LUCÍA SAT on the edge of a cracked porcelain tub, her shirt off, bandages peeled back. The wound looked clean. No swelling. But that wasn't the part that hurt most.

The mirror above the sink was warped. Her reflection stared back with tired, guarded eyes. Her skin was still pale, blood loss and tension working in concert.

Men like Gates didn't just show up out of the blue with tactical medkits and furnished safehouses. Ryan desperately wanted to believe that someone from his old life still gave a damn about saving him. But this didn't feel like rescue. It felt like bait.

She stood slowly and opened the narrow window above the tub. Outside, the coastal air blew cool against her skin. The SUV sat still, engine ticking faintly. But the driver's seat was empty.

Where the hell was Gates?

Something creaked. Not the wind. The floorboards. Purposeful.

Lucía stood instantly, grabbing her gun from the top of the toilet tank. Another creak. Closer now. Footsteps.

A gentle knock.

"You okay?" Ryan's voice, muffled through the door.

Lucía exhaled slowly. Her grip eased. "Fine," she called.

"You don't have to do this, you know," he said.

She pressed her palm to the door. Didn't answer.

All the heat from earlier—from that kiss, from the way his big hands had wrapped around her waist—it all hung in the air still. But so did the doubt. After all, trust was still the most dangerous currency in her world.

———

The boat barely whispered across the water, its small outboard motor hushed beneath a custom silencer Gates claimed was "borrowed from a narco seizure." Ryan didn't want to ask. The less he knew about where Gates sourced his equipment, the better.

He crouched at the bow, eyes narrowed against the salt-laced wind, one hand wrapped tight around the edge of the fiberglass hull. The heat from the kiss still simmered in his veins like whiskey. He shoved the memory down into the same corner where all his other weaknesses lived.

The moon hung low and distorted behind wisps of cloud, casting broken silver ripples across the dark inlet. Beside him, Gates navigated, guiding them toward a dark, indistinct smear of land ahead: the coastline just beyond the Altamar Compound.

Behind them, Lucía sat hunched over her laptop, her face lit in ghostly blue from the maze of open windows. Her injured arm was strapped to her ribs, but her good hand worked with mechanical speed.

"You're clear for another hundred meters," she said into the headset, her voice clipped but controlled. "No active comms from the perimeter. But two sentries rotated through the northeast fence line two minutes ago."

Gates gave a nod without taking his eyes off the dark shoreline. "Copy that. Adjusting heading. Hold the drone until we reach cover."

Ryan barely looked back at her. It was easier that way, easier to stay sharp if he didn't dwell on how pale she looked in the screen glow, or how much blood she'd lost the night before.

"Another minute," Gates murmured. "Get ready to move."

They steered the boat into a natural break in the inlet, a narrow cove flanked by rocks and thick coastal scrub. It was shallow enough to wade. Gates killed the motor, and Ryan was the first to move, sliding over the side and dragging the boat onto a muddy rise beneath a collapsed dune.

The wind tugged at his jacket as he surveyed the terrain. The ridge above them was dark and quiet.

"Looks clean," Ryan said, voice low.

Gates followed, tossing two packs onto the gravel. He handed Ryan a soft rifle case and shouldered a second, then unzipped a pouch to reveal a compact set of bolt cutters wrapped in cloth. Gates's local contact, Reyes—a stocky *federale*, with small round glasses and a buzzcut—joined them without a word. He gave Ryan a nod and dropped into a crouch.

Lucía's voice returned in their ears. "Drone's airborne. I've got you from above. No vehicles in the outer yard. Thermal sweep shows three bodies at the north end. Still no chatter. You're in the window."

Ryan, Gates and Reyes slipped into the dunes, following the winding scrub path that led them around the perimeter. The ground was uneven, coated in wiry brush and shells that cracked beneath their boots despite every effort to stay silent. Ryan led, checking angles, counting seconds between light sweeps.

The fence emerged like a phantom out of the dark: chain-link half-hidden by tangled vines. No barbed wire. No IR cameras. It looked too easy.

Gates knelt and retrieved the bolt cutters, moving with deliberate care. The metal links gave way with soft crunches. Within seconds, they'd peeled back a wide enough section to slide through.

Lucía's voice came again, more urgent. "You're good. Still no movement on internal thermal scans. But there's a motion sensor tripped near the truck bay. It might be a raccoon but stay sharp."

Ryan ducked through the fence first, pistol ready, followed by Gates and Rojas. They pressed into the shadows of a storage silo, then crossed open ground in short bursts.

A guard appeared near a cargo trailer—lean, bored, rifle slung loose. Ryan signaled. Gates tilted his head. Reyes vanished left, silent as a shadow.

There was a low *thwip*, and the guard crumpled without a sound. Tranquilizer dart. Ryan dragged him into cover.

They pushed forward.

Ahead, the warehouse bulked against the skyline. A few lights glimmered in the office wing, but the bay doors were shut. They reached the south entrance, a rust-pocked steel door with a keypad. Gates produced a slim device and wired it in, tapping commands with one hand.

Lucía's voice crackled again. "Override window opens in seventy seconds. Once I engage jamming, you've got ten minutes before backup systems reinitialize."

"Roger that," Gates muttered. The lock unit blinked.

Ryan's heart kicked. He checked his weapon, eyes sweeping the compound's layout. No motion yet. No sounds beyond distant waves and the clicking of Lucía's keys in his earpiece.

"Drone picking up two more heat signatures inside the central corridor," she added. "If they're guards, they're not patrolling."

"Sleeping?" Ryan asked.

"Maybe. Or waiting."

The decoder beeped. Green.

Ryan exchanged a look with Gates. They both understood: once they crossed that threshold, it was game on.

He grasped the door handle, breath steady.

"Ready," he whispered.

Lucía's voice: "Timer starts now."

And with that, they slipped into the dark.

Ryan crouched beside a rusted barrel, his breath coming low and steady as he scanned the warehouse wall. In his ear, Lucía's voice: soft, precise, tethering. "Northwest quadrant is still blind. Your entry window is about ninety seconds. Perimeter guards have begun rotation. No new signals."

"Copy," Ryan muttered.

Gates stood a few feet away, checking his watch. Reyes was already slipping through shadow, moving toward the fuel storage tanks along the western fence. That's where the distraction would go down. Not flashy enough to call in reinforcements, but loud enough to make security take notice.

Lucía's voice again, cooler this time: "Heat bloom near the motor pool. One… No, two guards heading west."

"Reyes," Gates said into his comm. "Light it. Now."

Three seconds later, the quiet cracked with a dull whump. A flash of orange lit the far side of the compound, followed by a column òf smoke and shouting in Spanish. Boots scraped pavement, voices barked orders.

"That's our cue," Gates said.

Ryan moved first, low and fast. They skirted along the corrugated siding of the warehouse, each footstep calculated. At the service entrance, Gates rested his hand on the door handle and gave a subtle nod.

Ryan took point. The keypad had already been disabled by Lucía on the boat, and the moment the latch clicked, he eased the door open. Darkness inside. The smell of solvents and mold.

Inside, rows of dusty crates stacked high, forklifts idle in the corners. No guards in sight.

"Clear," Ryan whispered.

They slipped in, weapons raised. Gates motioned with two fingers, sweeping left. Ryan mirrored right, sweeping between crates, eyes sharp.

Lucía's voice returned. "Perimeter's thinning. One signal

headed toward your sector, but he's not close. You've got about four minutes before full comms come back online."

Ryan moved deeper into the shadows, past crates stamped with false shipping codes. Each step was muscle memory, the old rhythm of tactical movement, reignited.

Then: footsteps. Muffled. Close. Gates paused at a corner, raised a fist. Ryan held.

A guard rounded the corner, rifle low.

Pfft. The guard crumpled before he could speak. Silencer smoke curled from Gates's weapon.

Ryan exhaled and moved forward. They were close now.

Lucía again, this time with urgency: "One of the perimeter guards just turned back. He'll be at your twelve in thirty seconds."

"Copy," Ryan said.

He signaled Gates. They picked up speed.

Beyond the final stack of crates: a secured interior door. Heavy-duty. Likely where they'd stash sensitive cargo—or a child they didn't want anyone to see.

Gates stepped forward, pulled a pry tool from his vest.

The door creaked open just as another distant bang echoed outside. Reyes again. Another distraction.

They slipped inside, silent.

Phase Two: complete.

Showtime was coming.

———

Ryan pressed deeper into the warehouse interior, his breath steady, PPK low but ready. The scent had shifted—less industrial now, more damp and sterile. Like something had been wiped clean in a hurry, then left to rot beneath the surface. The faint echo of his boots on concrete reverberated off high ceilings. It made him feel more exposed than armed.

Lucía's voice crackled through his earpiece, threaded with

tension. "I found a manifest in the compound's internal storage logs. Room 18, east wing. Marked as 'personal holding' with restricted access. No other details."

Ryan's pulse kicked up a notch. "Could be him."

Lucía again: "There's a comms burst from that quadrant five minutes ago. Someone checked in. Not security, internal operations code."

Gates's voice joined in, calm and clipped. "I'll continue sweeping the west wing. Make sure our exfil is clean."

Ryan grunted his assent and adjusted course, angling down the east corridor. The air grew heavier. Metal grates gave way to old tile, the grout stained and cracking. A disused wing, maybe, one that wasn't meant for foot traffic. He passed a security checkpoint—abandoned. A tipped-over chair. The eerie silence of a place forgotten by oversight.

He ghosted down the hallway with the surety of a man who'd done this before. Who used to train men to do this before. Door by door, he passed rooms marked with alphanumeric codes, storage bays, a shuttered infirmary. But something about this stretch of hallway made the hairs on his neck rise.

Lucía again, voice sharper now: "One heat signature inside Room 18. Small. Still."

Ryan's heart thudded once, then went silent. The door was reinforced but not military-grade. Newer than the rest. A retrofit.

He knocked twice.

Nothing.

Then a shuffle. Quiet, hesitant.

"Noah?" he said, voice rougher than he intended.

A pause. Then a boy's voice, hoarse and wary: "Who is it?"

Ryan exhaled. The tightness in his chest cracked just slightly. "I'm a friend of your mom. I came to get you."

There was a keypad beneath the handle, but it too was disabled. Ryan pushed the door open, trying to kept his movements slow and steady to not spook the boy.

He looked smaller than Ryan was expecting. Pale and thin. But his eyes were wide and familiar.

The boy blinked at him, confusion on his face. "Are you here to take me?"

Ryan knelt to meet his gaze. "Yeah, buddy. We have to go. Right now."

He slipped out of his jacket and wrapped it around the boy's narrow shoulders. Noah leaned into him without hesitation. Ryan swallowed hard and scooped him into his arms. The kid barely weighed anything.

Lucía's voice returned: "Thermals lighting up. Movement on the north wall. They're responding to the fires. You've got maybe ninety seconds."

Ryan pivoted, heading back down the corridor at a dead run. Every step felt like walking through water. The walls too close. The shadows too thick.

"Hold tight," he whispered to the boy.

Through comms, Gates again: "Exfil route secure. Southeast hatch unlocked. I'm waiting."

Ryan's grip on the PPK tightened as he moved faster, boots hitting tile, then concrete. Noah's breath warmed the side of his neck.

The compound ahead was no longer quiet. Somewhere distant, a siren wailed—short, sharp, localized. Not an alarm. A signal.

And behind him, far too close, came the sound of a door slamming open.

Ryan didn't look back.

He just ran.

FORTY-TWO

RYAN TORE THROUGH THE CORRIDOR, boots pounding, Noah cradled against his chest. The boy had gone silent, his breath shallow and uneven. Every step Ryan took echoed in his skull like a countdown, every footfall a grim metronome ticking off what little time they had left.

Lucía's voice cracked through his earpiece, laced with tension. "You've got movement behind you. Four, maybe five heat signatures. They're closing. Fast."

Ryan didn't break stride. "Exit status?"

Gates voice came through, calm as ever, like he wasn't knee-deep in a firestorm. "Southeast hatch is clear. I'm in position. Route is green for another sixty seconds, max."

Smoke from the diversion fire bled into the ventilation system, cloaking the corridor in an oily haze. The air reeked of scorched plastic, extinguishers, and fear made tangible.

Ryan rounded a corner, nearly losing his footing, and hit the main junction.

A steel access door loomed ahead, slightly ajar.

Then the siren began.

Not the blaring kind—this one was subtler. Controlled. A

proximity ping. Short, rhythmic chimes, like a heartbeat pulsing through the walls.

Lucía's voice cut through his earpiece, taut and focused. "External trip. Motion sensors on the north ridge just went hot. You've been made."

Ryan ducked low, rammed the door with his shoulder, and burst out onto a loading platform washed in the flicker of distant fire. The moon hung low behind the smoke. Gates and Reyes were crouched behind a stack of pallets, rifles up.

"Here! Move!" Gates barked.

Ryan sprinted toward them, Noah clutched tight against his chest. The boy's arms locked around his neck. Behind them came shouts, boots, and the metallic echo of gunfire in the building.

Gates keyed his comm. "Lucía, status on exfil?"

Static cracked, then her voice came through, louder now, wind rushing in the background. "I'm inbound. Two clicks out. Hold for sixty seconds."

Ryan slid in behind cover, panting. "You're cutting it close."

Lucía didn't miss a beat. "Change that. New contact. SUV on the ridge. Six armed men. They're heading straight for your exit. You need to move now or you'll lose the beach."

Gates cursed softly. "Copy. We're moving."

Reyes rose and fired a short burst into the dark, forcing the advancing shadows to scatter. Ryan took the opening and bolted, lungs burning, boots hammering asphalt. Noah's weight dragged at his arms, but adrenaline kept him moving.

"ETA thirty seconds," Lucía's voice came again, the boat's engine roaring behind her words. "You'll see my light."

"Go!" Gates shouted, falling in beside Ryan.

They tore downhill, gravel and ash skidding underfoot. The loading dock gave way to a stretch of uneven dirt, then to the edge of the inlet, jagged rocks and coarse sand.

Ryan pushed forward, breath ragged. His shirt was soaked with sweat, and every muscle screamed. The wind carried the crackle of fire and the shouts of pursuit. Ahead, through smoke and salt spray, the faint beam of a running light cut across the dark water—Lucía's boat charging toward the shore.

He saw her at the boat's console, eyes wide, scanning the shadows. She gunned the engine, veering the craft toward them through shallow water.

"Incoming!" she shouted.

From the ridge above, muzzle flashes burst like fireworks.

Ryan dove, twisting mid-air so that Noah was shielded beneath him. The sand exploded in a spray of dirt and pebbles as bullets chewed into the shoreline inches from where they landed.

Gates was already pivoting, firing back in short, disciplined bursts. His stance was clean, no panic. Every shot was a message.

"Board now!" he barked.

Lucía swung the boat closer, the hull grinding over rocks and sand. Ryan pushed up, grabbed the edge of the railing, and shoved Noah aboard. Then he followed, pulling hard until his knees hit the deck. Reyes went next, then Gates vaulted in last, landing with a thud and immediately scanning their rear.

Lucía jammed the throttle forward. The boat roared and peeled away, throwing a wake of white water behind them. More shots rang out, wild now, chasing ghosts.

Ryan fell back against the bench, chest heaving, Noah held tight. He could feel the boy's heartbeat against his ribs. Lucía turned from the wheel. Her mouth was drawn, but her eyes searched his with desperate clarity. "Are you okay?"

He looked at her. Then at Gates, who was crouched near the bow, watching the compound vanish into the smoky dark.

"Yeah," Ryan said, though it didn't feel true. "We're okay."

FORTY-THREE

THE BOAT RIDE BACK HAD BEEN quiet. Gates piloted with eerie calm, the small motor cutting a low drone through the black water. Lucía sat in the back, watching the wake stretch behind them like a scar. The air was salt-thick and humid, but she barely felt it. Her gaze kept slipping to the bow, where Ryan sat with Noah curled against his chest.

The boy hadn't said a word since the compound. He clung to Ryan like a lifeline, his small hands twisted into the fabric of his shirt. Ryan kept one arm around him, protective and still, his free hand resting lightly on the boy's back. There was a softness in his face Lucía hadn't seen before, something she hadn't known he was capable of.

For some reason, it unsettled her.

After docking in darkness, they walked. A long, cold trek through scrubland to where Gates had stashed the SUV, hidden beneath a camouflage tarp in a dry arroyo. Noah shivered in Ryan's arms the whole way. Gates drove them in silence, headlights off, one hand on the wheel, the other drumming his thigh with a strange, patient rhythm.

By the time they crested the final ridge and the safehouse came into view, a familiar unease had settled in Lucía's chest.

Inside, the place was untouched. The trauma kit still lay open on the kitchen counter. The bloodstained rag from Lucía's earlier wound had dried stiff. The chair Ryan had sat in, watching her sleep, remained angled toward the bed.

Ryan carried Noah in and laid him gently on the couch in the living room. The boy stirred but didn't wake. Lucía watched as Ryan knelt beside him, brushing the boy's hair back with an unconscious tenderness that caught her off-guard.

Gates moved efficiently, setting his gear near the door, then checking the perimeter through the warped blinds. "We'll stay here until first light. No chatter. No lights."

Ryan didn't answer. He stepped into the kitchenette, opened a bottle of water, and drank half in one go.

Lucía lowered herself onto the kitchen chair, her body still protesting the motion. Everything ached. Her bandages were soaked with sweat, and her skin prickled beneath the gauze.

"Kid needs electrolytes," Gates said. "And rest." He pulled a small packet from his bag and held it up. "I'll mix this into water. It'll help."

Ryan returned to Noah's side, handing him the bottle once Gates had added the powder. The boy drank, eyes still foggy with fear. Ryan murmured something low. Lucía couldn't make out the words.

She turned her attention to Gates.

His bag was pre-packed. Everything in place for a quick getaway. "You planning to get him out tonight?" she asked quietly.

Gates met her gaze. "Soon. The longer we stay, the more exposed we are."

Ryan looked up sharply. "You're not taking him anywhere without telling us where."

"Of course not," Gates said.

Lucía caught Ryan's eyes. Weariness was written into the lines of his face. He nodded once. The look he gave her was intimate but distracted. Like he was still halfway inside that compound, still hearing footsteps and gunshots.

———

The overhead fan stirred the humid air, but not enough to stop the sweat from collecting in the hollow of Lucía's throat. She'd washed the grime and blood and salt spray from her skin in the bathroom with a washcloth, careful not to aggravate her wound. But no sooner had she dressed in fresh clothes than she was damp with sweat again.

She sat cross-legged on the edge of the bed, elbows resting on her knees, her ghost laptop closed in front of her. She hadn't let herself think about the ledger in days. The hunt for Noah had occupied her attention completely and forced it to the periphery of her mind. Maybe that was why she'd been so quick to offer to help. Distraction as a form of protection.

Through the door, she could just hear the soft murmur of voices. Ryan and the boy. Noah's voice, light and tentative: a question about the safehouse generator. A joke from Ryan, followed by a quiet laugh.

The boy was safe now. Her role in the rescue mission was over. Her gaze fell to the laptop. And there was nothing to shield her from the thing she had to face. The ledger. Javier's empire in 1s and 0s. And the digital noose she'd been carrying around for over nine years.

She dragged a hand through her hair. Her shoulder still ached. It was healing, but slow. Every jolt of pain reminded her of Ryan, of how he'd tried to patch her up on the side of that road outside Salina Cruz. Of how he'd risked his own freedom to accept help from Gates. Of how he'd sat by her bedside, the worry etched on his face.

Of how he'd been so gentle with her when he'd kissed her…
And the *kiss*…
Lucía closed her eyes. She could still feel the heat of it. The

grip of his hand at her jaw. The feel of his tongue in her mouth, hot and wet and so hungry for more.

But that had been adrenaline, she told herself. Fear. Relief. Biology.

Distraction, as a form of protection.

She wasn't foolish enough to imagine a life with a man like that. Not with what was coming. Because tomorrow they'd go their separate ways. Gates would take Noah north, back over the border and hopefully back to his home. Ryan would face whatever consequences awaited him for putting his trust in Gates.

And she—

She would become smoke again.

Literally. Because she had no real plan. Just the ledger and the long shadow of Javier Esquivel.

She leaned forward, pulled the laptop closer, and flipped it open. The screen lit her face in blue. She needed to finish what Mateo died for. She needed to bring it down.

Even if it meant burning everything with it.

A soft knock at the door broke her concentration. Ryan's voice, low and cautious, filtered through. "Lucía?"

She quickly wiped her hands on her jeans before opening the door. Ryan stood there, looking at her with quiet concern. She forced a smile, though it didn't reach her eyes. "I'm fine."

He stepped into the room, his gaze flicking to the laptop on the bed, then back to her. "You don't look fine."

Ryan's boots scuffed softly against the wood floor as he stepped into the room. "Want to talk about it?"

Lucía shook her head once, sharp and dismissive. "There's nothing to talk about. I'm okay, I'm just thinking."

"You're shaking."

She looked down. Her fingers were clenched so tightly that her knuckles had gone white.

He crossed his arms but didn't move closer. "I've seen this before. When the pressure gets high enough—"

"You think this is me being emotional."

"No," Ryan said quietly. "I think this is you being human."

She wanted to snap at him, to throw something—maybe the laptop—and march out. But instead, her throat tightened. She looked away, blinking fast. "The final piece of the ledger..." she started, then stopped.

Ryan didn't push. He waited.

Lucía swallowed. "It's not just data. It's not just some string of characters. It's tied to my past. My mistakes. Everything I built, everything I destroyed. It's in me, and I can't take it out without tearing something open."

She hadn't meant to say that much. The room felt suddenly too small. "It was supposed to be justice. But it feels like grief now. All of it."

Ryan unfolded his arms and stepped forward, slow, careful, like she was a wire about to snap. He didn't touch her; he just stood close enough to make her feel it. "What happens if you use it?"

Lucía's jaw clenched. "Everything changes."

His voice softened. "And what happens to you?"

She didn't answer.

———

Lucía sat on the bed and folded her arms. "What about you, cowboy?"

Ryan looked down at her, reading between the faint lines on her face that she'd shut up shop in the sharing-her-feelings department. "What about me?"

"You can't just force me to spill my guts and not reciprocate."

He arched a brow. "Firstly, I didn't force you to do anything."

She arched one back. "And secondly?"

Ryan sat on the bed beside her, head tilted like he was weighing whether to actually say the thing or just let the silence pass.

He chose the thing. "There was a woman."

Lucía rolled her eyes. "There's always a woman."

"She was a federal witness living in Florida. Working as a stripper. She was the kind of beautiful that made people underestimate her. Her testimony put eight Sinaloa guys behind bars."

Lucía's eyebrow arched. "Impressive résumé."

"I was relocating her to a safehouse in Baton Rouge. Then Hurricane Petra hit. I took a detour, ended up sheltering us in a falling-down farmhouse west of Mobile. No cell signal. Storm surge rising."

She gave a small smile. "Let me guess. You fell for her."

Ryan's mouth twitched. "She was sharp. Funny. Said she wanted to be a dance therapist, whatever the hell that is." He looked down at the floor. "I started thinking...maybe I could disappear. Off-grid. New name. Her, me. She had a way of making you forget the walls were closing in."

Lucía's amusement faded just slightly. "But they were."

"Yeah," he said. "Because I'd sold her out."

The words dropped with weight, not volume.

Lucía sat still.

"They had my ex-wife, Kylie. I hadn't spoken to her in months. Last I knew, she was using again. Living with Noah in a cockroach-infested flat in Philly, bouncing between rehabs. Then I got a call."

He paused. "It wasn't her voice on the line. It was a man. He said he'd grabbed her off the street after he'd found her shooting up on his doorstep. He said she was safe, for now. But I'd need to do something for him."

Lucía's expression darkened.

"Kylie had told him I was a U.S. marshal. He seemed to think I could assess WITSEC files, and he wanted one in particular: Jessica Meeks's. Said she'd been a dancer who'd flipped on the Sinaloa boys. Wanted confirmation. Location. Said they'd cut Kylie into pieces if I didn't do it."

He looked down, his voice tight. "I pulled some strings. Big ones. Got my hands on her record. Told myself I was saving a life." He exhaled through his nose. "I told myself a lot of things."

Lucía didn't interrupt.

"I gave him the file. Then I tried to fix my own mess by trying to get Jessica to safety. The storm got in the way. So did the truth. Needless to say, we never made it to Baton Rouge."

Her brow furrowed. "She figured it all out?"

"She did. Afterwards, she vanished again. Last seen headed for Texas, I think." He gestured around the room. "I did the same. But for different reasons."

Lucía leaned back, studying him. "So you're the dirty cop in every movie. The one who sleeps with the witness, breaks protocol, and blows up his whole life."

Ryan didn't smile. "Except I didn't even get to sleep with her."

She tilted her head. "Did she at least get a goodbye kiss before you ruined everything?"

He finally looked amused. "You really want me to answer that?"

Lucía's eyes softened, though her mouth kept its edge. "And now you're here. Still running."

Ryan nodded once. "You, too."

She didn't deny it.

———

Lucía's gaze held his for a long, loaded second. The room was still. The whole world seemed to have exhaled and not yet breathed in again.

She reached out, slowly, and let her fingers rest against his forearm. Light, tentative. Not an invitation. Just contact.

Ryan didn't flinch.

Her hand moved upward, barely tracing. She paused at the bend of his elbow, then let her palm settle flat against his bicep. It was steady there, like she needed the solidity beneath it. Or like she was checking to see if he'd disappear.

He didn't.

She could feel her pulse beating thickly under her skin all over her body. She tried to remember the last time a man coaxed this kind of a response out of her body just by looking at her. Actually, she knew exactly when that had been, and it was a very long time ago.

His hand came up, brushing a stray lock of hair behind her ear. The movement was hesitant, gentle. As if he knew he'd only get one chance to do this right.

The tension between them was so taunt it almost hummed. Without breaking eye contact, she leaned over until her mouth was a breath away from his. There was a moment of pure, crystallized silence.

Then he closed that tiny distance and kissed her.

Their lips met in a soft press. Testing. But then he placed a hand on the back of her neck, and her head fell back and her mouth opened for him.

His tongue dipped into her mouth. Then there was no stopping it. Not now. There was only one way this was going to end, and they both knew it.

Most men treated kissing like something that had to be gotten over quickly so they could get to the main event. But not Ryan. He took his time, his tongue gliding against hers, like he could do this all night.

But after a while, urgency began growing. She could feel it in the way his fingers dug into her hair above her ear. She had twisted herself to face him on the bed and he had mirrored her. It was awkward and uncomfortable, and as soon as they broke off the kiss, their bodies automatically sought more user-friendly positions.

He moved across the bed, his back to the wall, pulling her with him. She swung herself onto his lap so her butt was pressed against his thighs. They didn't make eye contact while they were doing this, just in case either saw something in the other's eyes that made them rethink the consequences of it.

Regretting this was for later.

He reached up, fumbling the buttons of her shirt free. Because of her shoulder wound, she wasn't wearing a bra, and at the sight of her bare breasts, he gave a low moan.

He cupped the left one, then the right. The sensation of his hands on her sent currents of pure pleasure over her skin.

She leaned over him, making short work of his shirt buttons. Pushing the fabric apart, she found what she'd only been able to admire from afar: hard muscle, hot skin and a fine dusting of golden hair that trailed all the way down…

He watched her eyes slide down to his belt buckle. "Get my cock out," he whispered.

A pulse of white-hot heat went straight to her core. Holy fuck, she wasn't going to need to be told twice. She unclasped his belt and unzipped his fly. She slipped a hand into his briefs and pulled him out. He was big, and so thick that if she wasn't already sopping wet between her legs, it would hurt. "Damn," she murmured. "It's always the quiet ones."

As she ran her hand up his shaft, he drew in a sharp breath. "Lucía," he said on the exhale. The word was both a question and a plea. "You want it inside you?"

She gave a breathy laugh. "If it'll fit."

He gripped the back of her neck, pulling her ear close to his lips. "Oh sweetheart, we can make it fit."

His words made her almost moan out loud.

He unfastened the button fly of her pants and pushed them down her thighs. Then he slid his hand into her panties. When his fingers discovered how wet she was, a slow smile spread across his face.

"Is all this for me?" he said, gliding up and down her slickness.

The feel of his blunt fingers working their magic against her clit made her almost speechless with desire, but she managed to contain it long enough to give his chest a little shove. "Hey. It's been a long time, okay?"

He smirked. "For me too. I almost came when you wrapped your hand around it."

"Mmm," she said. His cock was still jutting out above the waistband of his underwear. She gripped it again, massaging the tip with her thumb. "You mean when I did this?"

He sucked in a breath and dropped his head back against the wall. His big hand closed around hers, stopping her from continuing her exploration.

When he looked at her again, his eyes grew serious. "I don't have a condom."

She gave a quick shake of her head. She'd had an IUD for years. "It's okay."

Climbing off him to kick her pants away, she straddled him again, bracing her hands on his shoulders. He dropped his hands to her hips, angling her so her pussy was pressing right against his cock. They were both panting now, partly in an effort to keep quiet, but they both held their breath as she lowered herself down onto him.

They expelled those breaths simultaneously in a heavy sigh. He leaned forward, wrapping his hands around her lower back and pulling her all the way down onto him.

She gave an involuntary gasp and wrapped her good arm around his neck, pressing the side of her face against his. "Oh my God, Ryan," she whispered, squeezing her eyes shut.

"Am I hurting you?" he said, right in her ear.

She shook her head, even though he was hurting her, a little. But the pressure felt better than the pain. "You feel incredible."

His grip on her waist was tight and damp with sweat. "You feel pretty damn incredible yourself."

She nestled herself closer to him. "I just hope we're driving tomorrow and not walking."

He laughed and she could feel the vibration of it in her own chest.

Slowly, she eased herself off him, then back down again as he lifted his hips to meet her. They formed a rhythm, still tightly gripping each other's bodies, their movements both urgent and steady. He was taking sharp breaths and exhaling slowly, like he was trying to slow himself down.

As she got used to the sensation of him moving inside her, their rhythm picked up pace. His fingers dug into the flesh of her hips, pulling her flush against him, again and again. Her arm was still hooked tightly around his neck, her cheek against his, their bare chests pressed together. She felt so close to him in that moment—this man she barely knew, this man she shouldn't trust. Somehow, that only made it hotter.

One of his hands slid up her back to grip her braid, and she knew he wasn't going to last much longer. Neither was she. He was hitting about three different spots inside her, so when she came, it was almost painfully intense. She lifted her hand from around his neck and gripped a handful of his hair and sunk her teeth into his shoulder.

He groaned, his abdomen tensing. Then he released inside her with a shudder that she felt travel through his whole body.

He crushed her against his chest and held her there. She could feel his heart thumping in his chest. Hers was beating just as hard, right against his. Like they were both trying to knock something down in there.

He was still breathing hard, his hand hanging onto her braid like it was a lifeline. Ripples of pleasure continued to spread through her. She hadn't come that hard in…maybe ever.

They stayed that way for a long time. His arms wrapped tightly around her, her cheek resting against his jaw. His breath washed over the skin of her neck. He smelled like soap and under it, his own warm male scent. That moment felt so perfect, so right, she never wanted it to end. She wanted the rest of the world to just blow away and leave the two of them there like this forever.

FORTY-FOUR

GATES SAT ALONE in the kitchen of the safehouse, the old oscillating fan ticking back and forth above him. The boy was asleep on the couch, and Ryan and Lucía had retreated to the bedroom to… Well, he knew what they were doing, and it wasn't something he wanted to contemplate.

He'd seen the way Lucía had watched him during the boat ride back. Not with thanks. With calculation. She hadn't asked him anything directly, but her eyes had. *How did you get here so fast? Why did you have supplies ready? Why are you always one step ahead?*

He could feel her questions like pinpricks against his back.

Ryan hadn't said much either, just kept one hand on the kid, the other close to his sidearm. Protective. Guarded. Watching Gates like he was still trying to decide if this was a trap he'd just walked into willingly.

Fine. Let them wonder.

Gates didn't need their trust. He just needed a little more time.

He turned his attention back to the device in his lap—a matte-black satellite communicator, smaller than a paperback and far more dangerous. The screen glowed faintly, casting green light across his face. He typed without hesitation, fingers quick and efficient.

ASSET SECURED. FINAL TRANSFER PENDING.

He stared at the message for a moment before hitting **SEND**. The burst was encrypted, untraceable, routed through two proxy chains. No one reading it would know what or who the asset was.

But they would know Gates had delivered. Or was about to.

The message disappeared, burned by the device's failsafe protocol. He watched the cursor blink three times. Then nothing.

He closed the cover and leaned back, exhaling through his nose.

This was the part he hated.

Not the lies. Not the covert drops or fake names or burner networks. Those were just tools. What he hated was the flicker. The thing that caught in his chest when the mission stopped being clean.

He'd told himself it was still about the job. Still about justice. Getting the ledger back into the right hands. Ensuring no more people died.

But the edges had started to blur. Ever since Inglis had walked back into the picture. Ever since Lucía Duarte became more than a name on a file.

He rubbed a hand down his face, then he stood, stretching his back, and crossed to the window. Outside, the moonlit coast was still. The ocean whispered in the distance, waves lapping against the rocks. It was almost peaceful.

He scanned the line of the horizon, checked the angle of the shadows. No movement. No lights. He waited another moment, then closed the curtain.

Tomorrow, everything would change.

FORTY-FIVE

RYAN STIRRED, his cheek pressed against the back of her shoulder. Her skin was warm and smelled so good it made his mouth water. Her hair tickled his nose but he didn't move.

Her breathing was slow and even. And for once, his was too.

The ceiling fan above them kept up its sluggish rhythm. Outside, no birds yet. Just the hushed quiet of desert pre-dawn.

Ryan closed his eyes again, letting it wash over him. Last night hadn't been planned. And it sure as hell hadn't been smart. But it had been real. Not just the sex—the heat of her on top of him, the soft murmur of her voice against his neck—but the moment after, when she didn't move away. When she stayed curled against him, her fingers pressing against his skin like she was checking he hadn't vanished.

His arm was draped over her waist now, his hand resting on the bare slope of her stomach. Her skin was soft there, still warm. He could feel the rise and fall of her breath. Slow. Safe.

He didn't feel safe often. But now—

A thought tugged. He frowned faintly.

Something felt wrong.

He shifted, carefully lifting his head. His eyes adjusted to the dark. He sat up slowly, trying not to jostle Lucía.

Ryan stood, bare feet hitting the cool floor. He yanked the door open and stepped into the hallway, bare-chested.

The front room was empty. Couch still sagging, the throw blanket folded too neatly.

"Noah?" he called, low and sharp.

Silence.

His heart thudded once, hard. He moved through the kitchen fast—eyes darting, mind already clocking anomalies. The fridge door hung slightly ajar. A half-drunk water bottle sweated on the table. He turned toward the back bedroom.

Empty. No duffel. No boots. No Gates.

His voice came rough: "Jesus Christ."

Lucía's voice floated in from the bedroom. "What's wrong?"

She appeared in the hallway, barefoot, shirt unbuttoned, hair still tangled from sleep.

"They're gone," Ryan said. "Noah. Gates."

"Gone?" She blinked, like trying to clear a fog from her mind. "Why wouldn't he wake us?"

Ryan didn't respond, just strode past her and yanked open the front door.

Outside, the pre-dawn haze clung to the scrubland. Ryan crossed the dirt lot in long strides, his bare feet kicking up dry dust. The SUV was still there—Gates's.

He yanked open the driver's side door. Keys still in the ignition. A half-empty bottle of water in the cupholder. The map they'd used to plan the compound breach lay folded on the passenger seat, edges curled from handling.

Lucía caught up to him, breath uneven. She took one look and frowned. "Wait. He left the vehicle?"

"Looks like it."

She moved around to the passenger side and opened the door slowly, as if something might leap out. Her brow furrowed. "He couldn't have gone on foot."

"No." Ryan stepped back, thinking. Faint tire tracks trailed toward the road. "He had help." He crouched near the tire grooves, fingers tracing the shallow tread. "They didn't rush. Didn't peel out. No signs of struggle."

Lucía stood still, arms wrapped around herself. "Then it wasn't a kidnapping."

"No," Ryan muttered. "This was a decision."

He rose, jaw flexed, rage flickering behind his eyes. "Three of us went into that compound," he said, voice low and cutting. "We got the kid out. We got him safe. And Gates just…decides to disappear without a word? Doesn't ask. Doesn't explain. Just takes him?"

Lucía crossed her arms. "He was never going to let you keep him. You know that, right?" Her voice turned gentle. "He's not your son. He has a grandmother. A legal guardian. A home—"

His voice dropped again, low and sharp. "You think I don't know that? I was ready for that," he said. "What I wasn't ready for was this. A nighttime extraction like we're the problem."

Lucía swallowed hard. "Maybe he thought he was protecting the kid."

Ryan laughed bitterly. "From what? From us?"

"No. From Javier. From whatever's still coming."

Ryan shook his head, the fury cooling into something else. Disgust. Betrayal. "He just…left."

Lucía looked away, toward the horizon, her voice quiet. "Maybe he thought we'd try to stop him."

Ryan didn't answer. He just stood in the doorway. The wind picked up, stirring the dust in ghostly little spirals. In the distance, the faint glint of daylight began to creep over the horizon—bright, merciless, and indifferent.

He yanked open drawers. Pulled aside throw pillows. Kicked open a cabinet door. Not looking for anything in particular, just something. Something to *break*.

Lucía stood near the front door, still silent, watching him unravel in real time.

He opened the last cabinet near the kitchen.

And froze.

There it was. The burner phone. The one he'd left behind in the Sierra Norte cabin. He'd left it on the table, as a final *fuck you* to the men who'd been using it to order him around. He knew he'd left it.

But it sat there now on a folded dish towel like it had been waiting for him. Screen dim but blinking.

He picked it up. One message. Timestamp: two hours ago. From: Unknown

He opened it.

If you ever want to see the boy again, bring the woman. Hotel Punta Roja. Room 6. Noon today.

His breath left him in a slow, bitter drag.

Lucía stepped closer. "What is it?"

Ryan held the phone out wordlessly.

She read the message once.

Then again.

She stared at the message, her fingers brushing the screen like maybe it would change if she touched it again. "This doesn't make sense. That phone was gone. We left it in that cabin in the mountains."

"Exactly." He looked at her. "Which means it didn't find its way here on its own."

Lucía's expression tightened. "Gates. *Shit.* He was playing us this whole time?"

He shook his head. He had no idea anymore. Nothing made sense. He set the phone down carefully, like it might detonate. Then leaned back against the counter, arms folded tight.

Lucía frowned. "But why help us at the compound?"

Ryan's jaw clenched. "Maybe that was part of his play."

"You think he's been stringing us along just to get the last fragment?"

"I think…" He exhaled sharply. "I think we've been dancing to someone else's rhythm since the start. Every lead we chased, every clue that looked like a breakthrough—it all led here."

"To this," she murmured. "A trade."

Ryan nodded. "That's why he left the car. The keys in the ignition."

They were both silent for a long moment. Then Ryan said, "He knew you wouldn't hand it over. Not willingly. So he took the boy to force your hand. Or force mine."

He looked at her, the weight of what he was saying settling over them both. *Force him to extract the last fragment from her to save Noah. Force him to make a choice between the two of them.*

"I won't do it," he said, voice low. "We won't do it."

Lucía swallowed and looked down at her hands. "We thought we were ahead of them. Turns out we've been behind the whole time."

She moved to the window, peeled back the curtain, stared at the line of dull horizon. Silence stretched between them again.

Finally, Ryan spoke, voice hoarse. "I don't give a shit who's holding the leash. If they've got Noah, I'm going."

"You're not going alone."

Ryan didn't respond. Just looked at her, something softening in his expression.

She stepped closer. "We go together. We get Noah back. And we end this together."

He didn't speak. Just reached for the burner phone and turned it off, the screen blinking out. Then he slid it into his pocket and said, quietly, "Then we've got until noon to figure out how not to die in the process."

FORTY-SIX

THE ROAD BLURRED into heat shimmer, flat and endless, the horizon bending like light through a glass. Gates's abandoned SVU was one of the smoother rides they'd procured on this Odyssean journey, but Lucía still gripped the passenger armrest like it was in danger of flying to bits at any given moment.

Maybe it wasn't in danger of flying to bits, but she felt like she was.

Beside her, Ryan drove with one hand, the other resting on the curve of the wheel. His jaw was tight. He hadn't said much since they left the last gas station. Not since they'd filled the tank and restocked their water supply.

Her throat tightened. She adjusted the sun visor, even though the glare didn't touch her. "I've been thinking," she said.

Ryan glanced over but didn't speak.

"I could just give it to them," she said softly. "The fragment. I could just give it to Gates."

He didn't answer right away.

The tires hummed. A stretch of road passed.

Lucía went on. "That's what all of this is about, isn't it? It's why they took Noah. It's why Gates turned. They want what I have."

Ryan's voice was quiet. "It's more than that. They want what it means."

"I know." She looked down at her hands. "The plan was to finish it. Leak the full ledger to the right channels. Let it blow apart the cartel's financial spine. Take down the whole rotten infrastructure."

Ryan was silent.

Lucía turned her head toward him. "But what if it's not worth it?"

He frowned. "What do you mean?"

She shook her head. "What's the point of toppling empires if I let a little boy die in the process?"

His eyes flicked to her again. More carefully this time.

"I've spent years holding onto this thing like it was the last thread keeping me connected to Mateo," she said. "Like if I pulled hard enough, the whole world would unravel and maybe he wouldn't have died for nothing." Her voice caught. She swallowed hard. "But now? There's this kid. This terrified little boy, stuck between monsters. And I could end that. I could give Gates what he wants."

Ryan didn't look at her. "He's a liar."

"But he's also strategic," she said. "He won't kill Noah if he still thinks he can use him. But if I don't give it to him…"

She trailed off. They both knew what came next.

After a long pause, Ryan said, "If it were me, I'd give it up in a heartbeat." He glanced at her. "I'm not saying you should. I'm saying if it were me—if it were my ledger—I wouldn't hesitate."

She stared at him. "You'd throw away the only chance to dismantle an international cartel network?"

"Yes. I'd burn the world down for one person," Ryan said. "That's not the right answer. But it is the truth."

Lucía looked away. The desert stretched on around them, flat and empty.

Ryan wasn't looking at her. But his hand had moved—just barely—between them. Not touching, but close enough that she felt it. "Whatever you choose," he said, "make sure it's something you can live with."

———

The road twisted through low hills, pocked with scrub brush and scattered cactus. Ryan took the next curve and saw it, about eighty meters ahead.

Two men in uniform. A sagging cone barricade. An old navy-blue patrol car parked off to the side.

"Shit," he muttered.

Lucía shifted in her seat. "Checkpoint?"

"Looks like."

She leaned forward, sharp. "Those aren't *federales*."

Ryan narrowed his eyes. The man on the left wore a sun-faded uniform with a badge stitched askew. His boots were too new for rural patrol. The man beside him had a patch that didn't match the shoulder emblem. Something about the way they stood, like they were posing as law enforcement, not acting like it.

Ryan let the SUV slow, not brake.

Lucía's voice was low and even. "Shoes don't match. And that badge is upside down."

Ryan exhaled through his nose. "Cartel proxy?"

"Or local muscle playing uniform."

He adjusted his grip on the wheel. "Either way, they're watching for someone."

Lucía's hand slid toward her Colt. She didn't draw, just rested her fingers near it.

The man on the left raised a hand, flagging them down.

Ryan rolled to a stop, one hand still on the gearstick. "Here we go," he said under his breath.

The man walked up slow, one hand resting near his belt. Not on a weapon, not yet. His other hand lifted lazily in a greeting.

Ryan rolled the window down halfway.

"*Buen día,*" the man said. His voice was smooth, almost cheerful. "*¿A dónde van?*"

"*Sur,*" Ryan said, thick accent intentional. "Just…Salina Cruz. Vacation."

The man smiled. "American?"

Ryan nodded. "*Sí.*"

The man leaned in slightly, looking past Ryan toward Lucía. His gaze lingered a second too long. "*Y ella?*"

Ryan glanced sideways. "Cousin."

Lucía didn't blink.

The man's eyes slid back to Ryan. "Papers?"

Ryan shrugged. "Lost wallet. *Rentamos el camión de un amigo. No tenemos problemas.*" He kept the smile thin. Friendly. Useless.

Behind them, the second man was moving now, walking slowly along the passenger side, pretending to look at the tires, the bumper.

Ryan heard the soft click of Lucía slipping her Colt free, low against her thigh.

The first man tilted his head. "You look like someone."

Ryan chuckled. "I get that a lot."

The man's smile didn't move.

There was a long pause. Then the second man called something from behind the truck—too soft for Ryan to catch.

The first man didn't react. Not yet. The air between them turned solid.

Ryan's thumb tapped the wheel. Then he said quietly: "You ever work with Delgado? DEA logistics, south branch?"

The man blinked.

Ryan leaned slightly toward him. "Tell him Langston says he still owes me a bottle of mezcal."

The man stared. For a breath too long. Then he stepped back.

"*Buen viaje,*" he said flatly. He slapped the side of the truck.

Ryan didn't wait. He eased off the brake and rolled forward.

Lucía waited five more seconds. Then he saw her slide the Colt back into place.

The SUV hummed as it picked up speed, gravel crackling under the tires before the road smoothed again into cracked asphalt. The fake checkpoint faded in the mirrors, just a blur of heat haze and too-long stares.

Lucía kept her eyes on them for another thirty seconds before turning forward again. "That was a bluff," she said flatly.

Ryan nodded, jaw tight.

"There's no Langston."

"Nope."

"No Delgado."

"Could be. But if there is, he definitely doesn't owe me mezcal."

Lucía smiled, if only faintly. They drove on in silence for another stretch. Then she said, "Your Spanish is terrible."

Ryan let out a short breath through his nose. "It's part of the charm."

She leaned her head back against the seat, exhaled slowly. "They weren't cops."

"No."

"They were waiting for someone."

He didn't respond. Because they both knew who.

After a moment, Lucía said, "How'd you know he'd let us pass?"

"I didn't," Ryan said. "But guys like that don't shoot until they're sure you're a threat. Uncertainty buys time."

Lucía turned her face toward the window, her reflection fractured in the dusty glass. "He saw my face."

"He saw mine, too."

And that was the part neither of them said aloud. Whatever just happened at that checkpoint, it was already being passed up the chain.

Someone knew they were coming.

———

Ten minutes past the checkpoint, Ryan pulled the SUV off the road and killed the engine. Dust clouded up, drifted, settled.

He leaned forward, resting his forearms on the wheel, exhaling through his nose.

Lucía stayed still beside him, hands in her lap. For a minute, neither said a thing. Then, quietly, she asked, "Are we going to talk about it?"

Ryan didn't look up. "About what?"

Her voice sharpened. "Don't."

He leaned back slowly, jaw tight. "What do you want me to say?"

Lucía looked out the window. "That it wasn't just adrenaline. That it meant something."

He rubbed his face, winced as his hand brushed the healing cut near his temple. "It did."

Lucía turned to him, eyes unreadable. "Then why do you look like you regret it?"

"I don't," he said.

She leaned closer, just slightly. "You think I'm a mistake, Ryan?"

He met her eyes. "No. I think you're a fuse. And I already lit you once."

Her breath caught, just faintly.

His hand was still on the wheel. Hers came up, brushing the edge of the seat between them, not quite touching him, but close. "You didn't have to come this far," he said.

She blinked, turned toward him slightly. "What?"

"Our deal. Back in the cabin. You were supposed to help me find Noah. After that, you were free to go."

Lucía didn't speak.

"I've dragged you halfway across México. Gotten you shot at. Got you sleeping in dingy motels."

Still nothing from her. But her jaw tensed just slightly.

Ryan exhaled. "I guess I just wanted to say…thank you."

Lucía scoffed. "You really think I'm still here because of a deal?"

"I don't know why you're still here."

Her eyes held his. "Neither do I."

He nodded, slow.

"Still," he said, voice low. "You stayed."

Her mouth parted—maybe to argue, maybe to soften. But whatever she was going to say disappeared when he leaned in.

Their mouths met, tentative for just half a second. Then it turned hungry. Lucía's hand came up to his jaw, fingers curling against rough stubble. Ryan's fingers found the side of her throat, then her waist. She pulled him closer over the center console, and for a breathless moment, it felt like they weren't in an SUV on the side of a dangerous highway. It felt like they were the only two people in México.

The kiss deepened. Then she pulled back, chest rising fast.

Ryan rested his forehead against hers.

Lucía didn't move. "We're not making it easy," she said, voice unsteady.

"No," he agreed. "We're not."

FORTY-SEVEN

THE LIGHT through the motel blinds was washed out and yellow, streaking across the cracked linoleum floor in slats.

The man sat on the edge of the bed, a disassembled Glock in his lap and a towel beneath it. His movements were steady. Practiced.

Barrel. Slide. Spring. Wipe. Oil. Reassemble.

Beside the bed, the boy sat on a worn cushion, thumbing through a battered comic book. Bare feet. Quiet. No complaints.

Good. Quiet kids were easier.

He checked the chamber, racked the slide, set the pistol aside. And waited.

The memory scratched at him: standing in the hallway at that safehouse last night, watching the door crack open just enough to see them tangled together—Ryan and Lucía.

Sleeping. Her head on his chest. His hand curled protectively at her waist.

He could have taken her then, and he almost did. But Ryan wasn't the kind of man you crossed when he was half-awake and holding something he cared about.

That would have been sloppy. Risky.

The boy was the better play. A clean grab, no noise, maximum leverage.

He stood slowly, walked to the window, tilted the blinds to scan the lot. It was empty. He checked his burner phone again. One unread message: **They're on their way.**

A smile tugged at the corner of his mouth. He slipped the phone back into his pocket and turned toward the boy.

The boy looked up at him, eyes wide but calm. "Are we going somewhere?"

The man shook his head, almost gently. "Nope." He picked up the pistol again. "But I am."

FORTY-EIGHT

RYAN PULLED the SUV to a stop beneath a scraggly mesquite tree, a good thirty yards from the faded motel sign.

MOTEL PUNTA ROJA. *Bienvenidos. Habitaciones con A/C.* The "A/C" part was scratched out.

He killed the engine, and the silence that followed was almost loud. There were no dogs barking, no TVs buzzing behind open windows. All he could hear was the thud of his own pulse.

"This is it," he said, eyes fixed on the motel's peeling stucco exterior. The place looked like it hadn't seen actual occupancy in years. There was a half-burned trash barrel near the front lot, and a vending machine in the breezeway with no logo left.

They sat in silence for a moment, the engine ticking as it cooled. Lucía scanned the balconies, the breezeway, the cracked asphalt. "Looks empty."

Ryan looked across at her. "Are you sure you still want to do this?"

She exhaled slowly. "I'm sure. We'll go in, check it's legit and Noah's safe. Then I'll give him the laptop and the password and this will all be over."

They got out, doors clicking soft behind them. The sun was brutal. The pavement shimmered.

Ryan reached for the PPK in his waistband, checked the slide with a quick snap, then tucked it beneath the hem of his shirt. Lucía mirrored him, drawing her Colt. She checked the chamber, thumbed the safety, then slid it back into her waistband at the small of her back.

They crossed the lot on foot, quiet, deliberate, eyes constantly moving. An old pickup truck sat at the far end of the parking lot, cab empty. A stack of broken pallets leaned against the office wall.

Ryan looked up at the middle level of the motel. One open curtain fluttered for a moment, then stilled. They moved down the breezeway, shoulder to shoulder, scanning the windows and doors.

Room 6 was dead ahead. Paint peeled in jagged flakes. A damp towel hung from the railing. The wind shifted. Heat pressed in close.

Lucía reached for the door handle. Ryan stopped her. "Let me."

She stepped back, gun drawn low and tight. He turned the knob slowly, gun in his other hand, ready.

Unlocked.

He pushed the door open.

It was dark inside. Ryan took two steps in, gun sweeping left to right.

The room was empty. Just a bed, rumpled like someone had sat on it and left. A table and a broken chair. A half-filled ashtray. A comic book lying abandoned on the floor.

Lucía's throat went dry. "Something's wrong."

"Yeah," Ryan said, already backing toward the door.

That's when the first window exploded.

They both dropped instantly, glass raining down like razors. A burst of suppressed fire tore through the wall. Ryan took cover beside the door frame, heart hammering.

Lucía dove for cover near the bathroom door, bracing herself on one elbow, gun up.

Ryan fired back once through the open doorway, fast and low, forcing the shooter to duck.

Another burst cracked from the stairwell outside. Dust and drywall ripped into the air.

Lucía pressed her back to the wall. "This wasn't a trade. It was never a trade."

No, Ryan realized. *It was a kidnapping.*

A figure in dark clothes ducked behind a support column at the edge of the breezeway. Too far to see clearly, but the rifle silhouette was unmistakable.

He counted seconds.

The shooter fired again, controlled bursts. Not cartel spray-and-pray. Tactical.

Ryan breathed through the pain in his ribs. "They brought pros," he muttered.

Then he took a deep breath and, keeping his back to the wall and his gun tight to his body, angled himself around the doorway.

From inside the room, he heard a sudden crash. Lucía must've tipped the table, made cover for herself.

More shots from the breezeway slammed into the door frame. Wood splintered. Ryan's thigh stung—he'd been grazed. He pressed his hand against it, felt warmth.

Blood.

"Son of a bitch."

He leaned out again—one eye, one arm—and fired three more shots.

This time one of them hit.

The shooter staggered back with a grunt, dropped to one knee. Rifle clattered. Ryan took the chance and limped down the breeze-way, gun leveled. He kicked the weapon away and shoved the man onto his back.

Bald. Bearded. Pale-skinned. American.

The man coughed wetly. "You're...Ryan Inglis."

Ryan aimed the PPK square at his forehead. "Wrong day to be a fan."

"Wasn't supposed to be you," the man gasped.

Ryan's jaw locked.

"It was always the woman. You were…the variable." The man blinked blood. "They want her alive."

Ryan's trigger finger twitched. "Who's they?"

The man smiled. It was ugly and red.

"You don't want to know."

Then he died.

Ryan rose, chest heaving, shoulder screaming. He grabbed the dead guy's rifle and whirled back around. "Lucía!" he shouted, voice raw.

No answer.

But he had a feeling the worst part hadn't started.

Not by a long shot.

———

Lucía burst out of the bathroom just as Ryan stumbled back into the room, his jeans soaked in red. The rifle in his hands wavered, then steadied as he saw her.

"Breezeway," he rasped. "One down."

She crossed to him fast, catching his elbow, guiding him down. He tried to wave her off but his legs were already buckling. They ended up crouched behind the flipped table she'd dragged from the wall.

"Stay down," she whispered. Her head snapped toward the window. She crept low and peeked between the blinds.

A black SUV. No plates. "Shit."

Ryan struggled to his knees. "They probably have us surrounded."

Lucía turned toward the bathroom. There was a small window above the toilet. She didn't wait. "Come on."

She dragged him up. Ryan bit off a groan and leaned on her as they half-hobbled, half-sprinted to the tiny bathroom. She slammed the door behind them and twisted the lock. Then she grabbed the edge of the window and started to shove it open.

"Go," Ryan said, pushing her forward.

"I'm not leaving you—"

"Lucía, now!"

Something in his voice cut through. She hesitated one second too long.

The bathroom door exploded inward.

Ryan spun toward the sound, rifle coming up. The shot should have gone off, but his wounded leg gave out beneath him. He fell hard, the muzzle veering high. The round punched harmlessly into the ceiling as the man burst through the doorway.

It wasn't Gates. It was a gringo in combat boots and civilian clothes barreling straight at them. Ryan tried to swing the rifle again, but the man was already on him, slamming the weapon aside and driving him to the floor.

Then the attacker was on her. He hit her full force. She crashed into the sink, shoulder screaming. Her hand went for the Colt. But he was fast and strong.

She got one elbow in—sharp, under his chin—but he twisted her sideways and drove her back into the wall. Her head cracked against tile. His gloved hand clamped over her mouth.

Ryan shouted—her name, she thought—but the sound was dim over the roar in her ears. Through the blur she saw him trying to rise again, blood pooling under him, one hand still reaching for the rifle.

She kicked hard. Fought. But he had the weight.

The man dragged her out. Past Ryan, who clawed toward her, rage written across his face, the rifle slipping from his grasp as the tiles ran red beneath him. Through the busted door.

Lucía twisted, thrashed, but the world turned sideways. There was a burst of hot air, then gravel underfoot.

Then: the SUV. Door open. Black interior.

She fought harder. Bit down on the man's hand. He cursed,

shoved her in. A cloth bag came down hard over her face. Then the door slammed. The locks thumped into place.

She bucked once, then again, but the engine roared, and inertia yanked her back. The tires spat gravel.

The back seat was stifling. The cloth over her head pulsed with every breath she took. Her lungs burned. Her shoulder was on fire. Her wrists had been zip-tied tight behind her, and her arms had already gone numb.

She twisted, tried to sit up.

A voice barked something from the front. *"Despacio—algo se mueve."*

Lucía froze, panting. Her body vibrated with adrenaline, with panic, but her mind stayed sharp. She counted seconds. And then faintly, from outside—

"LUCÍA!"

Her whole body stiffened.

Ryan.

Gunshots cracked, wild and close. She rammed her feet against the seat. Screamed against the bag. Kicked harder.

The SUV jerked to a stop. She heard a door open, and boots scrambling. A voice yelling, *"¡Baja! ¡Vamos!"*

Gunfire again, a long volley, thudding against metal. She flinched.

Then more scrambling. The doors slammed shut, the engine revved. They were moving again but faster this time.

She was thrown sideways again, ribs slamming into the door. She caught one last sound, just barely—Ryan's voice, hoarse and broken: "NO!"

Then nothing.

The vehicle peeled away into the desert.

———

Ryan didn't remember crawling out the bathroom doorway. Only that the blood trail was his, and it didn't seem to be slowing down.

He made it to the motel room door and, using the door frame for support, clambered into a standing position. Down in the lot, he saw Lucía, a bag over her head, her arms tied together, being shoved into the back of the SUV by two black-clad men.

He screamed her name, the word ripping free from his throat like a wild thing desperate to escape.

The SUV closed its doors and shot forward.

With shaking arms, he aimed his rifle in the direction of the tires and pulled the trigger. When the vehicle pulled to a stop and three of the men got out, he thought for a wild, hopeful moment that he'd been successful in stopping their getaway.

But that hope immediately died in a hail of returning gunfire. It exploded in the wall beside him, and he was forced to duck back inside the doorway. No sooner had the echoes faded than he heard the slam of doors, the spit of gravel as the SUV resumed its escape. It paused only long enough for one of the shooters to aim his rifle out the window and spray a wave of bullets at Ryan and Lucía's vehicle as it passed by.

He may have screamed, or maybe it was the pain screaming inside his head.

His gun hand trembled. His vision kept doubling. He pushed himself upright with a groan. Pain flared through his leg, his arms, his whole body.

On hands and knees, he crawled, out the door and down the breezeway. Finally, he collapsed beside the vending machine, cheek pressed to sun-warmed concrete.

The shooter in the breezeway was still there, dead now, eyes open. Ryan forced himself up, panting, and moved closer. He studied the man's clothes. Dark tactical pants. Civilian shirt. Armored chest rig. No tattoos. No gold. No cartel bling.

Ryan rifled through his pouches, searching for ID, and found instead a concealed pistol. He grabbed it, turning it over in his hands. The serial number had been filed away.

There was a half-torn velcro patch still clinging to the chest rig.

The letters were scuffed but readable: PHALANX SECURITY GROUP.

Ryan sat back hard on his heels.

Private. Fucking. Military.

He'd seen them before—in Afghanistan during federal training exercises. Third-party security vendors that no one talked about in briefings.

This wasn't just a betrayal. This was *sanctioned*.

So who the hell was Gates really working for?

FORTY-NINE

THE DESERT STRETCHED out from the ruined motel: flat and endless. A vulture circled lazily overhead, not even pretending to not notice him bleeding out against a crumbling wall.

Ryan sat on the ground where he'd fallen, back pressed to the motel's outer wall. His jeans were stiff with blood. His left arm was trembling so badly he'd finally let the rifle slip from his fingers.

He was done. He had nothing left but a gunshot-riddled vehicle in a ruined motel at the ass-end of nowhere and a wounded body that wasn't going to carry him much farther.

For a moment, he wondered what would happen if he just let it go. Leaned back. Let the blood run. Let the desert take him.

Maybe it wouldn't even take long.

He laughed, a rough, ugly sound that caught in his throat. When did he become this man? This wreck of a marshal, a traitor, a liar, a failure. Betrayed by his own friend. Unable to keep even a child safe.

Unable to keep Lucía safe.

She'd trusted him. She'd felt things for him. She'd given a part of herself that he knew she didn't give to just anyone. And she'd stayed when she didn't have to.

And he'd failed her, too.

A breeze kicked up, rattling a broken motel sign above his head. In the distance, the heat shimmer blurred the horizon until sky and ground became one pale smear.

There was no rescue coming. No fallback plan. And worse—he didn't even know who he was fighting anymore. Because it wasn't just the cartel, and it wasn't just Gates. It was something bigger. Darker. Faceless.

He leaned his head back against the concrete and closed his eyes. For the first time since it all began, he couldn't see the way forward. There was just dust, and heat. And the soft brush of wind that smelled faintly of death.

His head lolled to the side, scraping rough stone. He couldn't outrun it, couldn't outfight it. Every road he took curved back to the same place: this feeling. It was the same helplessness he'd felt when Kylie left him all those years ago. When Jessica fled from him on that road in Mississippi because he'd handed her name to men who'd vowed to kill her.

Kylie. Jessica. Lucía.

His badge hadn't protected any of them. His skills hadn't saved them. His instincts, his grit, his reputation—none of it meant shit.

All it had done was give him the tools to prolong the inevitable conclusion: that he was the bad variable in every equation.

The one who failed. The one who lost people. The one who got them killed.

He looked down at his shaking hands, the palms rough and cracked, smeared with his own blood. They didn't feel like hands that could save anyone anymore.

They felt like tools built for ruin.

———

Lucía came back to herself slowly. The canvas bag cinched around her neck was coarse and tight, thick enough to muffle sound but not pain. The zip ties around her wrist were too tight, they bit into her skin with every bump in the road. Her mouth dry and sticky. The SUV's interior swayed as they took another turn. Or maybe she was imagining it. Time felt unreliable.

Her knees ached from how they'd stuffed her into the back-seat. The familiar lump of her Colt against her hip was missing. Of course they'd taken it. They had stripped her of everything. Of Ryan. Of her weapon. Of her freedom.

No, not everything. The ledger fragment was still in her mind. It was still hers.

But what did that mean now? Even if she gave up the frag-ment—even if she revealed the last key—they'd still kill her. Then they'd bury her somewhere no one would ever find her. And use her data to enrich and empower the same structures she'd thought she was destroying.

Her pulse drummed at her throat, but there was no adrenaline surge this time. No clarity. Just a fog of exhaustion and futility.

A fresh ache spread through her ribs. She'd fought for so long. And for what?

Noah was still missing. The cartel still ran Sinaloa. And Ryan...

Her throat closed. She didn't let herself think about what state he was in. But it didn't matter. All her wars had collapsed into this single, airless space.

Lucía let her head sag forward.

For the first time since Mateo's death—since the moment she'd sworn she'd burn it all down—Lucía Duarte felt empty.

Hollow. And she thought maybe that was what surrender felt like.

FIFTY

RYAN'S HEAD lolled sideways against the pockmarked stucco, breath shallow, the pain in his leg growing by the minute. He'd torn a strip from his shirt to slow the bleeding, but it wasn't doing much anymore. His throat was dry as bone. His tongue felt cracked against his teeth.

Every muscle ached, but it was his stomach that clawed hardest: an emptiness deep and gnawing, twisting beneath his ribs. He couldn't remember when he last ate. When he last drank more than a sip of lukewarm water.

He was slipping.

The motel loomed hollow around him, windows shattered, walls cratered by gunfire. A gust of wind rattled a loose panel somewhere, like a coin spinning on tile. He barely registered it.

Then he heard a soft crunch.

Footsteps.

His hand jerked toward the rifle lying near his thigh, fingers numb and slow.

Another crunch. Then—

A small voice. "Don't shoot."

Ryan blinked, vision smeared.

"It's just me."

A shape came into focus. Gangly limbs. Red hair. A familiar, wary squint.

"Noah?"

The boy stepped out from behind the burned trash barrel. He was clutching a water bottle in one hand. "You're bleeding," he said.

Ryan let out a long, broken sound. Not a laugh or a sob, nothing that contained a recognizable emotion. Just something tearing loose inside him. Relief, maybe, although it felt a million times stronger than any relief he'd experienced before.

He tried to sit up, wincing hard. "Jesus. Kid. What—what are you doing here?"

Noah stepped closer, gaze wary but unafraid. "They left me."

"Who did?"

"The man with the glasses."

Ryan pushed his palms flat against the concrete, biting down a grunt as he forced himself upright. His leg buckled.

Noah stepped forward, then immediately paused, as if he didn't know whether or not to help. As if he didn't know whether Ryan was friend or foe. In the end, he just held out the water bottle, at a distance too far for Ryan to reach it, but clearly still intended as a gesture of goodwill.

Ryan nodded at him. "Thanks, buddy."

Noah finally came forward and passed him the bottle.

Ryan took it with shaking fingers. He uncapped it and drank in down in three gulps. Then he tossed the bottle aside, and bent double, hands on his knees and just breathed. Noah was alive. So was he. Lucía, though...

He forced himself back into a standing position and looked down at Noah, squinting through one eye. His time for self-pity and wallowing was over. He had a kid to look after, one who looked like he needed food and water and whatever else kids needed to survive. A hug, probably, given what this one had already been through.

Maybe it was the fog of dehydration slowly lifting, or the pain from his leg slowly easing, but something else pushed to the forefront of his brain. "Man with glasses?"

Noah nodded.

Something cold slithered through Ryan's veins. "Was he Mexican?"

Noah nodded again. "He told me to wait. Then he just left, right before the gunshots started. I think he forgot I was still in the room. I hid under the bed."

Ryan stared at him. "Was he with the other man? The tall one? The American?"

Noah shook his head. "No. It was just him."

Ryan swore under his breath. Pain sharpened behind his eyes. "Are you sure, Noah?"

The boy nodded. "He's the one who took me from the beach house. He said we were going to see my grandma."

Ryan exhaled. He felt like he'd been punched in the guts. It was Reyes. Not Gates. Not the man Ryan had spent the last day cursing in his own head. Not the old friend he'd accused. Reyes had set this whole trap. He'd taken Lucía and had left the boy behind like a duffel bag he didn't feel like carrying.

Ryan let his head fall back against the scorched wall, a hoarse laugh escaping his throat. It wasn't funny. Not even close.

That sly little bastard. *He'd been the asset the whole fucking time.*

———

Lucía had no idea how long they'd been driving. There were no voices in the back with her. Just the hum of the engine, the occasional static crackle of a comms radio up front, and the muted percussion of tires over pitted tarmac.

She pressed her cheek against the seat and tried to orient herself by sound. The tires had changed tone. Less crunch, more hum. Asphalt. They were still moving at speed. Still somewhere rural. She counted trees by the rhythm of shadow through the canvas. One-two. One-two. Sparse.

"Almost there," someone muttered from the front seat.

A second voice. "She still out?"

"Who knows? She hasn't said a word."

"She's got the code, right?"

"That's what Reyes says." They didn't speak with fear. They spoke with confidence. Like she was a solved problem. Like the rest was just procedure. "They say it's all in her head. That *she's* the passphrase."

Lucía let her head slump. But her mind was racing.

Reyes. The little *federale*? *He* was behind all this?

Bile burned the back of her throat. She forced it down.

It's always the fucking quiet ones.

She heard the buzz of a cellphone beside her. The third man— the one closest to her—answered it immediately. She recognized Reyes voice. "Yes, sir?"

There was a pause, then Reyes said, "No, she's intact. A little banged up, but breathing. That's what you wanted, right?"

Another pause. Someone was speaking on the other end of the line. She strained to hear the voice coming through the speaker, but it was too faint.

"Yeah, she's tougher than she looks. Tried to bite one of my guys. Nearly succeeded." A dry chuckle.

Lucía's fingers clenched. The zip ties bit deeper.

"Understood," Reyes said. "We'll be at the safehouse in five. Minimal exposure. No comms until then."

Then: a click. The line went dead.

The SUV hit a pothole. Her head cracked softly against the seat frame behind her. She forced herself to stay calm. Think. Her legs were free. A mistake? Or intentional?

Maybe they didn't see her as a threat. And maybe they were right.

Maybe she really was helpless.

The vehicle slowed. Turned. Gravel crunched under the wheels.

She braced herself. Outside, a gate groaned open. Chains

rattled. The SUV drove through. Somewhere outside the canvas hood, a new sound rose: the sharp bark of a dog.

She could smell salt in the air again. Ocean. Not far from the coast, then. Not far from where it all began.

She curled her fingers slowly. Felt the blood moving back into her wrists. Every inch ached. But it was better than numbness.

Because pain meant she was alive. And as long as she was alive, so was the fight.

FIFTY-ONE

RYAN HAD NEVER HATED his own body more. Every step was a goddamn war.

He leaned against Noah, who was barely tall enough to reach his ribs as he hobbled toward Gates's SUV. He forced himself to take one step at a time, both physically and mentally. The blood had reached his boot and soaked into his sock, making every footstep feel like he was rubbing away the skin of his heel.

Finally, they reached the bullet-riddled vehicle. The damage was worse than he'd feared. The windshield was a spiderweb. The rear panel had taken two slugs. The front tire was flat, the rubber shredded like cardboard.

He yanked open the driver's door, then climbed in, wincing as pain shot up his leg. The keys were still in the ignition, and he stared at them for a moment, offering a silent prayer to whatever gods were left in these parts.

Then he reached forward and turned the key.

Nothing. No power. Not even a flicker.

He slumped into the seat and stared at the dashboard. "Fuck."

Noah stood by the open door, arms wrapped tight across his chest. "You know you're bleeding, right?"

Ryan looked down at his leg. Most of the blood had dried,

but a new wet patch indicated it was still seeping out. Which meant the wound needed stitches, or a bandage at the very least.

He leaned back against the seat, exhaled hard through his nose, and forced himself to focus.

One thing at a time. Stop the bleeding. Keep the kid alive.

Think.

He popped the glovebox with a trembling hand. The med kit that he'd used on Lucía was still there. Partly used, but intact.

Remembering how scared she'd been after she'd been shot—how scared he'd been at the thought of losing her—brought back a wave of fresh guilt. Guilt that felt like it was starting to crystalize into grief. Which meant his mind was already starting to think of her as…

He gripped the door frame and swiveled himself around to face Noah. "Help me out."

"What are you gonna do?"

He gripped the boy's bony shoulder. He was at that age where he hadn't filled out much. But he also looked like he hadn't eaten a decent meal in weeks. It was yet another thing to add to the list of infractions he wanted blood for.

I'm gonna make someone fucking pay for this, he thought.

———

There was an old, cracked mirror bolted crookedly above the sink in the motel room. Ryan forced himself to his feet, grabbed the edge of the counter, and leaned in close.

The man staring back looked a hundred years old: skin gray beneath the dirt, beard scruff thick and uneven, eyes sunken.

But he was alive.

Supposedly, that was something.

He washed his hands at the rusted sink, then dug through the med kit until he found what he needed: gauze, iodine, a needle and thread.

Tequila would have helped. But there wasn't any. So he worked raw.

He removed the cloth from the wound, wincing as it stuck to the skin. He uncapped the iodine and poured it over the wound. Sweat broke on his upper lip as he forced the needle through the puckered edges of torn skin.

Once. Twice.

Again.

His hands shook, but he didn't stop.

When he finished, he wound the gauze around his leg with shaking fingers, cinching it tight enough to make his vision swim for a second.

It was done. He allowed himself a moment of rest, bracing himself over the sink. Then he turned and hobbled out of the bathroom into the bullet-strewn main room.

Noah sat on the bed, cross-legged, nibbling the protein bar Ryan had found in the glovebox. It looked rock hard, but the kid wasn't complaining. Ryan had a brief flare of concern about how much all of this was going to fuck him up in the future. Most kids his age only saw blood and bullets and the insides of safehouses from behind a gaming console on their sofa. He was seeing it all for real.

He forced himself to shelve that thought for another day and focus on the more pressing issues.

Okay. Leg bandaged. Water and food found, sort of. What's next?

Get this damn boot off. His blood-soaked sock has caused a blister on his heel to form. And he wasn't going anywhere if he couldn't walk.

He braced one hand on the chair, bent forward, and tugged at the laces. The motion was slow, mechanical. When the boot came free, he saw that his sock was stiff with blood, the edge crusted brown. As he went to set the boot aside, something caught his eye.

Inside, near the heel, something glinted faintly—just a flash of gray plastic under the insole.

He frowned. Reached in. His fingers brushed something smooth and foreign, wedged beneath the liner. He pried it loose, pulling it into the light.

Small. Flat. Black casing.

Ryan froze, the air leaving his lungs in one long, silent breath.

It was a tracker.

He turned it over in his hand, thumb brushing the thin seam along its edge. A GPS beacon, military-grade, maybe, or federal. This wasn't cartel tech.

He knew this kind of thing. He'd *used* this kind of thing.

"Gates," he whispered. "You motherfucker."

He should have known the marshal would've pulled a trick like this. The man's paranoia had always run deep. The bastard had never trusted anyone, least of all Ryan. He hadn't been the one to betray him, but he had been keeping him on a little digital leash.

And this time, Ryan had never been more relieved to be the object of his suspicions.

Because it meant if Gates was still out there—and if he was still alive—he'd probably be following the signal. And if he was, it would only be a matter of time before he showed up here.

It was a lot of ifs, but for the first time, he felt that maybe not all was lost.

———

Ryan pushed to his feet, biting back a groan as the stitched-up thigh protested every inch. He limped to the doorway, stared out at the lot.

On the opposite side of the lot from the ruined SUV was that battered pickup. Hood warped, tires soft. A relic of someone else's bad luck.

He could try it. It might even run.

Gas would be a problem. Food, too. But he could load Noah

in, point them toward the Sierra, or hell, even north. Pick a direction, any direction, and vanish.

Start over. Again.

He leaned against the doorframe, exhaling heavily. He didn't want to admit how tempting it was. Because what else was left?

Lucía was gone. Taken by mercenaries working for someone he still couldn't name. Phalanx Group didn't play small games, and Ryan couldn't even guess where they'd taken her.

He rubbed a hand down his face. Grit clung to his skin. He could take the kid, head for Belize or somewhere. Trade the last of their cash for a ride. Get them both new names. Try to carve out something quiet and human for once in his goddamn life.

But even as he thought it, he knew.

He wouldn't leave her.

Lucía had put her life on the line—for Noah, for the truth. For him, even when she shouldn't have. She had every reason to run, and she'd stayed. Again and again.

He looked down at the tracker, still clenched in his hand.

So maybe now it was his turn.

FIFTY-TWO

THE SUV SLOWED. Lucía felt it first in her stomach: that familiar shift in gravity, the dull lurch of motion bleeding into stillness.

Then the brakes hissed, and the engine settled into a low, uneven idle.

For a long moment, nobody moved.

The canvas hood clung to her face, hot with her breath. Sweat stuck to her hairline and trickled down her neck. Her wrists burned where the zip ties had rubbed the skin raw.

She counted the heartbeats between breaths. Four. Five. Six.

Then the doors clicked open.

Gravel crunched under boots. Two of them got out first, their movements sharp and purposeful—they were soldiers, not thugs. Reyes stayed inside. She could hear his steady breathing beside her, smell the nicotine on his clothes.

A door slammed. Then the metallic scrape of something heavy being dragged—chains? No. A gate, maybe.

The voice outside barked something in Spanish she couldn't catch. Another voice answered. Male. Clipped. Military.

Lucía's pulse spiked.

A hand grabbed her arm, hauling her upright. Pain shot

through her shoulder where the bullet wound had barely begun to heal. She stumbled, her knees buckling as her boots hit dirt. The gravel was loose, jagged. She could smell dust, diesel, and the faint chemical sting of jet fuel.

"*Cuidado,*" one of the men muttered.

She heard Reyes's voice again, over to her left. "She's fine. She knows what happens to people who make trouble."

He'd smiled at her once. Over Gates's shoulder, back at the safehouse. He'd brought her water. Told her he was glad she'd survived the tax office hit.

And now he was delivering her like cargo.

The heat pressed down in waves. Even through the hood, she could tell it was late afternoon. The air was heavy, the wind dry enough to sting her cracked lips.

Somewhere ahead, she heard the distant whine of machinery, the echo of voices. Maybe they were closer to civilization than she'd hoped. Close enough that if she screamed loud enough, someone might even hear her.

But not close enough for them to help.

One of the men shoved her forward and she stumbled. She caught her balance, breathing through her nose, forcing herself to think.

Information. Always the information.

She counted steps, estimated distance. The ground shifted from gravel to compact dirt. The air cooled. Echoes changed.

They were inside.

The bag was whipped from her head. The room wasn't bright, but the sudden change in light made her squeeze her eyes shut. Slowly, she reopened them. The room was hollow, big. A warehouse, or maybe a hangar. The floor was stained in places with oil, and something darker. Overhead, chains hung from ceiling trusses like abandoned nooses. A decommissioned plane sat gutted in the far corner, its stripped fuselage casting a skeletal shadow across the room.

There were no windows. Just the metallic stench of fuel and

rust, and the cold certainty that whatever came next wasn't meant to be seen by the outside world.

There was one man behind her, still gripping her shoulder; two a few feet away, both armed with rifles and watching her with blank but alert stares. Like she was a mildly interesting creature in a zoo. Potentially dangerous, but more of an oddity than anything.

She opened her mouth to say something—anything—but the sudden feel of a blade at her back made her shut it immediately. A loud *zip* followed, the sound of fabric being sliced with a sharp knife. Her t-shirt was pulled away in pieces, and then she felt blunt fingers tug at the back of her bra. He didn't unclasp it; instead, there was another zipping sound, and it too was cut away.

Her indignation barely had time to register before it was done, and she was standing there half-naked. It turned immediately to fear, as the man behind her sliced away at the back of her pants, the tip of knife skimming lightly against the backs of her thighs. The rags of her cargo pants joined the remains of the rest of her clothes on the ground.

Fear and rage and humiliation formed a hot soup in her stomach. She tried to pull away, but the man behind her tightened his grip on her shoulder. Pain seared through her wound as he jerked her back, in anticipation of her trying to break free.

The other men were still staring at her, their expressions having sharpened. Like the zoo creature was now something they wanted to pet.

Well, if they did, they would soon find out this one bit. Fear and adrenaline were making her whole body shake, but she forced herself not to panic. Yes, her arms were still bound, but she had both legs free and if any of these fuckers tried to touch her, she knew exactly where she was going to aim the first kick.

But neither of the men made any move toward her. One dragged a metal chair over, its metal legs screeching against the concrete. The hand on shoulder tightened again, forcing her down onto it.

"Take a seat."

A zip tie cinched around one of her ankles, securing it to the leg of the chair, then the other. Both her hands were then tied to each arm.

The footsteps moved away. The door slammed. The lock turned. Silence fell again.

She tried to shift her weight, but the chair legs grated loudly.

She could hear the men outside now, faint through the walls. Talking, laughing. And under it all, the low hum of a plane engine winding down.

Someone had just arrived.

Her heart leapt painfully. She thought of Ryan when she'd last seen him, bleeding, furious. She thought of Noah, just a kid and yet trying so hard to be brave through things that would make most adults shit their pants.

And of Javier: his voice smooth as polished glass, promising that she would always come back to him, one way or another.

Lucía inhaled, slow and quiet. She could taste rust in the air. And something else—cleaner, sharper. Disinfectant.

Someone had prepared for her.

She rotated her wrist, slow, careful, testing the friction of plastic against skin.

She wasn't done yet. Not by a long shot.

FIFTY-THREE

THE SUN WAS LOW, bleeding red across the horizon like an open wound. Long shadows stretched across the cracked parking lot of the motel.

Ryan leaned against the hood of the old pickup, one boot resting on the bumper, the other pressing into the dirt. His PPK, loaded with the last of his ammunition, was back in his hip holster. The truck coughed behind him, engine idling unevenly. He'd found a jerry can of gas stashed beside a collapsed shed earlier that afternoon. It was only half full and likely siphoned off a decade ago. It reeked, but it ran.

He'd stripped the truck of anything unnecessary: a rotted bench seat, a pair of fuzzy dice, a CB radio that hadn't chirped in years. The tires held air. The brakes were spongy, but they worked. Noah sat curled in the cab, clutching a bottle of tepid water.

Ryan's leg throbbed, a steady, radiating pain that pulsed with every heartbeat. The stitches he'd put in earlier were already puckering. He'd splinted the thigh with a piece of cabinet slat and some duct tape, but the wound was deep, and he was burning through his limited painkillers fast. They had to move. As for where, he didn't know. He had a set of tire tracks from the

Phalanx SUV heading north and following them was about as good a plan he had. For now, anyway.

The tracker still sat in his palm. He turned it over once more; lips pressed into a line. The idea of walking away burned. But maybe that was the only play he had left. Gates might still be on his way. But he might not. For all Ryan knew, Reyes had killed Gates, and taken Lucía halfway to Guatemala by now, and the dot in his boot was just a goddamn breadcrumb no one was ever going to follow.

Hell, maybe Gates had been part of the plan all along. Maybe this was just another layer in the con. Maybe he was, as he'd always been, on his own. He flicked the tracker into the dirt and crushed it under his heel. Then he reached for the driver's door, muscles screaming with every movement.

And that's when he saw it.

A shimmer on the horizon. Dust kicked up from a small vehicle speeding along the gravel road. The sun had dropped just enough to turn the oncoming shape into no more than a silhouette.

Ryan froze, fingers still resting on the truck door. He squinted into the distance. The vehicle crested the low ridge. It slowed as it approached the edge of the lot, tires crunching. As it came closer, Ryan could see it was an old Volkswagen Beetle, bright orange.

He slid his weapon from its holster.

The car stopped. Noah stirred behind him. "Ryan?"

"Stay in the truck," Ryan murmured.

The driver's side door of the car creaked open. A figure unfolded himself from the vehicle, his movements stiff. It would have been a comical sight—a big, broad-shouldered man climbing out of such a tiny car. But Ryan found it unfunny enough to keep a firm grip on his weapon.

"Jesus Christ," he muttered as the man straightened.

"Miss me?" Gates rasped.

Ryan didn't answer. He just stared at him.

The marshal limped toward the truck, sweat-streaked and

unshaven. His shirt was torn down one side, caked with dust and what looked like dried blood.

"Where the hell have you been?" Ryan said finally.

Gates exhaled and rubbed at his jaw. "Cupboard."

"What?"

"Reyes clocked me after I stepped out of the shower," he said dryly. "Woke up zip-tied and stuffed inside a goddamn armoire. By the time I got free, you were gone. So was the boy. Took me a whole day to catch up."

Ryan's grip on the gun finally loosened. He holstered it, jaw tightening.

Gates shrugged and looked toward the pickup. His eyes landed on the boy in the window, and something shifted in his expression. "You have the kid."

Ryan nodded. "You sure you're not here to take him away again?"

"I didn't take him last time."

"No," Ryan said flatly, "but we thought you did."

Gates scrubbed a hand through his sweat-damp hair. "Can't blame you. Kid okay?"

"He's shaken. And hungry. But he's alive."

"What about your girlfriend?"

Ryan bit down on the inside of his cheek, hard. "They took her. Phalanx. A private security outfit. They wanted her alive."

The expression on Gates's face told him that he knew all about Phalanx. "For the ledger."

Ryan nodded.

Gates said nothing for a long beat. Just looked at the horizon like he was weighing something in his mind. Finally, he looked back at Ryan. "Then we go get her."

Ryan squinted at him. "Just like that?"

"Yep. Just like that." He took a step forward, limping. "I know all about those yahoos. I know how they operate and where, too. There's a place about half an hour from here, up north past the bad roads and into the real forgotten country. Name's Santa Loma. Not even on half the maps."

"And?"

"And it's where Phalanx likes to move people when they don't want them found. Old crop-duster runway turned covert ops zone. Secure perimeter, flat terrain, no local police to worry about. Last time we clocked it, they were running personnel drops and cold storage from there."

Ryan's jaw clenched. "You think that's where they took her?"

"I'd bet my badge on it. While I still have it."

"This is the part where you tell me you've got a plan?" Ryan asked.

Gates squinted into the light. "Something like that."

Ryan gestured at the Beetle. "Was that all Avis had?"

Gates shrugged. "I, uh, borrowed it from an *abuela* on her way to Salina Cruz. It drives like a pissed-off goat, but it'll get us there."

"You stole it from an old lady?"

"I said I was resourceful, not proud."

Ryan shook his head. "Then let's go get her." He turned to go get Noah from the pickup, but Gates called after him.

"One thing you should know about Santa Loma."

"Yeah?"

"It's not just guarded."

Ryan looked back at him.

"It's owned. Phalanx has muscle there. A lot of it. This won't be a sneak-in kind of job."

"Good. I'm tired of sneaking."

FIFTY-FOUR

THE ORANGE BEETLE rolled to a stop behind a low ridge, its engine ticking in the silence. Ryan stepped out slowly, jaw clenched against the pain in his thigh. The stitches were holding, but just. Every step felt like walking with a nail in his leg.

He reached into the footwell behind the driver's seat and pulled out the pair of binoculars he'd swiped from the dead merc, alongside his FN SCAR rifle and ammunition rig. What was a rescue mission without a little grave robbing?

The Santa Loma airstrip cut across the valley like a scar. Lights lined its edges, low and industrial, the kind that threw long shadows. To the east, the compound sat tucked behind fencing and floodlights. Tin-roofed structures. A hangar. Outbuildings and a squat tower. Armed men moved in regular paths.

"Two at the fence," Ryan muttered. "Another near the hangar doors. What do you bet that's where they've got her?"

Gates stepped up beside him, resting hands on hips. "No doubt."

He chewed his cheek for a moment, watching the pattern of the guards' movements. They weren't amateurs: they moved in tight formations covering each other's arcs.

Ryan dropped the binoculars. "Phalanx."

Gates gave a short nod. "And they're expecting someone. You don't pull in that kind of muscle for an overnight fuel run."

"They'll have her inside," Ryan said. "Somewhere with no windows. No exits."

Neither of them spoke for a moment, as they both contemplated the reality of Lucía's situation.

"She's tough," Gates said.

Ryan didn't reply. All he could think was *everyone breaks eventually*. And the thought of someone breaking her made him want to snap their bones with his bare hands.

The sun slid lower, dragging long shadows across the desert floor.

Ryan turned and looked at the boy asleep in the back of the car. "Noah's not going in there with us."

"No," Gates agreed. "But we can't leave him here either."

"There was a service shed about two clicks back." Ryan nodded at the road they came in on. "Cinderblock. Empty. Still has a roof. We leave him there. Give him my burner, tell him to lock the door and wait for us to come back."

"And if we don't?"

Ryan looked at him. "I'll preload a message on the phone to the U.S. embassy. We tell them where to find him. Who he is. What he's seen. If we don't come back in a few hours, all he has to do is hit send."

He unclipped a black handheld radio from his belt. It was still crusted in dried blood. "I took this off the guy back at Punta Roja. Might still be synced to their frequency."

Gates gave a dry smile. "Now we're talking."

———

They left Noah in the small stone building a few yards from the main road, with three water bottles, a flashlight, Ryan's burner, and instructions to contact the embassy if they weren't back in an hour. The boy just nodded solemnly, then settled himself in the corner with his comic book. He must have read it over a hundred times by now, but he wasn't complaining. Ryan wanted to say more, do more, *be* more for the kid but he had nothing in him left to give. Just survival. And then maybe a way out of this mess for all of them.

Back at the vantage point above the airfield, Ryan racked the charging handle on the salvaged rifle and slung it over his back, adjusting the strap so it wouldn't thump against his bad leg. Gates had a shotgun they'd yanked from the SUV's rear, plus his Glock.

Ryan crouched behind a boulder and slid the binoculars up. "Three on the gate. Two by the fuel tanks. Another doing circles near the hangar. No clear path in."

"Listen," Gates said, holding up the radio.

They both stilled. A voice came through—crackled Spanish, but clear enough.

"Bravo team rotating. East quadrant clear. Lights cycling in fifteen."

Ryan's eyes narrowed. "That's our window."

They watched for five more minutes. Patrols shifted. The east side—near the service access gate—dropped to one man. The lights along that section flickered, then went dark.

"Let's move," Gates said.

They ghosted through the brush, moving like shadows. The stolen radio buzzed again: routine check-ins, minor updates. No hint yet of trouble.

At the fence, Gates clipped the wire with bolt cutters Ryan had salvaged from the old pickup's toolkit. It took them less than thirty seconds to breach and slip inside. Once past the perimeter, the compound swallowed them whole.

Ryan knelt by a low crate, listening. The place was alive, but only in pockets.

Ryan said, "I'm going in. You cover me, keep eyes on the perimeter. Let me know when we have an out."

Gates nodded, and Ryan took off at a limping jog, heading for the cluster of attached buildings beside the hangar. The door he chose was half ajar, light seeping through. He moved room to room, through storage closets, mechanical rooms, a gutted kitchen. Finally, he reached a tiny guard post at the end of the corridor. It was empty, but terminal screens lit the darkness. They showed surveillance feed on monitors, from different locations around the airstrip.

He crept closer. There. Top left.

Lucía.

She sat in a hard-backed chair, completely naked. Her hands were bound again, her posture straight. A tall figure loomed in front of her.

Ryan didn't recognize the man, but something about the way he was standing over her suggested he wasn't some grunt tasked with extracting information from her.

No, he looked like this was personal to him, and that he was enjoying every moment.

The pistol grip of the rifle was sweaty in Ryan's hand. If he could have raised it and fired at the man through the screen, he'd have unloaded the entire clip, then reloaded and emptied that one, too.

But he couldn't. All he could do was watch.

FIFTY-FIVE

THE DOOR SHUT with a soft click.

Lucía didn't flinch, but her spine stiffened. She sat in the center of the large room, wrists bound to the arms of a metal chair, feet strapped at the ankles. There were no windows. Just one bare bulb above her and a drain in the floor that whispered its own implications.

She'd been waiting nearly an hour. The restraints bit at her wrists. Her shoulder throbbed where the gunshot wound had reopened during the struggle. Her mouth was dry, but her mind was clear. Sharp. She had catalogued every sound in the building: the scuff of boots on tile, the clack of a radio clipped to someone's vest, the low murmur of Spanish outside the door. But not his voice. Not yet.

Then: the latch had turned. The door had opened. And in Javier Esquivel had walked. Strolled, actually, like it was a wine bar and not a torture chamber.

He was alone, and he appeared to be unarmed. Somehow, he looked exactly as she remembered, and yet nothing like she remembered. The silver at his temples had grown and there were more lines on his face. And yet that squared-jawed, movie-star handsomeness was still intact. His shirt was custom-made, crisp and elegant, sleeves rolled with surgical precision.

And he was carrying her ghost laptop, which she'd last seen… Where? In their SUV back at the abandoned motel?

He didn't smile, and his tone was business-like. "Lucía."

She didn't respond.

He stepped closer. His cologne reached her: something expensive, citrus, cedar. Not the same as before, and yet so like him it seemed to slot into her memory of him with ease.

"You look…feral," he said. "I was worried the American had domesticated you."

Lucía stared at him. "Where's the boy?"

Javier cocked his head. "No pleasantries? I'm a little hurt." He crossed to a metal table against the wall and placed the laptop down carefully. Then picked up a blowtorch, inspecting it like he wasn't sure what its function was. The slight smile playing on his face said otherwise. "But maybe not as much as you're about to be."

Lucía's stomach felt like it had dropped out of her body. She gripped the armrests of the chair. "Where is he?"

He continued to ignore the question. "You're angry," he said. "That's good. It means you haven't given up yet."

Lucía's jaw flexed.

"I always admired that about you. You weren't like the others. Pretty, yes. But you didn't lead with it. You were smart. Hardworking. You wanted things."

"I wanted to matter," she said coldly. "I mistook you for someone who could give me that."

Finally, Javier smiled. "And I did, didn't I?"

"You gave me a cell with better furniture."

He placed the blowtorch down with exaggerated care, then stepped closer to her. "You remember how I work, don't you?" he asked, voice low. "You remember the nights you came to my office. How you used to look at me?"

She felt the air shrink.

"I remember," she said. "I remember trying to please you. Trying to survive."

He smiled. "You did more than survive."

She shook her head slowly. "I was young. I was hungry. And you knew exactly what to do with girls like me."

"Mmmm," he said, like he was remembering exactly that. "I did, didn't I?"

Lucía's cheeks flamed. Before she had a chance to respond, his hand whipped out, as quick as a snake, to grip her jaw. He squeezed hard. His black eyes looked bottomless, empty. How had she ever thought he was handsome? He was grotesque.

"Do you know what's beautiful about our history?" he said. "It's unfinished. This ledger, this vendetta, it's just a footnote. You and I? We're the real story." He leaned down until their faces were inches apart. "I'm offering you a way out," he said. "One last time. Give me the passphrase. The key."

It was hard to speak with his hand on her jaw. "And if I refuse?"

He let go, and stood, smoothed his hands down his suit. "I really hope you don't. You always had such beautiful skin."

Lucía swallowed. Her wrists burned. Her shoulder ached. Her whole body ached.

But what hurt the most wasn't from her bindings, or her wounds, or even from the fear of what he was about to do to her.

It was from recognition. From realizing that this was who he'd always been. This was who she had once bent herself around, like ivy curling around a poisoned tree. "You think I'll trade what's in my head for your mercy."

"I do," he said, in that low, certain way of his. As if to provide evidence of his certainty, he turned back to the table and picked up the blowtorch again. He clicked the igniter, and the bright blue flame flared to life.

He came back around to face her, squatting down so he was level with her. He didn't say anything, just looked up at her with an almost adoring expression, like he was trying to memorize her face. It was an expression a man might give the woman he loved, if this were a romance and not a horror story.

He lifted the blowtorch, but he didn't direct it to her skin. Instead, he aimed the flame at the metal frame of the chair near her thigh.

Lucía felt a tremble start in her legs and travel up her body. She could control her mind, she could lean into the fear, but her bones and tissue and sinews wanted no part of what was about to happen.

The metal began to warm beneath her. The hiss of the torch grew louder. The air shimmered with heat. Then the heat crept upward, slow at first, until her skin began to prickle, then throb. Then the metal began to tick, soft, irregular pings as it expanded under the flame.

The sound got inside her head.

Ping. Ping. Ping.

"You just need to say the words, Lucía, and it all stops."

Her mouth was dry, but somehow she managed to collect enough saliva in her mouth to spit on his face.

Javier didn't react; he just kept the gas flame directed at the metal frame. At the point of contact, the metal had turned white hot.

Her throat worked, but she refused to make a sound. The smell of something acrid reached her—burned oil, scorched dust, maybe fabric—and for a moment she told herself that was all it was. Then came the pain.

It didn't come as a wave. It bloomed. A flower of fire spreading under her thighs, into the soft places at the back of her legs, along the curve of her spine.

Her body jolted once, involuntary, and the zip ties at her ankles bit deep. Her breath came fast and short, the way it did before crying, but she wouldn't cry. She couldn't give him that.

Javier watched her, head tilted slightly, studying her face like a man assessing a work of art.

"Pain," he said quietly, almost conversationally. "It isn't the enemy, Lucía."

He shifted the torch a few inches. The blue flame licked along the frame. The heat climbed. The metal armrest began to glow faintly orange.

The smell changed. Stronger. Sharper. Meatier.

Lucía's stomach lurched. She bit the inside of her cheek until she tasted blood.

Another ping. The chair popped loudly as the welds expanded.

Lucía's mind fractured into two distinct planes—one screaming, the other counting. She counted her breaths. Counted how long it had been since he'd turned the flame on. Twenty seconds? Thirty? The air smelled of burned hair and something worse.

"Say the password," he said softly. "It's only a few words. Just words, *querida*."

The back of her legs felt wet now. *Sweat*, she told herself. *It's just sweat.*

"Fuck you," she whispered.

Javier watched her for a long moment, the torch steady, the reflection of its flame turning his eyes a hellish gold. Then, finally, he shut it off. The silence afterward was almost unbearable—her pulse roaring in her ears, her breath ragged.

He stood, set the torch on the table with delicate care. "I'll be back in an hour for round two," he said, almost tenderly. "And you'll beg before sunrise."

He straightened, checked the cuffs on her wrists as though adjusting jewelry, then walked to the door. Then he was gone. The door shut behind him with that same soft click.

Lucía sat in the stillness, panting, her body trembling uncontrollably. She stared at the flame-shaped shadow still dancing on the wall from the afterimage burned into her retinas. The smell of scorched metal filled her nose; the pain was so complete it felt almost distant now, as if it belonged to someone else.

FIFTY-SIX

THE SURVEILLANCE SCREEN FROZE MID-FLINCH. Lucía's body—naked, trembling—was caught in a sick stutter of pixels, her face twisted in pain, lips pulled back in a silent scream. Her thighs were blistered red where the metal chair had burned into her skin. Smoke shimmered faintly in the corner of the frame.

Ryan's pulse kicked so hard he thought he might black out.

Javier knelt beside her, blow torch still hissing in his hand, blue flame licking the edge of the steel frame as casually as if he were searing crème brûlée.

Ryan moved.

The chair scraped back, the legs shrieking against concrete. He didn't hear it. Didn't hear the clatter of the fallen radio, or the way his own heart sounded like a war drum in his chest.

He was already out the door, sprinting. Because that wasn't a video. That wasn't replayed footage. That was happening.

Right now.

———

The world came to Lucía back in pieces.

Pain, first.

Her nerves fired in waves, heat flaring along her thighs, her back, her wrists. Her tongue stuck to the roof of her mouth. The room still smelled like her own burnt flesh.

She blinked but saw nothing. Her eyes were open. It just didn't matter. A second later, light stabbed through her skull. The overhead bulb. Still on. Still humming.

She was still in the chair.

Lucía turned her head a few inches and screamed. Just once. Short. Sharp. The sound of her skin tearing away from the hot metal where her shoulder had fused to the backrest.

Then silence again. Her heart hammering in her chest. Her breath coming fast.

She looked down. The sides of her thighs were blistered—burned in the shape of the metal where the heat had radiated through. Her left hip bore the ugly red kiss of the frame. Her wrists were raw, the skin slick with blood where the zip-ties had bit into them during the convulsions.

He'd only been gone a few minutes. Or an hour. She didn't know. There was no time here.

Lucía pressed her head back and closed her eyes.

Through the fog of pain and thirst and hunger and exhaustion, she saw Ryan. His handsome face, his strong jaw. Eyes so blue they were almost clear. He didn't smile often, but the few times he had had been breathtaking.

He'd nearly been hers. Just like Mateo had. But for a trick of fate, a quirk of the universe, a *you go left and I go right* moment. If only she could have had one more go-around, one more chance to see him, she'd tell him she loved him, and that she'd known it since he'd first kissed her.

But there were no go-arounds. Real life didn't get a replay. All she could do was picture him in her mind, her Mills and Boon cowboy, and say it in her head.

I love you, Ryan Inglis.

In her head, he spoke back, but what he said wasn't what a Mills and Boon cowboy would say. Nothing like that at all.

In her head, he said, *Plastic weakens in heat. It gets brittle. A little leverage, it pops.*

She jerked upright in the chair as the memory hit her. A tremor ran through her arms as she tested the tie on her left wrist. The plastic stretched like hard taffy but it didn't give. She didn't have the leverage that Ryan had, nor the brute strength. She rotated her hand, slow and deliberate, grinding blood and sweat into the tie. The pain was so intense it was almost hallucinatory. But it wasn't everything. Not anymore. Not when rage was simmering behind her ribs, hot and clean and merciless.

Her fingers clenched. Twitched. Moved.

"Come on," she whispered.

With a final twist and pull, her left hand slipped free with a sick, wet sound. Her forearm flopped forward, nerves screaming as it fell slack.

She bit down on her own shoulder to keep from crying out.

Then the other hand. Then the feet.

By the time she collapsed to the floor, it wasn't victory she felt. It was ignition.

She lay still for a second, cheek against cold concrete. Her lungs burned with every breath. Her body wept from ten different wounds.

When she looked up, she saw her laptop sitting open on the dirty table, its screen dimmed but still alive.

Lucía dragged herself toward it, inch by inch. Every scrape of her palms left smears of blood on the concrete. Her body was an instrument of pain—burned, blistered, trembling—but her mind had gone diamond-sharp.

When she reached the table, she clutched at the edge and pulled herself upright, using her good arm. Her breath came in gasps. The scent of scorched skin and hot metal clung to her.

The screen flickered awake at her touch.

Lines of code shimmered faintly across the monitor: encrypted strings, her old algorithms looping endlessly, waiting for the final key.

Lucía's fingers hovered over the keyboard. They were shaking, slick with sweat and blood, but she found the keys by muscle memory. The phrase came to her all at once, like breath returning after drowning:

Tr3mbl_n0_c41g4_s0la.

She typed it slowly, carefully, each keystroke a small act of rebellion. Then she hit Enter.

The laptop hummed. The screen flared white, then filled with a torrent of data: names, transfers, coded transactions. The ledger was assembling itself.

For a heartbeat, she simply stared at it.

Then she saw the final prompt appear:

> Upload to distributed mirrors? [Y/N]

Her finger hovered. And she pressed **Y**.

The progress bar shot across the screen. Her fail-safes came online, one after another, a cascade of systems she'd built in secret over years—each one relaying fragments of the data through hidden servers, secure clouds, anonymous networks.

DATA PUBLISHED TO MIRRORS: 12/12.

It was done.

The silence that followed felt enormous. Her whole body shook, not from fear this time, but from release. The pain was still there, burning deep, but beneath it was something else.

Freedom.

Lucía exhaled. It came out as a laugh, hoarse and wet. She reached forward and closed the laptop with both hands.

Then she slid to the floor, her back against the table leg, breathing through the pain. The room smelled of burnt flesh and blood and victory. She whispered the phrase once more, softly, tasting the ash of it on her tongue. *Trembling doesn't make a leaf fall alone.*

And for the first time in her life, she believed it.

Ryan's bootfalls were muffled, but the corridor was quiet enough to make every breath feel like a cymbal crash.

He reached a corner. Paused. Listened.

Nothing.

Then, footsteps. Soft. Padded.

Ryan ducked into a shallow recess in the wall just as a soldier passed. Black fatigues. Sidearm holstered. No helmet.

He passed by without spotting Ryan, and without Ryan having to waste anymore of his precious bullets. Somewhere ahead was the hangar. He could feel it in his bones. And inside that…

Lucía.

———

The silence after upload didn't last. There were bootsteps outside the door, slow and heavy.

Lucía tensed. Someone was coming to check on her. She got back to her feet, burns stretching like fire across her skin. She needed a weapon now.

The table was littered with industrial odds and ends but her eyes went straight to a metal tray lined with what looked like surgical tools. Scissors. Forceps. A scalpel, sharp and bright, fresh out of its packaging.

Javier's next instruments of persuasion.

She picked up the blade. Behind her, the footsteps got louder, closer. Lowering herself to the ground, she ducked around the side of the table, blade in her left hand.

The lock clicked. The door opened.

A man stepped in—bored, distracted, adjusting his walkie. He looked like a grunt. One of Phalanx's nameless bastards.

Lucía didn't lunge. She waited, coiled like wire, letting him approach, letting him see her naked, bloodied body crouched beside the table.

He leaned in—

She struck.

The blade plunged up beneath the shelf of his ribs. He gasped. She yanked sideways. He went down hard, gurgling.

She followed him to the floor, hand over his mouth, eyes locked on his as the light drained out. When it was done, she rolled off him, chest heaving.

His gun was still holstered. With trembling hands, she took it and placed it on the tray. Then she quickly stripped his shirt, his boots, his pants. Every movement sent sparks of pain through her whole body, but she managed to shove feet into his pants, trying not to notice how they were still warm from his body. She had to roll the waistband over several times to make them stay up, and roll up the sleeves of the shirt, but at least she was covered. The boots were way too big, so she jammed her feet into his thick socks instead. They would provide both padding and muffle her footsteps.

Then she picked up his pistol, and stepped through the door, dressed in the borrowed skin of a soldier.

FIFTY-SEVEN

NIGHT HAD SUNK its teeth into the desert. The compound's outer floodlights threw jagged shadows across the perimeter fence, cutting the scrubland into sharp slices of white and black. Overhead, the stars hung cold and remote, indifferent to the war brewing below.

Gates crouched behind a rusted fuel barrel near the edge of the depot, breath low and steady, finger tight on the trigger of his Glock. Sweat slicked the back of his neck.

Stacks of chemical drums lined the fence. A broken forklift sat listing to one side. A rusted utility shack glowed faintly from a single overhead bulb. He moved past it, then heard footsteps ahead. Close.

He kept low, ducked between two barrels.

And saw Reyes.

The little bastard strolled like he belonged here now. Tactical harness, sidearm, the smug entitlement of someone who'd finally stopped pretending he was the help. Gates could feel it roll off him like heat.

He stepped out of the shadows, fast and silent. Grabbed Reyes by the vest. Slammed him into the barrel hard enough to make the metal clang.

Reyes gasped, reaching for his sidearm, but Gates already had the Glock pressed under his chin.

"You make a move, I turn your jaw into soup."

Reyes froze, breath wheezing. "You should've stayed in the fucking closet."

Gates shoved him to the ground, pinned him with one knee, forearm tight across the throat. The Glock didn't shake in his hand.

"Where is she?"

"Hangar," Reyes choked out. "North quadrant. Big one. They've got her restrained."

"Javier?"

"Been in there with her for a while."

Gates's stomach knotted. "Alone?"

Reyes tried a grin, blood on his teeth. "Don't act shocked. You knew how this worked when you signed on."

Gates's jaw clenched. "I didn't sign up for this."

"The hell you didn't," Reyes rasped. "You just thought you'd keep your hands clean."

He grabbed Reyes by the collar and dragged him upright. "You took a kid, then you tortured a woman for a password. What's your number, Reyes? What's the sum that makes you this kind of man?"

Reyes spat blood, half-laughing. "You tell me. You're still cashing the same checks."

The sound that left Gates wasn't a word, it was a low, animal growl. The shot rang out, hitting Reyes just below the chin, before ricocheting off the fuel tanks. His body slumped beside a leaking drum, blood pooling under his collar.

Gates stared at him for a moment, breathing heavily, then he stepped back. And that's when he saw it. A small flame licking along the ground, straight toward the chemical barrels.

"Shit—"

He backed up fast, just as the first drum ignited with a loud whoomph, sending a fireball skyward.

Flames burst out sideways, searing hot. Gates turned and ran like hell.

———

Ryan turned left down another hall, this one tighter, filled with stacked crates. He ducked through shadows, checked each door. One was ajar, marked with a faded "Hangar Access." He limped toward it, one hand trailing the wall for balance. The pain in his leg was building, hot and relentless. Then he thought of the pain Lucía must be in and his own immediately faded into the background.

He had to get to her.

Suddenly, a voice cracked through the radio on his belt. Static, then something low in Spanish. Ryan froze. The voice didn't repeat.

Somewhere behind him, he heard footsteps. Then shouting. He backed against the wall.

He waited a second more, his heartbeat slamming in his ears. The radio on his hip crackled again, louder this time. A flurry of voices. Then alarms screamed to life overhead.

Shit.

Ryan broke into a limp-run, teeth bared against the pain. A siren blared. The floor shook under his feet as a heavy door slammed somewhere behind him.

The doorway loomed up ahead. A few more yards, then beyond it, the hangar. His thigh felt molten. He tasted blood in his mouth. The pistol in his hand was almost empty.

But he was here. He was close. Lucía was close.

And he was going to burn this whole place down if they laid another hand on her.

———

The hallway beyond the torture room reeked of diesel, sweat, and the acrid tang of burning fuel. Lucía limped through it like a ghost from some ruined war, wrapped in a merc's oversized uniform, blood drying sticky at the backs of her knees.

She held the pistol in both hands. The hall curved left, toward a bank of utility lockers and a concrete washroom, its industrial sink stained with old rust. She ducked inside, breathing hard.

In the mirror, she looked like something unearthed from a grave. Blood crusted in the creases of her lips. Her eyes were too wide, whites showing all around. Her arms trembled. But under the wreckage, there was something clean and electric in her expression.

Focus.

Lucía tucked the pistol into her waistband and splashed cold water over her face. Then tore paper towels from the dispenser and pressed them to her skin.

The radio crackled, voices distorting through static.

"—repeat, fire's reached the generator shed. Containment's failing."

A burst of static. Another voice, higher-pitched, panicked. "North depot's gone! We've got chemicals burning, smoke in the hangar bay!"

A final voice, hoarse and breathless: "Where the fuck is Reyes?"

She stepped back into the corridor. She didn't know where Javier had gone, but she knew where he liked to be.

High ground. Surveillance. The seat of power.

She crossed into a long access hallway, moving slowly, staying to the shadows. Her footsteps were near-silent. A stairwell rose ahead, unguarded, dimly lit. She took the first step, then the second, each one dragging fire up her legs. By the fifth, her vision was swimming.

She paused on the landing, breathing hard. Her wounds were searing, hot from adrenaline, but she kept going.

Something scraped above her. A voice: low, male.

Javier.

She moved faster now, adrenaline eating through the pain. The stairs opened to a steel catwalk that wrapped around the edge of the wide hangar floor. The mezzanine office door stood open.

Inside, a glass wall looked out over the hangar, but it was covered by so many years of grime, the view was like staring into smoke. Javier stood by the desk. His jacket was draped over a chair.

She watched him from the doorway, gun raised.

And for a moment—just a flicker—her arms trembled.

Not from fear.

But because she remembered the way he'd once spoken to her. Looked at her. Like she was something rare.

It had been a lie, all of it. She stepped inside. "Don't move."

Javier froze. He turned slowly, hands just slightly raised. His expression was unreadable. Curiosity, maybe. No fear. Just calculation.

"Lucía," he said softly.

She kept the gun on him.

"I suppose this is when you say something noble," he said. "Some last words before you pull the trigger."

"No," she said. "This is when I make sure you never touch another girl like me again."

And then she fired.

———

The hangar was massive and crammed full of crates and rusted machinery. A work light hummed overhead. The big industrial kind. It swung slightly, as if someone had brushed it on their way past.

Then Ryan saw it: a body.

Face-down on the concrete, arms sprawled awkwardly. He'd been stripped nearly naked, and blood fanned out beneath him.

Ryan crouched, checked the pulse out of habit. Nothing. His

eyes scanned the rest of the space. The chair in the center of the floor stopped him cold.

The metal was scorched. Melted zip ties dangled from the arms.

He pictured her there. Writhing. Burning.

His gut twisted, rage flooding his chest so fast he could barely swallow it.

But she was gone. She'd gotten out. She was free. He looked toward the mezzanine office, a glass box suspended above the floor on steel supports. Lights were on up there. Movement. Shadows.

Then—

Gunfire. One shot. Close.

Ryan surged to his feet. "Lucía!"

FIFTY-EIGHT

THE METAL STAIRS to the hangar mezzanine groaned beneath Ryan's weight, one slow step at a time.

He kept his rifle raised, moving fast but cautious. Then he saw it. The office door at the top of the mezzanine was cracked open, a smear of blood trailing down its frame.

He felt like his whole body had ceased functioning, each and every cell frozen in time. With a trembling hand, he pushed it open. Lucía stood in the center of the room, her body still, one hand gripping the back of a metal desk chair. Her knuckles were white. Her eyes fixed on the man collapsed on the floor at her feet.

Javier Esquivel.

Blood pooled under his head, one eye still half-open, jaw slack in death.

Lucía wasn't shaking. She wasn't crying. But she was so still it made the air feel wrong.

She was wearing baggy mercenary gear cinched tight at her waist, a bloodied black shirt. Her cheeks were smeared with blood and sweat, her hair matted at the sides. She looked like she'd just crawled through hell and made it. Barely.

Ryan lowered his pistol. Relief poured over him, like hot water over freezing skin. "Lucía."

She turned, slow and deliberate. Her gaze found his. "You're alive," she said. Her voice was hoarse.

He stepped into the room. "Are you okay?" It was a stupid question. The things he'd seen on that surveillance video said that clearly she wasn't.

Her eyes flicked down at Javier's body. "I did what I had to," she said.

Ryan moved a little closer, but not too close. "I know you did."

She looked down at Javier again. "He thought I still belonged to him. That I'd fold the second he dangled mercy."

Her eyes found his again, and they looked hollow and empty. Like dead eyes.

"I was afraid we were too late," he said.

Her brow twitched. "We?"

He shook his head. "Doesn't matter."

She crossed the room, stiff with pain. "We need to get out of here," she said. "I think there's a fire somewhere."

Ryan nodded. He wanted so badly to reach out to her, to wrap her in his arms, but he couldn't. He didn't know how much pain she was in physically or mentally for that. So all he could do was gesture stupidly to the door and say, "There's a hole in the fence on the east side. We can get out that way."

She moved toward him, then paused and looked back at Javier's body. "I thought I'd feel something," she said. "Killing him."

Ryan didn't speak.

"I don't," she added quietly. "I just feel...nothing."

Then she stepped out the door and into the smoke-streaked dark.

Ryan lingered for a heartbeat more. Looked down at the man who had stolen so much from the woman now walking away. At least she'd finally gotten the chance to steal something back.

———

Ryan felt the blast before he heard it. A deep, concussive shudder ripped through the compound, rolling up from the ground and through his bones. A second later, the night went white, an eruption of fire from the far side of the hangar.

He staggered, caught himself against the railing, eyes narrowing against the glare. For half a heartbeat, everything held its breath—the floodlights flickered, the sirens choked silent—and then the world broke open.

Lucía stumbled beside him. He grabbed her elbow, steadying her as the grated stairwell groaned underfoot. Her eyes found his in the half-light, wild and confused.

"Shit," Ryan muttered, already turning toward the fire. The heat hit them like a physical shove. Another blast popped deeper in the compound, rattling the catwalk.

Smoke rolled in thick, black waves from the north quadrant. Below, the shouts began—men barking orders, boots hammering on steel. A floodlight cracked, sputtered, and went dark.

They bolted down the stairs, metal clanging beneath them, the air alive with heat and panic. Lucía gasped behind him, "What the hell happened? Is that—?"

"Don't know." He reached the landing and froze. A figure pushed through the smoke ahead.

He raised his weapon, instincts flaring, until the man's voice cut through the din.

"Thought you two had decided to stay."

Gates.

Lucía's breath caught. "How—?"

"No time," Gates snapped, pointing behind him. "Fire's spreading fast. Whole place is coming down."

Another fireball blasted skyward, shaking the hangar's skeleton. Ryan squinted into the light. "You started the fire?"

Gates gave a grim half-smile. "Let's just say Reyes and I had a disagreement by the fuel tanks."

The blaze was moving quick now, leaping from roof to roof,

swallowing the night. Mercs scattered in every direction, some shouting into radios, others running for their trucks.

Ryan jerked his chin toward the perimeter. "Fence. Now."

They half-ran, half-hobbled through the smoke, the ground shuddering beneath them. Lucía's breath rasped behind him. A final explosion went off somewhere close, metal clanging, glass screaming, and then they were at the fence.

Ryan kicked the loosened wire free, the metal groaning as it curled outward. Beyond it stretched the desert: black, endless, silent.

"Go," he said, shoving Lucía through. The heat behind them was almost physical now, pressing at his back. The airfield burned, painting the night orange. Alarms still wailed faintly over the crackle of fire.

Ryan turned and grabbed Gates's arm, hauling him through the gap.

They ran.

The ground sloped down from the fence line, loose gravel giving way to dry scrub. The orange Beetle waited where they'd left it, parked under a mesquite tree, its absurd color glowing like a target in the half-light.

Ryan reached it first, wrenching open the driver's door. "Get in—"

The word caught in his throat. Lucía wasn't moving.

She stood ten feet back, breath ragged, pistol raised. The wind tugged at her baggy shirt. Her hand didn't tremble.

She had the gun pointed at Gates.

Ryan's blood turned cold. "Lucía—?"

"Step away from the car," she said quietly, like she wasn't asking.

Gates blinked, once. Confusion gave way to wariness. "You're kidding me with this shit."

Lucía's eyes stayed on him. "Javier told me something, right before he died. He said you were playing us and had been the whole time."

Ryan turned to Gates, something heavy dropping into his stomach. "Tell me that's not true."

For a heartbeat, Gates said nothing. Then, finally, he said, "I wasn't working for Javier."

Lucía's voice was like ice. "But you were working with them. Phalanx."

The pause that followed was the wrong answer.

Ryan stared at the marshal. He'd known Gates longer than anyone in this nightmare. And while he'd never fully trusted him, he'd at least thought he knew him.

"I didn't know about the kid," Gates snapped. "I swear. And I didn't know Javier was the buyer until too late."

Ryan laughed under his breath. "But you thought you could play both sides. Sell the ledger, save the kid, get out clean."

Gates looked at him. The defensive expression on his face fell away and suddenly he just looked tired. "I thought I could manage it. That I still had control."

Lucía didn't lower the gun. "You made a deal to betray us," she said. "You came down here acting like the hero. And all the while you were just another bastard looking to cash out."

Ryan stared at him, something acid burning at the back of his throat. "You judged me," he said quietly. "You sat across from me and told me I'd betrayed everything we stood for."

Gates didn't deny it.

"Thing is," Ryan continued, "you were just better at hiding it. That's all. I knew I'd crossed a line. You just learned how to decorate yours with noble excuses."

Gates's jaw twitched. "We all crossed lines. I just crossed mine later than you."

"I'm not going to kill you," Lucía said, although she kept her finger on the trigger. "I probably should, but I'm not. But you're not coming with us."

Gates shrugged, holding up his hands like he meant no harm. Like he'd never meant them any harm. Then he stepped back from the car slowly, the firelight casting his shadow long across the gravel. Lucía didn't move until he was gone, just a shape swallowed by the dark.

Only then did Ryan feel his knees weaken. He leaned into the open door, gripping the frame hard enough to hurt. Everything in his head buzzed with heat and betrayal and exhaustion. He looked at Lucía, still clutching the gun. "You okay?"

She didn't answer right away. Finally, she said, "I'm just trying to figure out if there's anyone left I can trust."

———

The Beetle rolled to a stop on the shoulder of a desolate service road, its engine clicking in protest as Ryan cut it off. The headlights stayed dark.

Down the slope, a crooked service shed slouched beneath the stars, half-collapsed and hunched in a grove of mesquite. A faint yellow glow flickered inside.

Lucía gripped the passenger seat. The metal under her fingers was cold, even after the inferno they'd left behind.

She watched Ryan climb out, moving like every joint hurt. He crossed the gravel, disappeared inside. There was silence, then a creak of hinges and a small voice: "Ryan?"

Lucía's vision blurred.

She turned away from the windshield, forehead pressing to the cool glass. Her hands found her knees and clutched hard.

The chair.

The heat.

The sound of Javier's voice, telling her she'd beg before sunrise.

The way her own scream had echoed inside her skull.

She squeezed her eyes shut, but the tears came anyway, hot and wild. She bit the side of her hand to stifle the sob but it still broke. A single ragged breath pulled from deep in her ribs.

She folded forward. Her body shook. Not from fear. From the violence of staying alive.

It was the grief of not dying.

The passenger door creaked open.

She didn't look. But she heard the soft scuff of Noah's shoes as he climbed into the back seat. The gentle click of the seatbelt.

Ryan's voice, low: "He's safe."

Lucía nodded, still hunched.

"I didn't think we'd all make it," she whispered.

Ryan slid into the driver's seat, shut the door. "Yeah. Me neither."

She finally looked at him. Saw the dirt on his face, the fresh blood at his collar, the dried blood on his hands. And still, somehow, that steady blue in his eyes.

He turned the key. The Beetle groaned, coughed, then rumbled back to life.

"What now?" he asked.

Lucía blinked at the windshield. The road ahead was black and empty.

"A place no one can find me," she said.

Ryan adjusted the mirror. Glanced back at Noah, curled up in the backseat.

"That makes three of us."

The car rumbled forward as they drove into the dark.

FIFTY-NINE

TWO MONTHS LATER

LUCÍA STOOD UNDER THE SHOWER, steam curling around her, warm water streaming over her skin. Her burns were healing well, though she knew she'd carry the scars from each blister for the rest of her life. The gunshot wound on her shoulder wasn't fully healed yet, the skin still fleshy and red.

It felt like the first time she'd truly felt safe in years.

Ryan had an equally raw scar on his upper thigh, but that's not where her eyes were as he stepped into the shower beside her. She trailed her hand down his chest, over the rippling muscle, enjoying the way his body responded. Then she reached between his legs, hand closing around him, feeling him harden even more in her hand. "Good morning," she murmured.

He moved under the stream, forcing her back against the cool tile.

The heat of his body met hers, his chest pressing to her breasts, his breath warm against her neck. "Yeah," he whispered. "It is."

Her fingers slid over his forearm, tracing the scars, the rough skin, the ropy muscles beneath. When she tilted her head back, he took her mouth, slow at first, tasting her like she was a delicacy he couldn't get enough of. Then the kiss grew deeper, hungrier. His hands gripped her hips, and he spun her around. The swollen tip of his cock pressed into the small of her back, where her scarred skin was still so sensitive.

Her palms pressed against the wet tiles as his arms circled her waist, tightening, pulling her closer. His lips found the curve of her shoulder, planting a line of kisses up her neck to her earlobe. She moaned, her eyes drifting closed. He positioned her hips where he wanted them, them with one hand braced on the shower wall above her shoulder, he pushed into her with a groan. His other hand slid around her hip and down between her legs, teasing her clit until she gasped. His own breathing grew ragged as he started to glide in and out of her, slowly at first, but harder and deeper as she relaxed around him.

The water drummed steadily, the sound wrapping them in a cocoon. Every other sensation faded until the only thing she could feel was his hands and his cock, and the building pleasure that spread from where he touched her and where he filled her.

His other hand sliding up between her breasts, palm slick and hot against her skin. He bit gently at her shoulder. "You're mine now, Lucía," he growled. "No one else's. Just mine."

Lucía gasped, her back arching. His fingers circled her clit again, more insistently now, driving her closer.

"God, Ryan—don't stop—"

He thrust again, harder this time, and she nearly lost her footing. He caught her, held her tight against him, his chest slick against her back.

"Let go, sweetheart," he whispered. "I've got you."

And she did. Her whole body tightened, her vision going white at the edges as she came with a soundless cry, shaking beneath him. She clutched his forearm where it circled her waist, nails digging in. She could feel every inch of him, every beat of his pulse.

When she started to come down, he pulled her back against his chest and groaned, his thrusts slowing, deepening, then shuddering to stillness as he came inside her, hand splayed flat over her ribs.

They stayed like that for a moment, locked together beneath the spray. His forehead pressed to the back of her neck. Her eyes closed. The world outside the glass door didn't matter.

Only the sound of their breathing. The hush of water. The warmth of his arms. And the truth that, finally, they'd made it out.

———

Lucía lay on her stomach across the bed, cheek pressed to a cool patch of linen. Salt air drifted through the open balcony doors. They'd been in this little hotel on the Pacific coast for twelve days. Before that, a tiny rented room in a town called El Cántaro. They never stayed anywhere long. That was the only rule.

The place wasn't fancy, their budget was limited to what remained in Lucía's crypto wallets. But it still felt more like a home than any of the dingy dives she'd lived in for the past nine years. And she knew it had nothing to do with the décor.

On the nightstand beside her, Ryan's burner phone buzzed once then went still. She ignored it.

Instead, she scrolled slowly through the newsfeed on her own cracked screen, thumb tracing the same motion she'd made a thousand times in the past weeks. Another headline. Another quote from a man in a suit denying everything. Another face pixelated in shame. Somewhere between the corruption charges and the abrupt resignations, she'd stopped saving the links.

The ledger had detonated like she'd hoped. Spread like burning oil across dry land. But fire didn't always clean. Sometimes it just scarred things beyond recognition.

She set the phone down.

Her thighs still bore the faint, ridged outlines of the chair frame. The scars on her wrists were deep, and she'd lost some sensitivity along her left calf, and her shoulder ached when she lifted anything heavier than a wine bottle.

Ryan sat on the bed behind her, his weight shifting the

mattress. One hand slid up her bare spine and rested between her shoulder blades. She felt the heat of him, the steadiness.

Noah was back in the States now. Safe. Ryan had arranged it quietly, a phone call to a woman back in the States, with an assurance of no questions and no police. Two days later, Noah stepped into his grandmother's arms on the side of a sun-bleached highway. Ryan and Lucía had driven away before the old woman could even look over her shoulder.

She turned over, studying Ryan's face. She reached up, brushed a wet strand of hair off his temple. He leaned into her touch.

Lucía pressed her forehead to his collarbone. "You hungry?"

"A little."

"We should get food."

———

Lucía jingled the room key with theatrical impatience. "You've got two minutes to get dressed, or I'm leaving you for tacos."

Ryan didn't look up from his phone. "Just a sec."

She rolled her eyes. "Fine, I'll wait for you out in the hall."

Ryan watched her leave, closing the door behind her. They didn't talk much about the ledger. Or Javier. Or Gates. But sometimes at night, he'd feel Lucía tense beside him in the dark, just for a second, and know she was still there in that moment, standing in that hangar office, standing over a dead man.

He never asked if she regretted it. And she never said whether she did.

On the balcony, salt air greeted him, threaded with the distant scent of grilled meat and diesel fumes from the road below. He pulled out his phone again, refreshed his inbox. Nothing.

But then, just as he was about to pocket the device, it buzzed.

Blocked number.

He stared at it, a cold knot tightening in his stomach.

It rang. Once. Twice. Four times. Then it stopped. A red badge appeared.

1 new voicemail.

He didn't move at first. Just stood there, the wind brushing against his damp hair. Then he tapped "Play."

Static hissed then a voice he hadn't heard in months and didn't think he'd ever hear again.

Gates.

"Inglis. I know you don't exactly want to hear from me right now, or probably ever. And you're not going to like this, but I don't have time to soften it. Word came down from someone I trust. Cartel informants, stateside. Quiet channels. This isn't chatter, it's movement. They've found Jessica Meeks."

His heart kicked.

"They know she's living in Texas, Daniel Castaño, too. I don't know who's pulling the strings, but the timing's not a coincidence. The fallout from that ledger made a lot of people angry. They want blood, and those two have been on their hit list for a very long time. I thought you should know."

Pause.

"Do what you want with it."

Click.

The message ended.

Ryan stared out at the black water. His fingers curled around the phone, knuckles white. He closed his eyes. The shadows he thought they'd outrun were already catching up.

Because the war wasn't over. Not even close.

ALSO BY S.K. MUSKAT

Love on the Run

Jessica, Not Her Real Name

South of Justice

You Can Run

ABOUT THE AUTHOR

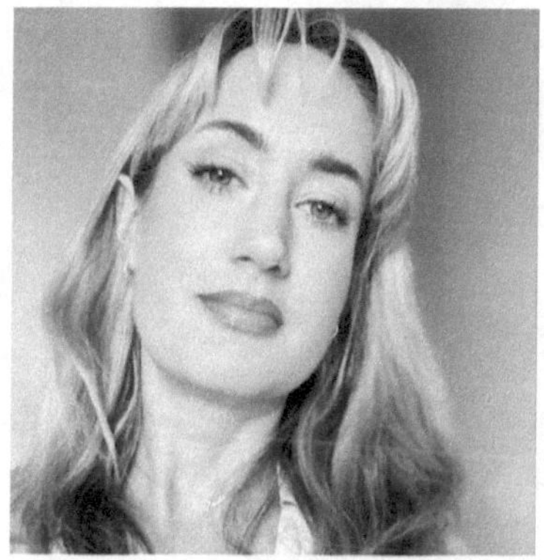

S.K. Muskat is the pen name for Shannon Hart. She writes romantic thrillers where love is risky, secrets kill, and no one gets out unscathed. With a passion for storytelling that has taken her around the world, she now calls New Zealand home—along with an ever-growing collection of plants that, unlike her characters, thrive under her care.

A small press bound by the belief that every voice matters.

Sign up for our newsletter to learn about new releases and more.
https://oliver-heberbooks.com/subscribe/

Follow us on social media:

facebook.com/oliverheberbooks
instagram.com/oliverheberbooks
amazon.com/oliverheberbooks
youtube.com/@OliverHeberBooksPublisher